Dangerous Disguise

An Allingham Regency Classic

Merryn Allingham

DANGEROUS DISGUISE

This novel is entirely a work of fiction. The names, characters and incidents portrayed in it are the work of the author's imagination. Any resemblance to actual persons, living or dead, events or localities is entirely coincidental.

First published in Great Britain 2019 by The Verrall Press

Chapter One

'Stand and deliver!'

The command shattered the stillness of the autumn evening and bounced from tree to tree in a slowly diminishing echo. Even as he struggled awake, the door of the carriage was being wrenched opened.

'Stand and deliver!'

He was looking down the barrel of a duelling pistol. An odd choice of weapon his mind registered, but fleetingly for the pistol was ominously close and waving him to descend. Very slowly he rose from the padded leather, the mists of sleep still clouding his vision. They were in an open space, rare amidst the thick canopy of forest, and a cloaked and booted figure astride a chestnut mare filled the carriage doorway.

The moon was riding high, glinting across the horse's glossy coat and lighting the silver braid of its rider's three-cornered hat. In the ghostly white light he saw that his attacker was unusually slight, hardly a match for the gruff voice issuing from behind a silk handkerchief. He calculated his chances of foiling this blatant piracy and decided they were good enough, despite the risk of the cocked pistol. He was carrying a substantial sum of money and had no wish to see it fall into the pockets of a gentleman of the road.

The chestnut was becoming restive, bucking and prancing at the side of the carriage, the white blaze between its eyes shifting in and out of the moonlight. With luck the mare's antics would distract its rider, since the one pistol must cover two men - his coachman as well as himself.

He made as though to descend as he'd been ordered, but then at the last moment shot his arm forward and grasped his assailant's wrist in a punishing grip. The wrist, as he'd suspected, was as slender as the form. The pistol faltered, drooped and fell with a thud on to the turf. He looked at the eyes behind the mask and saw them dark with dismay. The arm was pulled violently and suddenly from his grasp and the sharp tear of cambric filled the silent glade as the attacker's sleeve ripped apart. Then, in a breath, the highwayman had backed his horse, turned, and was riding into the distance as though all the demons of hell were on his heels.

And so they should be, he thought grimly. The scourge of ambush had all but disappeared from England's roads but not, it seemed, from the deeps of Sussex. He picked up the discarded weapon and a scrap of lace - the remains of a torn ruffle - that lay near by, then looked closely at the abandoned pistol. It confirmed what he'd thought. It was a strange choice for a robbery. The gun was beautifully balanced, intricately decorated and evidently expensive. Hardly a toy for a highwayman.

He slipped both pistol and lace into the capacious

pocket of his travelling coat and called to his coachman.

'It's all right, Fielding, it's quite safe to come down.'

The man arrived at his side in seconds, breathing hard and looking downcast. 'My lord, I had no choice but to stop.' His voice quavered slightly. 'He was threatening to shoot the horses – and then me.'

'He was indeed a desperado.' The tone was quietly ironic and there was a pause before his master continued, 'Although my guess would be a local youth out on the spree or intent on winning a wager.'

'I don't know about that, my lord.' Fielding puffed at the implication. 'He looked the real thing to me.'

'He would hardly win his wager if he had not.'

'Whatever he was, he's cut the traces,' the coachman remarked with something like a note of triumph.

His master strode to the horses' heads and retrieved the trailing leather. 'An intelligent move for a callow youth.'

'Yes, my lord, we're good and stranded.'

'You are stranded, Fielding,' his employer corrected gently, as he unhooked the broken traces from one of the leaders. 'I shall ride one of these expensive beasts to the nearest inn and hire whatever transport they can offer.'

The coachman sighed but his master affected not to notice. 'Tomorrow you will seek out the nearest saddler and arrange for the traces to be replaced. In the meantime we must find a home for the carriage and horses.'

The coachman sighed again a little more loudly and his master added in a kindly fashion, 'As soon as I find a hostelry, I will arrange for your rescue.'

⌒

Lucinda rode at breakneck speed, hunched low over the mare's neck, and threading a dangerous path in and out of the trees. She was losing time but she had to be sure she'd shaken off any likely pursuit. Now she was out of the forest and hurtling down the rutted lane she'd traversed so hopefully only an hour ago. She must put as many leagues as possible between herself and her nemesis.

Her plan had gone abysmally wrong. The man in the coach was not supposed to attack her. *She* was the assailant: she issued the commands and he was meant to deliver. Instead she'd found herself temporarily mesmerised by his powerful figure and urged into flight only when he'd grabbed her with such paralysing force that she had dropped the gun. Even now her left wrist throbbed sickeningly, and she was barely able to touch the reins without a shudder of pain. She thanked heaven that Red knew her way home and would take them there safely.

Only gradually did she slow her headlong gallop. A thicket of trees appeared in the distance, small but dense, climbing its way up the shallow hillside as though each set of roots was planted atop the trees beneath. Within their branches lay a secret, vital to her plans if she were to accomplish the task she had set herself.

But would she? Tonight had been a disaster and she could not afford another. It was only by the quickest of thinking that she had galloped free, a split second decision to abandon the pistol and run. If she had not had the forethought to cut the traces first... it did not bear thinking of.

The man would have taken the gun, she was sure, but he

would not know to whom it belonged. It was most unlikely he would ever trace its owner. And if by the very worst of luck he did, whose name would he find? – that of a young man left to rot in a verminous London gaol. Certainly no highwayman free and riding the road. Her brother! She could weep when she thought how badly she had let him down. There would be no escape for him now. He would remain, as she had seen him just days ago, thin and ill, surrounded by every kind of dirt and disease.

Lucinda slid from the saddle and walked towards a wall of greenery. Coaxing Red forward, she lifted the intertwined branches, one by one, to reveal a rough, wooden entrance built into the hillside. She tugged on the iron handle and the door swung smoothly back. She was safe but, thanks to her bungling, Rupert was still in danger.

Assuming the guise of a highwayman had been a crazy idea but, since her visit to Newgate, she had been unable to keep it from her mind. She'd been struck by one of Rupert's fellow prisoners, a giant of a man with shaggy, black bristles and laughing black eyes. He'd smiled at her saucily as the turnkey escorted her to her brother's miserable cell and she'd been impelled to ask his name.

'Black Jack Collins,' the gaoler had said, as though she should know. And then when she'd continued to look blank, he'd added helpfully, 'A gentleman of the road so called, who'll hang before the week is out.'

Despite this grim prediction, the image of Black Jack Collins had stayed with her. A gentleman of the road did not sound as brutal as a robber, particularly if the victim was stupidly wealthy and emerged unhurt. If she became a highwayman for just one night, she might rescue her brother. The idea held and she'd thrown herself into the adventure, relieved to be doing something, anything, to aid Rupert. All it would take was one successful theft. She would choose a wealthy traveller, a man who would hardly miss the money he'd be forced to surrender. It wouldn't be simple, it would need careful devising, but it was possible.

Lucinda had bubbled with excitement at the audacity of the plan and been filled with hope for its success. The black suit had been her brother's, a little baggy, but with Molly's quick needle, it fitted well enough. Molly's mother, a chambermaid at The Four Feathers, had found the tricorne at the back of a dusty cupboard, no doubt abandoned long ago by its nefarious owner. And the weapon had been simple – Rupert's duelling pistols had pride of place on his bedroom wall. She had taken one and prayed that she would not have to use it.

Meticulous planning but all for nothing. The adventure had started well enough: the coachman had been cowed by the sight of the pistol, his horses obediently still, but the man she had been tipped to rob, had not been as obedient. He had not read the same script as she and her wonderful scheme had crumbled before her.

⌒

A little ahead and at a point where the narrow stone passage branched in opposite directions, a dimly glowing lamp was being held high in the air. Red gave a gentle whinny at the sight of the waiting figure.

'Miss Lucy, thank goodness! You're here at last.' A

young girl rushed forward. 'I thought you'd be returned an age ago.'

'There was some trouble, Molly, and I had to take the long way home.'

'Trouble, miss?' The maid's eyes held worry. 'Then you didn't –'

'No,' Lucinda said flatly. 'I've returned with nothing.'

'But you found the coach – the one mother told us of?'

'Yes, I found the coach.' Her mistress's voice was faint with weariness. 'I even brought it to a halt. But its passenger was too strong for me and... ' She stumbled on her words. 'I was nearly caught.'

The maid gave a sharp intake of breath.

'You mustn't worry.' Lucinda gave her a quick hug. 'Red spirited me from the scene and, as you see, I'm safe and well.'

'Thank the Lord you're home, Miss Lucy. I've been that anxious. But –'

'But?'

'There's trouble brewing. Your uncle is fair beside himself.'

'Uncle Francis? What ails him?' Surely her uncle could not have got wind of this exploit.

'I don't rightly know, miss, but he's been demanding to see you this past hour. I said you were laid down with the headache. But he fell into such a tantrum that I'm afeared he'll be banging on your door before long and demanding to come in.'

'Then I must make sure I'm behind it when he arrives,' her mistress said, with a brightness she was far from feeling.

And before her maid had turned to lead the horse away, she was racing along the left hand passage, making for the concealed staircase.

Chapter Two

She had barely struggled out of the incriminating clothes and into her wrapper before there was a peremptory knock on the door and her uncle strode into the room. Lucinda tried to compose her face into one of suffering and hoped that her cheeks were not glowing too pinkly from the night time gallop. Francis Devereux planted his plump figure firmly by the window embrasure and stared at his niece.

'I understand from your maid that you have been indisposed. Did you not think to tell me? I waited dinner for at least half an hour.'

She should have remembered. Her uncle's mealtimes were sacrosanct and an attack on his food was an attack on him. 'I'm sorry, uncle. Molly was busy attending me else I would have sent her to you with a message.'

He harrumphed irritably. 'I trust her ministrations were successful. You are recovered?'

Lucinda decided that she had better be recovered. Even in the muted light of a branch of candles, she was looking far too healthy.

'Molly brewed me a wonderful concoction of her

mother's – Mrs Tindall is a genius – and since I have rested, the headache has vanished.'

Her uncle's small blue eyes peered at her short-sightedly. 'I'm glad to hear it. You certainly look well enough and it is most important that you do so.'

He began to pace up and down the room, the wooden floor occasionally creaking beneath his considerable weight. After a few minutes he stopped to face his niece and saw her puzzled expression. 'I wish you to look your very best.'

As an explanation it fell far short. Lucinda was beginning to think that perhaps her uncle had imbibed rather too heavily at dinner when he startled her by saying, 'As it happens, it is fortunate that he has not yet arrived – although I must say I find his tardiness difficult to understand.' Francis's tone was pettish and there was a frown on his face. 'I trust he will be with us tomorrow at the latest.'

'Who?'

'Do you never listen, Lucinda?'

She tried to look contrite but it was hard. She had no memory of a likely guest. In fact, guests at Verney Towers were as rare as hen's teeth and she could only imagine this was one of her uncle's little schemes. She seldom had time for them and tonight even less. Tonight she had almost been caught and the spectre of the gallows cast a dark shadow in her mind. She shivered as she thought of Black Jack's fate. She had risked the same terrifying destiny, but only to fail – her beloved twin was still imprisoned, still liable to succumb to illness or worse.

But she dared not allow her uncle to suspect for one

minute what she had been at and attempted to school her face to one of complacence. 'I'm sorry, Uncle Francis, you must have spoken of this some time ago and it has gone completely from my mind.'

If she humoured him sufficiently, he would go away. Reaction to her wild adventure was setting in and every limb felt leaden. Her wrist was throbbing more painfully than ever and her whole being felt as though weighted by iron. All she wanted was to sleep.

Her guardian shifted impatiently and when he spoke his tone was part irritation and part indulgence. 'I shall never understand how women can remember the precise shade of a ribbon, but ask them to remember something of importance and it is all hay with them.'

Lucinda felt indignation rising. Long ago she had come to the conclusion that her uncle was one of the most tiresome men she would ever meet: a combination of foolish pride and moral rectitude was not a happy one. But she needed to be rid of him and she forced herself to sound agreeable. 'Please remind me, uncle.'

'The Earl of Frensham is to visit us!' Francis Devereux said this with the air of a ring master about to produce his most celebrated lion.

'I see.' She knew her response was inadequate but her uncle appeared too absorbed by his own cleverness to remark on it.

He had resumed his pacing, the squeak of new boots now joining creaking floorboards in rampant disharmony. 'I received a message from Lord Frensham earlier today, but as I had no wish to unsettle you, I made no mention of it,' he said grandly.

You thought it best not to put me on my guard, Lucinda translated inwardly, but why her uncle had been so reticent she had no idea.

'The Earl of Frensham!' Sir Francis exclaimed again. 'Think of that. Such a splendid prize. It has taken a deal of time and persuasion to get him here, you know.'

Her head was buzzing. Her uncle's self-satisfaction was hardly new but what had this earl to do with her?

Sir Francis walked towards her. 'I won't hide the fact, neice, that on occasions I have not been entirely certain that it was the right path to pursue. I've had my doubts. Disquieting rumours from time to time, but they have turned out to be nothing but spiteful gossip – the usual scurrilous talk of the *ton* and I was right to dismiss them. All froth and no substance!' he finished triumphantly.

'So the earl is coming,' Lucinda ventured, hoping that her uncle would get off his chest what he needed to say and leave her in peace.

'He is. He is coming to meet you, my dear.'

'But he does not even know me.'

'Naturally he does not. That is why he is coming to Verney Towers – to make your acquaintance.' Her uncle's tone suggested a laudable patience in the face of a feeble mind.

'I am most flattered,' she managed, 'but why me?'

'Surely, Lucinda, you remember that much. His grandfather and my father made a promise to one another.'

She recalled hearing some such nonsense at the breakfast table one morning but she'd dismissed it as a triviality, unworthy of notice. Apparently her uncle was not of the same mind.

'If the old Earl of Frensham – that is the second earl – if he were to have a grandson and my father a granddaughter, they were to make a match of it.'

She stared in astonishment. 'But why?'

'It was their dearest wish that the two families should be joined. They were the very best of friends their entire lives.'

'It seems a little odd to be making plans for your grandchildren.' More than a little odd, she thought. 'What about *their* children – surely they would have fulfilled the family wishes much sooner?'

Her uncle looked fixedly at the floor. 'It pains me, as you well know, to talk of your mother. I believe the old earl's son proved similarly unreliable.'

'I'm sorry, Uncle Francis, but I still don't see what this has to do with me.'

Her uncle lifted his gaze. 'You are the granddaughter, of course.' He spoke slowly and emphatically, as though by intensifying every word, any objections would be blown away. 'I hope very much to see you marry into the Frensham family.'

'You wish me to marry an unknown man, years older than myself?' Truly her uncle had run mad.

'He is not old, foolish girl. He is the third earl and inherited the title and considerable estates when he was a very young man. He can be little more than thirty.'

'But I do not know him.' Lucinda realised she was repeating herself but felt too dazed to argue coherently.

'This is your opportunity to become acquainted. I

consider it a blessing that the two of you have not previously met. Your unspoilt charm will come as a delightful surprise, since he has been on the town for many years and suffered every kind of lure.'

Lucinda was too appalled to respond but it hardly mattered. Francis was in full flow. 'The earl is a very wealthy man.' He sounded inordinately proud of the fact. 'And has been much courted. I understand that he has grown tired of the attentions shown him. You have never mixed in high society and so will be the perfect antidote. His sisters – all three of them charming creatures – are as convinced as I that you will make an ideal couple.'

Are they indeed? And what about me, Lucinda wanted to yell. How ideal for me? I've no wish to wed – indeed, I loathe the very notion. But if I'm to be forced into marrying, how ideal is a man ten years older than me? One I have never met, a man who has scandal trailing his coat tails?

It was useless to argue, though. When Francis Devereux alighted on an idea, it would not be dislodged by even the mightiest earthquake.

Her uncle took her bowed head as acquiescence. 'I will not push you into any marriage you do not wish to make, Lucinda,' he said more amenably, 'but I will expect that you treat with courtesy a man who has travelled here to make your acquaintance.'

The door shut behind him and Lucinda sunk on to the bed, numbed by the string of disasters that had befallen her. Cherished hopes had been shattered tonight, a terrifying escape endured, and now the threat of an unknown husband had appeared out of nowhere, a poisonous cloud filling the air. Her uncle had said that he would not force her into an arranged marriage but she was not stupid. She would be pressured in all kinds of subtle ways, that was for sure. A man did not travel from London to be given a polite brush-off. He would expect an answer and in the affirmative.

'Is everything all right, Miss Lucy?' Molly had returned from the stables and was peering anxiously around the bedroom door.

'No,' she answered bluntly. 'My uncle wishes me to know that he has a guest arriving very shortly, a man I have never met but one I'm expected to greet with complaisance.'

'Does he come as a suitor?' the maid ventured.

'He may choose to call himself such. I do not. The idea is preposterous.'

'You may like him,' Molly said hopefully.

Lucinda was well aware of the romantic notions embedded in her maid's breast and tried to let her down gently. 'That is most unlikely. He will be as the rest of his tribe – wealthy, idle and over-indulged. From what Uncle Francis let slip, he may even be immoral.'

'That can't be true, miss. Sir Francis would never ask you to meet anyone disreputable.'

'I suppose you're right. My uncle is a puritan and if he has vetted and approved this man, he will be whiter than white and no doubt tedious beyond words. Prosy and dull. I shall probably fall asleep even as he talks to me.'

Before her mistress had stopped speaking, a sharp rap summoned Molly to the door. When she returned, it was to stammer, 'Your uncle has sent a message up, Miss Lucy. The gentleman has arrived.'

'Now! At this hour! What kind of person arrives at past ten in the evening?'

'I couldn't say for sure, but Sir Francis wants you dressed and downstairs immediately.' Molly opened a closet door as she spoke and considered the array of garments within.

'Shall I lay out the cream silk, miss? That compliments your skin beautifully. And we can do your hair *à la Meduse* – little ringlets, like so.' And she made a few passing feints in the air. 'I've been practising these past weeks and it shouldn't take long.'

Lucinda glared at her, shaking herself free of a depression that had begun to take strong hold.

'Lay out the drabbest gown you can find, Molly,' she commanded. 'And search for that dreadful shawl the vicar's wife gave me. I wish to look a complete dowdy! That should send him scuttling back to London in a hurry – he will want his money and title to buy something a great deal better than me.'

Chapter Three

When she saw who stood in the flagged hallway below, Lucinda almost turned tail and fled back to the sanctuary of her room. She faltered on the final two stairs and, but for her uncle's intervention, might have fallen. A state of frozen horror engulfed her. At this very moment she stood facing the man she had attempted to rob! She was incredulous, dumbfounded.

'Allow me to present my niece to you, Lord Frensham – Miss Lucinda Lacey.' Francis Devereux danced fussily around them. 'Lucinda, this is the Earl of Frensham.'

'Jack Beaufort,' he said, bowing low over her hand.

'My lord.'

Her tone was coldly formal and the curtsy she bobbed perfunctory. She was forcing herself to present an indifferent face but it was a titanic struggle. To maintain composure when her mind was besieged by terrors! Had he recognised her? She had recognised *him* immediately, but was it possible he saw in the badly dressed girl before him, the highwayman of a few hours ago? Please no, she prayed.

Slowly she emerged from the first sickening sense of shock and, under cover of her uncle's monologue, snatched a covert glance at their visitor. He wasn't what she'd expected. Nor, she was sure, what her uncle had expected. The man appeared completely at ease, his air of confidence pervading the vast hall and metaphorically rattling the suits of armour that punctuated its panelled walls in dreary sequence. Lucinda could see why he had overpowered her so easily, for though tall he was solidly built and his muscular form evidenced many hours of punishing sport.

Yet his dress was elegance incarnate, down to the last burnished tassel swinging from his gleaming hessians, and if not precisely handsome, he made a striking figure. A small scar punctured his left cheek and the way that a lock of dark hair fell across his brow almost meeting it, gave him the look of a pirate. He needed only the eye patch and he would be complete. Even his name – Jack Beaufort – had a piratical tang.

'We are delighted that you were able to visit, your lordship.' Francis Devereux oozed, his plump cheeks puffed with pride.

'I am delighted to be at Verney Towers and to make your acquaintance.' The words were right but the man's expression suggested otherwise. His was a smile of false pleasure, Lucinda decided.

'It is a great honour to welcome you to our house, Lord Frensham, no matter what the hour.'

Sir Francis, she noted, was unable to resist a rebuke even to his prize guest, but the earl seemed not to notice. 'I regret the necessity of arriving so late,' he said smoothly, 'but I was forced to hire a conveyance from The Four

Feathers, an inn a few miles from here.'

'Yes, yes,' Devereux said eagerly. 'We know The Feathers well. But why did you not continue the journey in your own carriage? I would have been more than glad to house your cattle.'

'That is most kind, Sir Francis, but unhappily it was not possible.' She saw a small smile appear at the corners of the earl's mouth and knew that he was enjoying himself. 'You see, I was set upon by a robber, a gentleman of the road as I believe they call themselves. He cut the traces and made it impossible for me to continue. I was forced to ride to the inn to secure help.'

'But that is dreadful.' Francis Devereux's face was stricken. 'Quite dreadful. A highwayman, you say. But we have not had highwaymen in Sussex for many a year.'

'You have one now,' the earl remarked laconically.

'But where did this dreadful event occur? Were you or your company hurt? What valuables were you forced to hand over?'

The questions rained down and Lucinda guessed their visitor was having to restrain himself severely from laughing aloud. The ambush had disturbed her uncle acutely and he had forgotten his society manners in the clamour to know every last detail.

'Please do not concern yourself. Nothing was taken and neither of us was hurt.'

'Neither?' Sir Francis looked puzzled.

'I was travelling alone except for my coachman.'

'Only a coachman!' This seemed to exercise the Honourable Francis even more than the attempted robbery.

'But my dear sir how could you be so imprudent?'

'Lynton, my valet, will follow in a day or so.'

Francis appeared to be working himself into a small paroxysm. 'This robbery – ' he began for the third or fourth time.

'Nothing was taken,' the earl reminded him.

'But it could have ended in disaster. We cannot have such a thing happening again, not in our quiet Sussex lanes.'

'In fact a quiet Sussex forest,' Jack interjected. Lucinda wondered if he was trying deliberately to annoy.

Sir Francis began to wring his hands. 'But to have this threat on our very doorstep...'

She could almost see Jack Beaufort sigh inwardly. His host was not going to let the matter rest. She was sure the man had mentioned his adventure to see its effect, no doubt a small amusement in a vale of tedium. But amusement was not now the first word that sprang to mind.

In an attempt to deflect his host, the earl said, 'I could always call in the Runners if you are seriously concerned. I have some small influence at Bow Street.'

The older man leapt upon the suggestion. 'Yes, Bow Street. That's the thing. I should be most grateful if you would do so, my lord.'

At these words, Lucinda felt her body stiffen. It was involuntary, the smallest of movements, and she prayed that her adversary had not noticed her recoil. She turned her head very slightly and met a pair of the deepest brown eyes. They wore a mere whisper of curiosity but they were fixed intently on her. He *had* noticed, she thought with misgiving, but what would he make of it?

~

It was clear that the girl had not liked the suggestion of a Runner. Jack could not imagine why that might be, but he'd hoped it might provoke her into speech. She had hardly said a word, standing mute and expressionless, beside her uncle. He was unused to such cavalier treatment, especially from a nondescript provincial. She was small and drab but what else had he expected? She appeared to be dressed in a brown sack for that was all he could call it: a shapeless, mud-coloured garment that looked as though it had been worn to clean the scullery. Beneath his fascinated gaze, she had pulled a shawl of the vilest magenta stripes more closely around her shoulders.

She appeared nervous, too, or so he'd first thought. That was hardly surprising, ill-dressed as she was and no doubt unused to company. She had almost tripped as she came down the stairs towards him. But straightening up from his bow, he'd been met by a pair of mutinous blue eyes. In the sparse candlelight of the bleak hall, they were pure sapphire. This was no shy ingénue, made uneasy by their meeting. Intrigued, he'd looked more intently at her. In response, she'd averted her glance and quite deliberately looked through him.

He had been taken aback. He had no intention of making her or anyone else an offer of marriage, but she could not know that. She would imagine he had come with courtship in mind and yet she was behaving as though he were the last man in the world she wanted to see. Miss Lacey was an enigma but there was something, too, that was strangely familiar about her. He couldn't put his finger on it.

Not that he wanted to since he was already cursing himself for having embarked on this journey. He must have been mad to agree to his sisters' suggestion. He'd risked robbery tonight – possibly worse – in order to visit a man he'd taken in immediate dislike and a girl who radiated disdain. Rescue could not come quickly enough. A fervid image floated in the air before him: Fielding racing his team of greys up the gravelled drive, halting the coach for a second only, while he leapt for its interior and made his escape. He could almost smell the cloud of dust.

He'd had to get out of town– that was clear enough. London was getting just a little too hot for him, the duel a step too far. And the constant scolding of his sisters had become intolerable. At the time it seemed a clever ploy, disappearing from London society for a few weeks to allow the gossip to quieten while at the same time fulfilling his family's wishes. But now it no longer seemed quite so clever. In fact, it was quite possibly one of the worst decisions he had ever made. The sooner he was on his way to Merry's and the congenial shooting party that awaited him, the better.

Verney Towers! The house was a barrack of a place, grandiose and uncomfortable in equal measure. Why had he allowed himself to be persuaded here? The scandal with Celia Burrage would have died a death soon enough. *Ton* gossip had a short life and after all he had done no more than many: his was not the first duel to be fought over an errant wife nor would it be the last. But in future he would eschew the married ladies of his acquaintance, accommodating though they were, and find his fun elsewhere. That shouldn't be too difficult. There were plenty of *chère amies* to keep the boredom at bay, barques of frailty more than willing to spend his money. As for his three taskmasters - he should be immune to his sisters' reproaches by now. That they should imagine he would honour some insane pledge of their grandfather's had seemed ridiculous when they'd told him. Now it left him speechless.

They would be rendered speechless, too, if they saw for themselves the bride they were proposing. It wasn't that she was bad looking. Indeed, he imagined that those eyes could be fascinating when they weren't so evidently affronted, and the straw blonde locks entrancing when not scraped into the most unbecoming bun he had ever seen. But they were of a piece with the rest of her appearance. Lucinda Lacey had made no attempt to attract, no attempt to interest or entice. Nothing, in short, that would persuade him to stay a minute longer than he had to. As soon as his travelling coach was roadworthy, he would make that escape.

Chapter Four

Lucinda woke early the next morning to the sound of creaks and rustlings as the old house settled itself to endure the coming winter. A sliver of bright light encircled the window frame and she threw back the curtains to a perfect autumn day. The sky was a blue sphere, untarnished by even a wisp of cloud. The air was still, the trees motionless, standing tall and proud, clothed in their last glowing leaves. It was a morning to be out, out and away from these musty walls and from the memory of yesterday's disasters.

She dared not think about Jack Beaufort and what he might do. If he were to recognise the figure that had ambushed him, she was powerless to save herself. He might have recognised her already – a splinter of fear pinched at her heart. He had certainly looked at her closely enough but that might have been simple curiosity. He would wish to inspect the woman his sisters were proposing he make his wife.

He must have suffered a gross disappointment. Even in her present dire situation, Lucinda had to chuckle at the likely effect of that hideous brown gown and the even more hideous shawl. If they had not completely repelled him, then her air of cold boredom should have completed the task.

She wished now that she hadn't acted quite so badly and not just because of her uncle's inevitable scolding. She had to confess that she found the earl fascinating. He was quite different from any man she'd ever met: he was fashionable, elegant, beautifully mannered. But then so were others. He was a rascal, she thought, that was what marked him out – the scar, those eyes, the wicked enjoyment of seeing Sir Francis and his pomposity deflate with fear. But she must tread warily: she must never forget that he could undo her at any moment. He might well hold her future in his hands.

But that of Rupert was in hers. She must plead with her uncle again to change his mind, to pay the money that would liberate her brother. It would be a final appeal to his affections, though in truth he had none. Once he had issued a decree, this soft and flaccid man was granite. Rupert had to be punished and more brutally than ever. Francis had failed to bring him to heel, to inculcate in him the imperative of family honour, and for that there could be no mitigation. It was terrifying to feel that she alone stood between her brother and an early death, but today was a morning to shake off such black thoughts. She would ride far and away and consign Francis, his house and his guest to oblivion.

⌒

In half an hour Lucinda was in the saddle and urging her mount along one of the chalk cart tracks which led to the Downs. The horse was in no mood to hurry and she had constantly to spur him forward. After her whirlwind ride last night, it felt unbearably slow. Once on the Downs, though, her mount grudgingly picked up speed until she was riding at full gallop along one of the highest ridges. In the translucent light of early morning she could see in the far distance the smudge of coastline. And the sea, a calm and fathomless mirror.

She galloped on until her breath was all but spent. Slowing to manoeuvre her way around a thicket of bushes, she heard hooves coming from the opposite direction. It was unusual to meet another rider on this vast expanse of downland, and particularly so early in the day. She dropped to a walk and rounded the bushes cautiously. Not cautiously enough for almost before she knew it, she had met the other rider head on. She began to apologise for her clumsiness but then found herself looking into the sardonic face of Jack Beaufort. Her apologies stuttered to a close.

'You!' she exclaimed ungraciously. 'What are you doing here?'

'Good morning, Miss Lacey. How delightful to meet you once more.' The irony was unmistakeable. 'You must forgive me for not realising that I was trespassing. I apologise for my ignorance.'

Lucinda's cheeks burned red. 'I am sure you know, Lord Frensham, that downland is rarely private. You startled me – I had not expected to see you here and so early.'

He sat back on his horse, perfectly at ease. Arrogantly at ease, she thought. The firm chin and the set mouth spoke a man who would not easily yield.

'My early ride can be simply explained. I could not sleep. I trust this is not an indelicate question, but does Verney Towers by chance play host to the spirit world?'

'There are no ghosts, if that's what you mean.'

'No murdered husbands or wives forever immured within its walls?'

'The house has led a blameless life.'

'Then the noises...?'

'It creaks and groans with changes in the weather.'

'How very disappointing! I have been imagining a hundred different tales, each of them more blood curdling than the one before.'

'The only death at the Towers is like to be from boredom,' she said tartly.

He could not prevent a grin lighting his face. 'And is that your opinion of Sussex society in general?'

'I imagine that society is everywhere much the same.' Lucinda's tone was dismissive.

'Where else have you known?' It was a sly question.

'I have lived a narrow and entirely parochial life, your lordship, as I'm sure you're aware. But I doubt that I would go on in London any differently than I do here.'

Jack's eyes gleamed with mischief. 'But if you have never partaken of London's attractions, how can you be sure?'

'I cannot, of course, but it is inevitable that given time they would pall.'

'In that case, let us do our small best to keep life's boredom at bay. I wonder if you would care to walk. The day is splendid and we ought not to waste it.'

She should ride on. Walking with him was dangerous, the

last thing she should do, but the grin had metamorphosed into the sweetest of smiles and Lucinda found herself acquiescing. He slid from his saddle and in seconds was at her side, helping her dismount. She was aware of the strong arm beneath her elbow, the strong fingers on hers, but she winced as his hand brushed against her wrist.

'You are hurt, Miss Lacey?'

There was a momentary pause before she replied. 'Yesterday I was in the garden and foolishly attempted to unearth a small bush without tools.'

'And what had the bush done to earn your displeasure?'

'It was in the wrong place,' she said shortly.

Jack gave a mock sigh. 'So often our troubles are down to that one small fact, don't you find – being in the wrong place?'

Lucinda gazed sharply at him, but his face was innocent of suspicion. She was tense, agitated, that was the trouble she chided herself, jumping at words that meant nothing.

They tethered the horses to the largest of the bushes and began to stroll along the ridge, their faces turned towards the sun with Lucinda always careful to keep her distance.

He appeared to ignore her deliberate aloofness, but his words when he spoke sounded a challenge. 'I hope that my visit has not incommoded you.'

'My uncle's guests rarely disturb me.' That was true since visitors were unknown at Verney Towers, but she had not meant to speak so rudely. She felt flustered and uncomfortable and had no idea why.

'I am greatly relieved,' he said, but the wry pull of his mouth undermined the sentiment. 'My stay will be brief, but I would not wish you inconvenienced.'

'How brief?'

The bald question left him unfazed. 'If I'd not had the misfortune to meet with some desperado on the road, I would even now be in the next county, enjoying the company of Lord Merrington and his friends.'

Was his mention of a desperado a tease? Had he guessed? Lucinda's heart was in her mouth and she dared not look at him, dared not speak since she knew she would be unable to keep the tremble from her voice. The only sound was the soft swishing of her skirts against the tufted grass. If only she had not chosen him of all people to rob...

'I am sorry your plans have gone awry,' she managed at last, 'but if your intention was to stay only one night with us, it seems hardly worth your while to call.' Once more she was sounding ungracious. No better than a badly raised schoolgirl, she thought.

'I would not be so harsh, Miss Lacey. If I had not called at Verney Towers, I would have forfeited the pleasure of meeting you and your esteemed uncle.' His voice was bland, but when she shot a glance at him she saw that his eyes sparkled with enjoyment.

He continued to talk, his voice smooth as caramel. 'My sisters, too, will be delighted to hear that I have called. They wished me to make your acquaintance and, as I planned to travel to Hampshire, it needed only a small diversion to find my way here.'

'I do not know your sisters, Lord Frensham, and cannot imagine why they were eager for you to meet me.'

'It is hard to credit, but their eagerness sprang from

some ridiculous story they were told. They had it from a very old aunt who died quite recently. I wonder if you have heard the same tale.'

'Are you referring to our grandfathers and the promise they made to each other?'

'Precisely. It is a fantasy, and maudlin beyond belief. But for some reason the story has taken hold of their imaginations and they will not let it go.'

The story *was* maudlin and should be buried as quickly as possible. For the first time since they'd met, Lucinda felt in charity with him. 'I fear that Uncle Francis is as enthusiastic as your sisters,' she was moved to confess.

He pushed the stray lock of hair from his forehead in an impatient gesture and she saw that he was frowning. 'It is amazing, is it not, that otherwise sensible people should concern themselves with such flummery? Such a proposition belongs to the last century – two people who have not a thought in common, to be pushed together only because their families wish to be united.'

'I believe that many people still find arranged marriages acceptable.' Lucinda did not intend to be too much in charity with him.

'That may be so, but I am not one of them.'

'Then you did not come as a suitor?'

'No, I did not,' he said gently. 'I hope that doesn't disappoint you. But from our brief acquaintance, I imagine not.' There was the shadow of a smile on his face.

It did not disappoint. Of course it did not. The last thing Lucinda wanted was to be forced into allying herself with a stranger – allying herself with anyone. If she were ever tempted to consider matrimony, she had only to remember her mother's history for the temptation to vanish as swiftly as morning dew. But still, in the back of her mind, there was a small wistful thought: Jack Beaufort would make a handsome husband. She felt unbearably confused.

'So why did you come – if you consider the story nonsense?' she blurted out.

'I confess that my visit was simply to stop my sisters' infernal nagging.'

'And will it?'

'I doubt it. Their mission is to find a wife for me and they seem unable to resist any opportunity. But by calling on you, I have done as they asked, and that surely must count for something.'

They had left the pathway and were strolling freely across the cropped grass, the sun warm on their faces. He was walking closer now and Lucinda was sharply aware of his proximity: the powerful athleticism of his figure, the lean, tanned face, the mocking dark eyes. She wished that she wasn't enjoying his company quite so much. Then she sensed he was watching her intently and the spell was broken. He was assessing her, appraising her, she thought indignantly. It was time to cause him discomfort if she could.

'I am beholden to my uncle for a home, your lordship, but you are free and independent. I cannot imagine why you would bend so easily to your sisters' demands.'

The slur on his manhood was brushed aside. 'That is because you have never met them. Georgina, the eldest, is overbearing and not easily gainsaid. Hester's ceaseless complaining drives me to distraction and now Maria has joined forces with them and, in the gentlest way possible, has indicated she wishes very much that I will soon bring a wife into the family. Together they are a formidable army.'

'Would it not be easier therefore to settle on a bride of your own choosing? I understand from my uncle that you have the pick of London beauties.'

'Surely Sir Francis could not be guilty of such vulgarity!'

Her unguarded remark had met the derision it deserved and she was left feeling gauche. But after several minutes he appeared to relent and stopping close, a pair of candid brown eyes fixed her with their gaze.

'I see I must make a full confession. The truth is, Miss Lacey, I have no intention of ever marrying. My sole hope in coming here was to secure a breathing space before the next onslaught.'

She looked up at him, wrinkling her nose in disbelief. 'It sounds as though you are fighting a battle.'

'It feels so. You have not experienced the full ferocity of a London Season, I believe, or you would understand.'

'I am grateful to my uncle for sparing me that at least. But I think you protest too much. I understand you are a grand matrimonial prize and courted avidly. It seems you cannot be that averse to *ton* circles.'

The earl shrugged his shoulders impatiently. 'You have that from your uncle, too, I imagine. What other morsels has he seen fit to communicate?'

'Only that your name is often linked to others. Would it not be sensible to marry one of your devotees as soon as possible?'

The grin was back but he schooled his voice to sound reproving. 'You really shouldn't listen to gossip, Miss Lacey. Come, we must walk on. The sun is warm enough but it doesn't do to be standing too long.'

They turned their steps and began heading back to the waiting horses. An unspoken accord had been reached and, this time, they walked together along the same path. It was rough and uneven in places with small clusters of broken chalk scattered at random and Lucinda unbent sufficiently to let him take her arm and steer her expertly over the crumbling stones.

'I could ask you the same question, you know.' Her brows rose enquiringly. 'Why not simply choose one of your admirers and marry him? It would stop your uncle importuning you further.'

'I have no admirer, Lord Frensham, nor do I wish for one.'

'Forgive me, but does that not augur a lonely future?'

'I shall not be lonely.' Her tone was defiant. 'I intend to live with someone dear to me.'

Lucinda had not meant to say as much and the earl immediately pounced. 'If he is not to be a husband, who is this mysterious person? I'm intrigued.'

Her answer was as brief as she could make it. 'My brother, Rupert.'

'I see.' But it was evident he didn't since he looked genuinely puzzled. 'And where is brother Rupert?'

She could not answer him directly, but said in a confident voice, 'He will be home very soon. And when he comes, we will make our plans.'

'Won't your brother have his own ideas of marriage?'

'No,' she said decidedly. 'Rupert and I are twins. We have always shared our lives and always will.'

'Then Rupert is a lucky man.'

They had reached the tethered horses and Lucinda knew she had stayed too long. Jack Beaufort was an attractive man, she acknowledged, but that was all. His confession that he was not about to make her an offer of marriage was a huge relief, one concern less, but he could still prove dangerous. She was sure now that he had not recognised her as his attacker, but at any moment she might give herself away without realising. Her safest path was to keep well clear of him. Safest for all kinds of reasons: the unexpected pleasure she'd felt in his company was a warning and she should heed it.

'I must return to the house and speak to my uncle,' she said quickly. 'But I wish you enjoyment of your ride.' She glanced across at the stolid beast belonging to Sir Francis. 'Though you might find it something of a struggle, I fear.'

The pirate's grin was back. 'You speak truly, Miss Lacey. A bigger sluggard you could not find.'

Chapter Five

The encounter had given Jack much to ponder. He could hardly believe the girl he'd met this morning was the one who had stood dumb and drab at her uncle's side last night. He wasn't sure what game she was playing but when he'd literally bumped into her, he'd been staggered at the transformation. A shapely figure had been shown to perfection by the close-fitting riding costume she wore – the dress of sapphire velvet a perfect foil for the cornflower blue of her eyes. Her complexion, untouched by any trick of the hand, was smooth and clear, delicately flushed from the morning ride, while wisps of golden hair escaped from a Glengary cap of blue satin. She was quite lovely – what a revelation!

Lovely and spirited, he thought, as he rode slowly back to the house. She was no simpering miss for sure: her eyes could dance with mischief and she was capable of the sharpest retort. When she'd thought herself being forced into an unwanted liaison, she had fought hard and he couldn't blame her; he knew how it felt to do battle with an intransigent family. Once she'd realised that she was safe from the threat of matrimony, she had relaxed into a different girl. He had enjoyed her company and found himself wanting more. But he should nip in the bud any interest she aroused, for spirited though she was, she was also young and inexperienced and no match for a worn lover such as he.

He wondered where the years had gone since Julia had left him humiliated. Years spent in every kind of sport. In travelling, drinking, gambling. In careless affairs. Not one of those so-called friendships had been meaningful. And here he was at thirty, still escaping the noose his sisters intended, still unable to put the past behind him. He gave himself a mental shake, keen to banish the shroud of gloom that had settled on his shoulders. He must make for Merry's as soon as he was able. He was missing all the fun.

Or was he? The gathering would be like every other exclusive house party he'd attended in the last eight years: he would play the congenial guest among the men, the attentive swain with the ladies, and return to London as bored as he'd arrived. The attraction of Hampshire did not seem quite so strong now and he fell to wondering why. Was it the girl? Had she got under his skin without his realising it? She was a beauty beneath that nonsense of last night, and she intrigued him. This business about living with her brother – but that would die a natural death when either or both decided on marriage.

There was more though. He sensed an unease that lay just below the surface of life at Verney Towers. The house was spartan, lacking all comfort, lonely too. Lucinda appeared to live a solitary life, her uncle enclosed in his own small world and her brother nowhere to be seen.

There had been something in her manner when she spoke of her twin that suggested trouble. That made him curious.

∽

The horses in the stable block whinnied softly as they picked up the sound of his approach. Only a single lad was at work, busily washing down the cobbled yard.

'Did you enjoy your ride, my lord?' he asked cheekily.

'No, I did not. There was never a more stubborn beast.' He slipped from the saddle.

'He has his notions, like his master.'

Jack thought it best not to enquire too closely of the boy's meaning. He pulled a cigarillo from his inside pocket and lit it with a sigh of contentment. The smoke curled upwards in the clear air and he stood for a while, leaning against the warm wood of the stable shutter. As always, smoking helped him think. What had possessed Francis Devereux to invite him when he must have known that his niece would react with hostility? Did the man genuinely believe in a foolish promise made years ago, or was his invitation more practical than that?

Lucinda Lacey had never been to London it seemed, never enjoyed a Season or had the chance of finding a suitable husband. Was the baronet hoping to marry his niece off with the least amount of trouble? If so, the man must have been delighted to receive Georgina's letter. Jack cursed his elder sister for her interference. She had always been too keen on minding other people's business and Hester had happily joined forces with her, chorusing together that their brother must marry, and marry soon to ensure the succession.

At an early age they had willingly agreed to the matches arranged for them, and had little understanding of their brother's revulsion at being bound to a woman he hardly knew. Now Maria had joined the fray. In her gentle way she had taxed him for showing no interest in the young women he'd met or at least not the kind of interest that led to wedlock. What could be better, she'd said in her soft, die-away voice, than to bring two old families together by choosing this young, unspoilt girl who had known nothing but a quiet country life?

The lad had almost finished rubbing down Sir Francis's mount and Jack sauntered towards him, gesturing at the row of partitions. 'You run a small stable.'

'Three horses, sir. Enough for me.'

'Three? Where is the third?'

'She's a little shy.'

Jack craned his neck and glimpsed a half-hidden stable at the far end of the long building. He walked towards it: an odd circular wooden door appeared to have been cut into its furthest white-washed wall.

'Where does that strangely shaped door lead?'

'I don't rightly know, sir. It's been locked since I started here.'

But it was the horse that interested Jack. He would have liked a choice of mount this morning but had been given none. 'What's her name?'

'That'll be Red. She's a real beauty. Belongs to Mr Rupert.'

Rupert Lacey's name seemed inseparable from this morning's conversations.

'Mr Rupert is Miss Lucinda's brother, I collect.'

'Yessir.'

'He lives here?'

'Not at the moment 'e don't,' the boy said carefully.

Jack knew better than to press a servant who, it was clear, had no wish to talk, so he said nothing but walked slowly towards the far stable and leaned over its open door.

The boy was right. The horse *was* a beauty. A tall chestnut mare, coat gleaming even in the weak October sun, and a soft white blaze down the centre of her forehead lending her the look of a magical creature.

A white blaze. Something rattled his memory. A clearing, a white diamond-shape blaze on a chestnut horse – moonlight silvering horse and rider. Surely not! This could not be the highwayman's mount! Yet when he looked closer, he was almost certain that she was. Jack's mind began to race, searching for an explanation. Had the mare been stolen in order to perpetrate the crime? But how do you steal a horse from private land, ride her like the wind, and then restore her to the stables without anyone being the wiser? It was hardly possible. More likely it was a member of the household – a servant, a groom perhaps? But who would have been so audacious and why?

He turned to the boy. 'How many grooms work here?'

'Jus' me, sir, with these horses. Dexter's the coachman but the carriage horses are kept in a different block t'other side of the house and 'e sleeps above their stable.'

So if a servant had staged a brazen attack, it would have had to be this boy and that seemed impossible. He gave the lad a small coin for his time and began to walk towards the house, eager to regain his room and think through the conundrum. As he walked, he extinguished his cigarillo and buried the butt in his pocket. His fingers touched something soft – a handkerchief? No. He brought the article into the light. A piece of lace torn from the ruffle of a shirt.

He stood stock still, his brain once more churning. It was a man's shirt but a gentleman's, not a stable boy's. A gentleman from Verney Towers. Apart from Francis Devereux, there wasn't one. Did Lucinda have a secret admirer who took to the road for fun? Hadn't he said to Fielding that he thought the ambush had been a jape gone wrong? But Lucinda had been adamant that no lover existed and, truth to tell, he could hardly imagine a foolhardy youth as her admirer. She was too careful, too considered in her dealings with men. He remembered the way she had pulled away when he'd touched her wrist.

Her right wrist! She had winced from an earlier injury, from pulling a recalcitrant bush from the ground, she'd said. But was that a cock and bull story? What if it had been her wrist that he'd grasped last night? If so, it would explain the fleeting sense of familiarity he'd experienced at their first meeting. The thought sent shock waves through him. He refused to believe it. What possible reason could she have to run such an appalling risk?

Once in his room, he spread his long form on the bed, thinking hard. Lucinda Lacey as his assailant! It was a ridiculous proposition: she was a lady. Ladies of his acquaintance might do many questionable things but holding up a coach wasn't one of them. He sat upright

– there was a way to find out. It wasn't only the scrap of lace that he'd picked up after his unknown attacker had disappeared into the night. He'd retrieved the gun and he had it still. He had been curious about it from the start, certain that it was a duelling pistol. If it was, it would be part of a pair, belonging to – not her, for sure, but this brother? Quite possibly.

He drew the weapon from the pocket of his travelling cape and took it to the light. It was as he'd remembered: the pistol sported a most intricate decoration, a crown in the shape of acanthus leaves. It looked like a family crest though not the Devereux emblem which was blazoned on every spare surface of Verney Towers. Did it perhaps belong to the Lacey family? In any case, it was not a gun that was easily replicated. If he found its companion here in this house, he would know almost certainly that the incredible was true. But then what would he do?

Chapter Six

Lucinda changed rapidly out of her riding dress, intent on seeking an interview with her uncle before luncheon. The darkest of clouds remained in her life but one threat at least had been removed: Jack Beaufort had no intention of pressuring her into marriage. In fact, he had no wish to marry at all. He had been candid and honest and Lucinda liked that in him. She wondered if he'd be as direct with her uncle or simply depart the Towers, thanking his host for a pleasant stay. Either way Sir Francis would be furious – he would not easily accept having his scheme frustrated.

The door to the library stood ajar and Lucinda slipped quietly into the room. Her uncle was dozing fitfully by a roaring fire but looked up as he heard her footsteps.

'What is it?' He sounded querulous and she feared she had chosen the wrong moment to make her appeal. 'I am about to write letters before lunch, Lucinda. You must come back later.'

There seemed little sign of this activity and she decided she would not be shrugged aside. Taking one of the room's least comfortable chairs, she sat ramrod straight facing her guardian.

'Uncle Francis, I wish to speak to you.'

His small blue eyes cast a baleful look. 'Indeed? Do you not think that *my* interests should come first? I have been wishing to speak to *you* on a matter of grave concern.'

She felt the stirrings of unease but counselled herself to be patient. Her uncle glowered at her for some minutes, fidgeting restlessly with the rings on his plump fingers, but at last he announced, 'I desire an explanation.'

'An explanation of what?'

'You dare to ask! After your disgraceful conduct last night!'

Lucinda was taken aback since she'd completely forgotten her first meeting with Jack Beaufort. In retrospect, her behaviour appeared horribly childish – it must be why she'd erased the encounter from her mind.

Her uncle's voice took on a cold anger. 'Did I not request that you look your very best when our guest arrived? Did I not ask you to meet him with courtesy and make him welcome? And what did you do but dress yourself quite deliberately in the most appalling gown you could find and then follow that outrage by treating him with unfeigned rudeness.'

Her uncle was prone to exaggeration but she could not deny his accusations. Every word he said was true and all Lucinda could do was keep silent and hope the storm would pass. But Sir Francis had more complaints. 'Not content with your shameful behaviour last night, you appear this morning to have abandoned Lord Frensham to his own devices.'

'I think you will find that the earl is as comfortable with

his own company as I am with mine,' she said levelly.

But her guardian was not listening. 'You made up your mind to dislike the man before he ever set foot in the door and you have conducted yourself towards him most shabbily. I did not expect it from you.'

Lucinda felt a stab of guilt. 'I'm sorry to have upset you, uncle. I may have behaved stupidly but the truth is that Lord Frensham and I would never suit.'

'How can you decide such a thing when you hardly know the man?'

'I do not need to know him. I'm sufficiently aware of the circles he moves in to recognise that I could never be happy with such a life. I don't accuse his lordship of personal involvement but his peers are the very people who helped Rupert to his ruin and I cannot imagine, uncle, why you should wish me to make a match with such a one.'

Sir Francis had risen from his chair and was stomping around the library, pacing to the window and back, shuffling papers on his desk as he passed and moving books from one shelf to another. Finally he stopped and faced her once more, his face mottled with vexation.

'You will have to marry, Lucinda. Is it not better that you secure for yourself a life of ease than be doomed to penury by wedding a half-pay soldier?'

She knew his thoughts were with his dead sister, that once beloved girl, who had abandoned everything including her life, to marry against her family's wishes.

'I understand your concern for me,' Lucinda said as mildly as she could, 'but I've no wish to marry, uncle, no wish at all.'

His face grew even redder. 'You must marry! You must forget this nonsense of setting up home with your brother. Rupert is a wastrel and always will be.'

His words stung but they also stiffened her resolve. She *would* live with Rupert one day and try in whatever way she could to compensate him for the unkindness he'd suffered at the hands of his family. But at this moment she could not allow herself to be deflected: she must make her plea even though it was likely to be futile.

'I know you consider Rupert to be a lost cause, Uncle Francis, and I know that in the past he has given you reason to think so, but –'

'He has – in full - and there is no more to be said.'

'I think there is. I must talk to you about him.'

'I will say only this, Lucinda, and then we will never speak of it again. While Rupert was a minor, I did all in my power to save the honour of the family – and to save *his* honour. Unhappily I failed. Now I consider my task at an end and I refuse to be troubled further.'

'You have been very good, uncle, more than good,' she soothed, well aware that for years he had treated her brother harshly and any benevolence her uncle had shown had sprung from inflated family pride rather than affection. 'You have done all you possibly could to keep Rupert on the right path.'

'And received scant gratitude! He has reached the age of majority and must now be responsible for his actions. It is quite simple.'

Lucinda's eyes were wide and pleading. She took a step towards her guardian, her hands raised in supplication.

'I'm sorry that I disobeyed you in going to London against your wishes but I had to see my brother. He is my twin and whatever he has done, I love him dearly. What I saw broke my heart. The prison is cold and dank and the treatment he receives severe. The stark loneliness of his life is more than any gently born soul can bear. If you would but see him, you would understand.'

'He has a lesson to learn and that is that he must live within his means.'

'I am sure he has learned it. Will you not reconsider your decision? If he needs further punishment, there must be other ways – but please, please, allow him to come home.'

'If he suffers, it is right that he should do so. He will be released in due time.'

'His release may come too late. Think how you will feel if that is so.'

'You have an unfortunate tendency to dramatise, my dear. Rupert Lacey is where he should be. Decency has not worked to make him an honourable man. Incarceration might.'

'But uncle –'

'No more! I have no wish to continue this conversation and no wish to speak of your brother again. While you live under my roof, Lucinda, you will observe my prohibition.'

Her uncle was immovable. As so often in the past she marvelled at the strange mix that was Francis Devereux: on the one hand a man willing to spend his fortune on the pleasures of life, fastidious in his choice of dress and food. On the other, a stiff and unyielding moralist, a man steeped in tradition for whom family honour was paramount.

Rupert had transgressed and was beyond forgiveness.

Not that her brother would care. The Devereux family meant nothing to him – he'd said often enough that, as Laceys, they did not belong. Without a doubt he'd been made to feel so from a very young age, punished for every small infraction of the rules, unjustly accused of every misdemeanour. Lucinda had tried very hard to protect him from their guardian's punitive regime but rarely succeeded. Realistically, in a world of powerful adults how could one young child protect another? But the knowledge that she had failed him was always with her.

She must not fail him now in the greatest crisis of his life. He had escaped Verney Towers and its petty rules as soon as he could, but it had been an escape to disaster. Uncle Francis, and their grandparents before him, had suffered a pathological fear that Rupert would follow in his father's footsteps and year after year had tried to beat the Lacey out of him. By all accounts, Eliot Lacey rarely had a feather to fly with and was more than happy to bleed anyone who came his way.

But the beatings hadn't worked. Rupert had become as big a gambler as ever Captain Lacey had been, though Lucinda knew that unlike his father he took little real pleasure in the turn of the dice. He'd gravitated to the tables because they represented rebellion and freedom rather than easy money. Yet there was enough of his father in him to keep him playing, even in the face of abject failure. Despite brutal punishment, Rupert had remained stubbornly a Lacey.

Chapter Seven

In low spirits she made her way to the dining room as the last chimes of the gong echoed through the cavernous hall. Their guest was already enthroned at one end of the massive black oak table. The room's velvet furnishings, once a majestic red, were now sad and faded and Jack Beaufort presented an enticing contrast. He had changed his riding dress to a coat of blue superfine, its cut expertly moulded across a pair of powerful shoulders, and his legs, when he rose to greet her, encased in a pair of tight-fitting fawn pantaloons. There were few men who could look as good in such revealing dress. He smiled lazily at her and unexpectedly she found herself flushing.

She hoped her uncle had not noticed her embarrassment but she need not have worried. Sir Francis had his attention firmly on the table as dish after laden dish arrived from the kitchens. For the baronet luncheon was not the usual modest meal and for some minutes he was wholly engaged in satisfying his appetite. Only after he had made his way through a considerable amount of food did he feel ready to converse.

'This is fine beef. It comes, you know, from a farm not

ten miles away – George Rutland's place. Do you have property in Sussex, Lord Frensham?'

Her uncle knew down to the last squire who held land in his home county, but he would be eager, Lucinda thought, for the earl to enumerate his vast possessions.

Their guest, though, was not playing the game. 'I own nothing in the county. In fact I have rarely visited Sussex.'

'Perhaps because it lies so close to London? That is most understandable. You have a splendid London house, I believe. In Grosvenor Square, is it not?' Sir Francis sat back and waited to be told of its glories.

'My home is not in Grosvenor Square. I live in Half Moon Street'.

His host looked shocked. 'But is it wise to leave such a beautiful house empty?'

'It's not empty,' the earl answered cheerfully. 'My sister, Lady Bessborough, fills the house with her four children. As a bachelor, I'm happy with something a little less grand.'

Francis was temporarily silenced by the need to taste several of the new dishes that had arrived at the table. When he spoke again, it was to say smugly, 'Of course, you will not have much of a garden in Grosvenor Square.'

The earl seemed disinclined to quarrel with this and his host went on, 'We have some splendid grounds at the Towers, you know – parkland which stretches for miles, a fine terraced garden and any number of succession houses.' He wiped his lips in satisfaction. 'Why do you not take a walk? The weather remains fair and I know that Lucinda will be pleased to accompany you and explain all that we are doing here.'

The earl had long since finished eating and seemed glad to rise from the table. 'It sounds a most delightful way to spend an afternoon.' His smile was only slightly wry as he bowed graciously in Lucinda's direction. 'If you are ready, Miss Lacey, shall we go?'

Beneath her uncle's implacable gaze, she had little choice but to surrender her seat and take the proffered arm.

The couple strode in silence towards the honey-coloured terrace at the rear of the mansion. Francis Devereux would waste no opportunity to throw them together, Jack thought, no matter how distasteful his niece might find it. No doubt the gardens were another step in his campaign. He felt sorry for the girl; sorry for himself. They had been put in an impossible situation.

'Your uncle was right – you have a magnificent estate. I can see why he was so insistent that we take a walk.'

Lucinda ignored his irony and said instead, 'My uncle is very proud of Verney Towers. You may have noticed.' There was only the slightest tinge of acid in her voice.

'He has every right to be proud,' Jack said dishonestly. 'It is a beautiful old house and surrounded by splendid countryside.'

She wrinkled her nose and he found it oddly charming. 'I might agree with you on the countryside, but the house could never be called beautiful. You flatter us, I think.'

'I never flatter, Miss Lacey.'

'I cannot imagine that is so or else how could you have made so many conquests?'

He did not feel sorry for her at all, he decided. She was

abominable.

'Whatever you may have heard will be an exaggeration. And I thought we'd agreed that gossip should be ignored.'

She let go of his arm and smoothed out her skirts of patterned muslin. She was looking as fetching as she had this morning, he noticed, a rich blue ribbon threaded through blonde curls and a blue velvet tippet around her shoulders. Yesterday's hideous rags had seemingly been consigned to the bonfire.

'You agreed. In any case I am not interested in gossip, but I do value the truth. I'm wondering why it is now that you've decided to visit us, Lord Frensham, since your sisters must have told you that silly story about our families quite some months ago.'

'I believe I mentioned that I was driving to Hampshire.'

'On the way to a country house party, yes, but I imagine you must attend many such gatherings not a million miles from Sussex. So why come to us now?'

He smothered a sigh; she was far too perceptive. 'Strictly in the interests of truth, I admit that this journey was convenient. Life in London was proving a trifle difficult.'

'Life – or was it a woman?'

The conversation was becoming more indecorous by the minute, but he still found himself answering. 'Yes. A lady.'

'A woman,' Lucinda said firmly. 'What happened?'

'Her husband happened.'

If he were to speak honestly, she might as well know the worst. There was a strange sense of satisfaction in for once talking candidly to a female, but he waited in some trepidation for her next question.

'Do you often have to deal with irate husbands?'

'No, I do not! This time I may have allowed myself to be pulled in a little too far and –why am I telling you this?'

'You are telling me because we've decided on the truth.' She pointed to the short scar on his left cheek. 'Did you get that from a similar "happening"?'

'I was foolish enough to walk down an unlit Venetian alley some years ago – I owe it to footpads, not an enraged spouse.'

'Then you escaped lightly. It must have been a most dangerous situation.'

'It was – particularly for them. Though I believe the canal was not overly deep and preferable, I imagine, to my sword. '

'And is it a duel that you've just fought – I mean with the angry husband?'

'You are far too inquisitive, not to mention brazen.'

'It's only right that I should know the kind of suitor my uncle is so eager for me to accept. He has been worrying over your moral suitability until your sisters put his mind at rest. Now if he'd been privy to this conversation...'

'I cannot pretend to be proud of the life I've led. But neither do I feel undue guilt. There are ladies,' Jack said carefully, 'certain ladies, who need little flattery or persuasion to extend their hand in friendship.'

'I am not so innocent that I don't know something of the world. I believe they are what Rupert calls lady-birds.'

He supposed he should look shocked but he wanted to laugh. 'Rupert may call them so, but you should not.'

'What should I call them then?'

'You should not know about them.'

'That is ridiculous.'

He had to agree but thought it wise to steer the conversation into safer channels. They had reached the small archway at one end of the terrace and strolled through into the rose garden. The central fountain had been shut down for the winter and there were gaps here and there where plants had died or bushes lost their leaves. The weather, though, was still mild for late October and a sprinkling of blooms added colour to the grey flint walls.

'This must be a wonderful retreat in high summer – the sound of tumbling water and the sweetness of so many flowers.'

He sensed her quick glance and saw that she was looking surprised. Evidently gossip had not credited him with an appreciation of nature. She bent down to sniff at a last apricot bloom. 'Do you grow roses on your estate? This is a Buff Beauty – it still smells divine.'

'I've tried to create something similar at Beaufort Hall, but in comparison my rose garden lacks maturity even though the Somerset climate is temperate. And the manor house in Yorkshire will never match the exacting standards of the Towers, I fear. It is situated on a hill and exposed to every extreme element.'

'Do you enjoy having so many properties?'

'I've never really thought about it,' he confessed.

'I suppose that comes of being rich.' It was clear that she set little store by this and the conversation limped to a close. He hoped they could talk more for she was delightfully unusual: though she had a face and a figure that seduced, she had a mind to match.

His hope was realised when they headed towards the cluster of hot-houses which lay on the far side of the rose garden and she threw him a challenge. 'I must pick flowers for the church today. Are you likely to be of any help?'

'I doubt that flower picking is one of my better skills.'

'What are then?'

'I can box.'

Lucinda could not prevent a giggle. 'I can't see flower arranging being the greatest use in the ring. But where do you box?'

'At Jackson's saloon in Bond Street.'

'Rupert followed the Gentleman's career with great interest, although my uncle never allowed him to go to a prize fight. I know for a fact, though, that he sneaked away several times when the rumour of a likely meeting reached him.'

Her brother seemed a continuing presence, though as yet there had been no sign of him. 'Was he permitted any sport?' Jack asked curiously.

'He wanted to learn to fence but our grandparents thought it dangerous. Do you?'

'Do I fence? Yes, frequently – at Angelo's. One never knows when skill with the sword will come in useful,' he added wickedly. Then seeing her reproving expression, hurried to say, 'I compete in curricle races, too, and that is one of the roughest of sports!'

'Then flowers will make an agreeable change.'

The succession houses were everything that the mansion was not – freshly painted, brightly lit and warm. Inside swathes of pelargoniums, fuchsias and heliotrope filled the space with such brilliant colour that he blinked, but it was their overwhelming perfume that caught him in their toils and played on his senses. He was filled with a mad desire to press Lucinda to him and dance with her around the flower-filled space.

His companion was not so easily distracted. 'We must pick quickly before Latimer discovers us. He is the head gardener and considers everything he grows to be his and his alone.'

Jack tried to do as she asked but her nimble fingers had filled two trugs to the brim before he'd managed to gather even a puny handful of chrysanthemums. 'Do we drive them to the church or does the coachman also have a proprietorial attitude?'

She looked at him astonished. 'I'd not call out the coachman to take a few handfuls of flowers little more than a mile. You are spoilt, my lord.'

'Evidently,' he murmured, picking up the heaviest basket. 'Show me the way, Miss Lacey.'

Jack Beaufort was not addicted to walking and his town attire was hardly suitable for a rural hike; he could only hope that his hessians would survive. They were already beginning to lose their champagne sparkle and a tramp along a dusty lane was unlikely to improve them. But he was enjoying himself far more than he'd thought possible.

༄

The village of Verney turned out to be very neat and very small: a cluster of white washed cottages around the green, a solitary shop which sold everything from shepherds' smocks to a side of ham – and a church. It was Norman in design, its square tower looking proudly over the Sussex countryside, and its flint walls cradling several vividly stained glass windows. Once through the huge oak door, the contrast in light was stark and for a moment he was blinded by the gloom. But as they walked towards the altar, pools of coloured light lit their way and the scent of flowers filled the air. He slid into a pew and watched as she arranged the blooms.

'Do all the flowers come from the house?'

'The cottagers provide them when they can, but it's more important for them to grow vegetables that they can eat.'

'And you do this regularly? The church flowers, I mean.'

She straightened up as she put the last vase to rights. 'When you live in a village, Lord Frensham, there are obligations.' Her tone was crisp and it was clear that she considered him incurably selfish.

'It's a very attractive village, a very attractive part of the country,' he said placatingly.

'There's a splendid view from the church tower. If you have a head for heights, that is. When the air is as clear as it is today, it's possible to see to Climping and the coast.'

The last thing he wanted to do was to climb steep stairs, but he responded gallantly to the invitation. 'What an excellent suggestion. Will you accompany me?'

If he were sensible, he would have cut their walk as short as possible. Her uncle had thrown them together but that didn't mean he had to go along with it. It would be better by far if he did not. But the sight of her slender, young figure in the simple sprig muslin, concentrating so hard on her task, had filled him with an unknown pleasure. He found that he wanted to stay longer with her.

Chapter Eight

Lucinda led the way up the spiral stone staircase. It was a climb of at least two hundred steps and, by the time they reached the square turret, her eyes were sparkling with the effort. He clambered up the last few stairs and joined her on the tower. Despite the steep climb, neither was out of breath and they looked at one another with respect.

'You did well, Lord Frensham. Normally visitors to the church need reviving by the time they make the tower roof.'

'I do my best. But after sharing such a punishing experience, do you not think you could call me Jack?'

'Jack,' she said experimentally. 'Is your name not James?'

'It is – James Mountford Gillespie Beaufort. But I answer to Jack.'

She looked at his powerful form, the glint in his eyes, the scar which enhanced rather than marred his face. 'I can see why,' she decided.

They walked to one side of the tower and looked out over the crenellated wall towards a distant sea.

'It's a perfect day.'

'Yes,' she agreed, 'perfect.' And for that moment it was.

'And you're right, you can see all the way to the coast. Every detail is clear – see that convoy of wagons to the right, making their way northwards. They are travelling very slowly. Weighed down with treasure, no doubt,' he joked.

'Do your sisters call you Jack?'

'When I was small I believe they did, but I am always James to them now.'

'You are the youngest of the family?'

'I am the long desired heir.'

'And did they spoil you – your sisters?'

'I can't recall they ever did.'

'But your parents must have, if they waited so long for a boy.'

'I hardly knew my parents,' he mused. 'They died when I was ten and before that I rarely saw them. From an early age I had my own quarters, my own staff. They came to see me on occasions and I visited the main house, but it was hardly an intimate family life.'

He had never been loved, but he was not about to confide that. He'd been born to a role and that was his value. As a child he was uninteresting to his parents; as a future earl, he was cherished. He understood that now, but as a small boy he'd longed for a kind word, an affectionate hug, a loving smile. They had not been entirely absent – a succession of nurses had done their best – but he'd looked in vain for a similar reward from his parents.

Lucinda looked aghast. 'It sounds horrible.'

'Not so horrible. I had the best of everything – the

61

best clothes, the best food, the best tutors. Every wish was granted.'

'That cannot have been good for you.'

'Alas, no. As you see...'

'And when did you become the earl?'

'That, too, was not good for me. My godfather held the reins until I reached twenty-one and then it was all mine – the title, the houses, the estates. No wonder I'm deplorable.'

'No wonder.' But she was smiling as she said it.

He touched her arm. 'Let us go down, Lucinda. I may call you that? I have a mournful fear that my boots will begin to pinch if I don't soon start back to the house.'

She turned to go but then, without warning, dashed to the far wall and almost threw herself over the small parapet, or so it seemed to him. She was leaning at an acute angle, hanging dizzyingly in the air.

'It's still there. Look Jack! That's where Rupert and I climbed to and placed a little red banner we'd made – my goodness, we must have been mad for there are no sure footholds on the tower.'

Jack, racing across the turret towards her, hardly heard. Frantically, he grabbed the folds of her muslin dress. 'You seem to have changed little,' he panted, clinging hold of her while straining to keep his footing. 'Move back, Lucinda. We are both in danger.'

Gradually he managed to shuffle his arms upwards until he could clasp her firmly around the waist and return her to an upright position.

'Did I worry you? I was quite safe, you know. The

parapet is high enough.' She was laughing at him and he felt a ripple of anger. He tightened his arms around her, holding her close to his body. 'I know no such thing. Never do that again!'

He looked down at her upturned face and was met by a pair of blue eyes glimmering with mischief. He could drown in those eyes, he thought, and for a moment he stood motionless, lost in their gaze. He felt her body warm against his, her soft curls tickling his chin. Her lips were close; he had only to bend his head a fraction and he could taste that full, smiling mouth. He wanted to with an urgency that took his breath away. Somehow he resisted and with a light brush of his lips to her cheek, he set her down on her feet.

Her carelessness had vanished and her breath seemed to be coming in short spurts. She was looking flushed and flustered and he could feel her body trembling beneath his touch. She was finding his closeness unsettling and that pleased him – it would teach her not to play games. When he dropped his arms, she turned away and walked to the stairs without another word.

In silence, they found their way back to the nave. 'Will you walk with me to the house?' It was courtesy that made him ask. He wanted to be alone and he thought she did, too – he sensed relief when she refused the invitation.

'You will have to excuse me. I have calls to make in the village,' she said.

'Your diligence is most impressive.' His voice was deliberately teasing.

'When you live in a small community, there is little

choice.' It was a sharp reproof, a signal that Lucinda had recovered her composure.

'Naturally, I wouldn't know.'

'You could always learn,' she threw over her shoulder, as she walked towards the church door. 'But not this morning, I think. I'm to call on a very sick old lady and the sight of your town bronze could well be the death of her!'

With a rueful smile, he watched her, basket in hand, trip up the aisle and out into the sunshine.

Jack strode towards the Towers in an unsettled frame of mind. He might be stranded in Verney for several days but he must keep his distance from Lucinda. For a man intent on remaining heart free, their recent encounter had been far too intimate and he must be careful not repeat it. He'd only once been in love, only once thought of marrying, and it had proved calamitous. He had no intention of repeating the experience, even with Lucinda's obvious charms so close at hand: she was lovely to look at, lovely to hold, he thought guiltily. She was spirited, bold even, to the point of recklessness, with an immense energy for life despite the cramped existence she was forced to lead. They were enchanting qualities. Yet they could also be dangerous, as he'd found to his cost. He was uncomfortably aware of how much she reminded him of that long ago love affair. Was Lucinda also a woman addicted to excitement?

The incident on the church tower loomed large in his thoughts and reignited his earlier suspicions. He could no longer dismiss the idea that she might have been his assailant on that moonlit night – from what he'd seen of her, he guessed that she'd be quite capable of riding out as a highwayman. But if she had dared such an exploit, and he still doubted it, what could be her reason? There appeared to be no motive – unless she was indeed one of those rare women who took risks simply because they were there, risks that could spiral into disaster.

Jack wanted very much for that not to be the case and a strong compulsion to prove Lucinda's innocence bubbled into life. While he walked, his mind considered the possibilities. If he looked for the matching pistol in the house and failed to find it, it would suggest the gun he had in his possession had never belonged at Verney Towers. Of course, Lucinda could have hidden its companion but that seemed unlikely. Why would she unless she felt herself to be under suspicion? And he'd been most careful not to betray his distrust.

If the matching gun *were* in the house, Jack was as certain as he could be that it would be in Rupert Lacey's room. He could only pray that it was not. Searching might prove difficult since the servants were up and down the grand staircase twenty times a day. But this afternoon he could be sure that at least his hosts would not disturb him: Sir Francis was immured in his library and Lucinda would not return from the village for at least an hour. It was unlikely that he would get a better chance. He took a deep breath – he would do it!

He was about to walk through the cavernous entrance of the Towers when he heard hasty footsteps crunching over the gravel towards him. It was Fielding, wearing an apologetic expression, his hat being nervously passed backwards and forwards through his hands.

'I found a saddler, my lord,' the coachman began uncertainly.

'And...'

'It took some time,' the man said defensively, 'but I ran him to ground in Climping.'

'And...'

Fielding must have decided to spill his bad news in one burst. 'And he's too busy today to see to the traces, or tomorrow or the next day for that matter. The earliest he can do them is Saturday.'

'Did you not mention my name?' He sounded arrogant, Jack knew, but the thought of another five days in this freezing mausoleum was not a happy one.

'Yes, your lordship, but he weren't to be budged. He said others were before us and he'd take them in turn, earl or no earl.'

The servant looked scared and the hat was achieving a new momentum.

'The man is a scoundrel, no doubt. Don't look so terrified, Fielding, it is hardly your fault. You best send a messenger to Lynton to join us here. I cannot do without his services indefinitely. And a message to Lord Merrington telling him I won't be joining his party until next week.'

'Yes, my lord.'

'How is your accommodation?'

'It's comfortable enough.' The servant's tone was diffident.

'I'm sure they would be happy to house you here if you would prefer, though I doubt you'd find this crumbling place any more comfortable.'

'It's not the accommodation, my lord, it's the clientele.'

His master looked enquiringly. 'The kind of people they entertain at the The Four Feathers,' Fielding explained.

'And what kind of people would they be? I noticed nothing untoward.'

'With respect, my lord, you were there but several minutes.'

'I took The Feathers to be a quiet country pub, rundown it's true, but hardly a hive of mischief. What is going on there, Fielding?'

'Nothing seemingly, leastways not that I can tell for sure. There are some locals, farmers and labourers, who drink there and they seem respectable enough. But there are others I'd swear who don't bear too close an inspection.'

'You interest me. Go on.'

'People visit at all hours, for one thing. Some of 'em knock at the back door rather than using the front entrance. And Mr Partridge, mine host, entertains them in a private room where no one else is allowed. I wandered in that direction by mistake the first night and was told to clear off in no uncertain terms.'

The whole neighbourhood appeared to be infested with villains, Jack thought grimly. Aloud he said as reassuringly as he could, 'What the innkeeper gets up to is not your business. Keep your head down and look to the horses. And make sure you get to that saddler! I cannot be on the road any later than Monday next.'

'Yes, my lord.' The coachman grinned. 'Lord Merrington's will be a piece of cake after this.'

꙳

Jack watched Fielding disappear from sight before he walked through the iron-studded front door towards the enormous staircase which bisected the house. He took its steps two at a time for he'd lost precious minutes and must be swift. The first floor could be discounted. He had been given a guest suite there overlooking the rose garden, a vast and glacial room, and his host's chamber was at the opposite end of the same landing. But he was not interested in Francis Devereux's room – his goal lay above.

He began the climb to the next floor where he knew Lucinda had her bedroom, and it was a good bet that her brother's was not too far away. His search began with more than a few false starts as he opened door after door to enough spare rooms to house a battalion. At the end of the corridor he found himself standing at last on the threshold of an occupied room. It was hers and surprisingly bare – the furnishings, as with the rest of the house, had seen better days, but it was the absence of pictures, trinkets, mementoes that struck him. It was a room to sleep in and nothing more. Lucinda could never have felt sufficiently at home in this house to make a haven for herself. He closed the door quietly behind him.

Where next? Working on the same principle as the floor below, he guessed that the room at the far end of the landing would be Rupert's. And he was right.

Here and there were suggestions of a male occupant – a silver snuff box, a pair of driving gloves, several discarded cravats – but the room had a forsaken air and it was clear that no-one had slept there for many months. He considered where best to begin: it should not take long if the cupboards and drawers were as bare as the rest of the room. He must search rapidly, he told himself, for at any time he might be interrupted.

He walked towards the large mahogany cupboard which had been rammed hard against the exterior wall of the building and tugged at its door. It resisted. Locked! Why lock a cupboard unless there was something you wished to hide? He considered what best to do. He could look for a key but it was unlikely he would find one. Or he could break down the heavy wooden door – he had the strength – but he was reluctant to do so. The noise might bring people running; the carnage would certainly advertise that someone had been here. But his desire to know, to absolve Lucinda of any wrongdoing, had become insistent. He moved away from the cupboard and bunched his shoulders ready to ram the door.

Then he saw it – an unmistakeable shadow on the opposite wall. Two shadows in fact, shadows which clearly traced the outline of crossed pistols. There had been guns hanging from that wall and what guns would decorate a young man's bedroom but a treasured pair of duelling pistols – pistols that were no longer there? He was sure that if he fetched the weapon he held in his room, it would fit the shadow precisely. His heart sank. He had not been wrong about the horse or the gun. They both belonged here at Verney Towers.

'What exactly do you think you are doing?' Lucinda was in the doorway and her voice was ice, freezing him where he stood. He needed to think quickly.

'This room affords a spectacular view of the Downs and I hoped you wouldn't mind my small intrusion.'

Her face was a study of disbelief. 'Have you not had your fill of landscape?'

'You must remember I am a lover of nature! After you were kind enough to show me the splendid vista to the coast, I thought to glimpse something of the countryside which lies north.'

'Whatever your reason, you are trespassing.' The curt tone cut his eulogising short.

'That was certainly not my intention, I assure you. The room was empty and appeared not to have been inhabited for some time.'

'You are mistaken, Lord Frensham. The room belongs to my brother and is private.'

"Jack" had disappeared, he noted. She was very angry.

'I'd not realised. I hope you will forgive my small mistake.'

'A small mistake?' There was no doubting the fury in her voice. 'I'm unaware of the manners pertaining in town society, my lord, but here you are trespassing.'

'Then please accept my sincere apologies and believe me when I say I had no wish to upset you.'

'You haven't.' She nodded at him coldly and stood back for him to leave.

But he knew that he had. He had not missed her furtive glance towards the incriminating wall, nor the flinch when she noticed the outline of those missing guns.

Jack had found what he'd searched for and wished that he hadn't.

Chapter Nine

Molly was in the bedroom, brushing the velvet riding habit into smartness, when Lucinda burst through the door.

The maid looked up and smiled at her mistress. 'I thought you might still be walking with the earl, Miss Lucy.' Molly's romantic dream was not about to die easily.

But Lucinda was oblivious, consumed by her anger at Jack Beaufort for daring to pry, and anger at herself for being taken in by him. He was the spoilt and arrogant man she'd first thought him, but a dangerous one, too. He was used to getting his own way, and she'd encouraged him. She'd relaxed her guard and allowed him to come too close. Allowed him to put his arms around her and keep them there – she had even, dear God, wanted to feel his lips on hers.

What had she been thinking? That was the trouble. She hadn't been thinking; her feelings had run riot and with what result? He'd felt sufficiently at ease to meddle and snoop in the worst possible way. He had found her out! Or at the very least, was in the process of putting two and two together.

She castigated herself for being so careless. She had been in too much of a hurry when she'd snatched the guns from the wall to notice the tell-tale shadow they'd left behind. But how could she have imagined that a stranger to the house would find his way to Rupert's room? What had led Jack Beaufort there? It was possible he'd pocketed the pistol she'd been forced to abandon, but what had made him suspect a connection to Verney Towers? She walked over to the window seat and for minutes on end sat motionless, staring blindly into the distance and trying to make sense of this new disaster. Then, in a sudden movement, she leapt to her feet. Molly's gentle gossip came to an abrupt halt and she looked at her mistress in astonishment.

It was the horse, Lucinda thought It was Red! She had ambushed the earl on the brightest of nights. A full moon had illuminated the clearing as though it were a stage set. He must have seen the distinctive blaze on the mare's nose. Why hadn't she thought of that? All he'd had to do was to wander to the stables and the evidence was there before him. How could she have been so stupid? Red had saved her that night but now the mare looked likely to unmask her.

Lucinda paced up and down the room, her maid watching her, open-mouthed. What would the earl do? What could he do? If he accused her outright, her uncle might not believe him, might even think he'd run mad. And if he tried to prove her guilty, what good would it do him? She had stolen nothing and both he and his coachman were unhurt. She was the one who had suffered – her wrist still bore the marks of his grasp. All he could point to was the inconvenience of broken traces and they would soon be mended.

In a day or two, perhaps even tomorrow, he would leave the Towers without another thought for its inhabitants. Until then she must make sure they were never alone together, make sure he had no opportunity to confront her. In a few days, she would be safe.

So why were her spirits drooping in this alarming fashion, why did she feel like a balloon that had been pricked and not seen the pin coming? This afternoon had been wonderfully exhilarating, that was the truth, and now she had come down to earth with a sickening crash. Jack had aroused her senses in a way she had never known before. She'd found herself melting into the warmth of his arms, felt a wild tingle flaring over the whole of her body, little shoots of pleasure swirling in crazy unison with the thud of her heartbeat. It had been the strangest feeling, but she'd not wanted it to stop. In her mind's eye she saw again his laughing eyes and the grin which crinkled his mouth so attractively.

It was fortunate he would soon be on his way, for he was dangerous to her. She must remember that, dangerous in all kinds of ways. She forced her mind to repeat the small phrase several times. She had come perilously close to forgetting her mission and she needed to focus. When Jack Beaufort left the Towers, she must be ready to act.

'Molly,' she said quietly, 'do you know how your mother was aware that Lord Frensham was travelling nearby?'

'What do you mean, miss?'

'Mrs Tindall told you that a stranger, a wealthy man,

would be travelling in this part of Sussex. Not just this part – she knew his precise route. How did she acquire that information?'

'She wouldn't tell me.' Molly looked uncomfortable. 'Ma's not involved, miss, but there's more goes on at that inn than meets the eyes, you can be sure. She overhears things – Humphrey Partridge ain't just a landlord, if you know what I mean.'

'I don't.'

'The Four Feathers don't make much money yet Mrs Partridge never wears the same outfit twice,' the maid said bluntly.

'You mean Partridge is involved in crime.'

Molly took a while before she answered. 'I couldn't definitely say so, but not everything he dabbles in is above board, I'll be bound.'

'What kind of dabbling?'

'The men he entertains for instance. Ma says they're on the shady side.'

'Shady? Thieves?'

'Mebbe. Leastwise people who know thieves, people who need to get rid of stolen goods.'

'Are you saying that Partridge is a fence? Isn't that what such men are called?'

'I believe so, miss. And he runs games for money.'

The mention of gaming sent a cold prickling down Lucinda's spine. If it were not for gaming, Rupert would be here with her now. That was something to remember if she were in danger of being dazzled by Jack's charm. He may have played no part in her brother's ruin, but he belonged to the same glittering circle of men who'd not lifted a finger to save a young man from his stupidity.

'Gambling isn't legal for a public house, is it?'

'I don't think Mr Partridge is too worried about the law. No one bothers him overmuch. Ma says,' and Molly lowered her voice to a whisper, 'that before the turnpikes were set up and made things difficult for 'em, The Feathers was a safe haven for gentlemen of the road.'

'Then the tricorne Mrs Tindall found was a relic of those days?'

'Happen so, miss.'

'So Mr Partridge was aware of the earl's journey, but how?'

'He has spies all over the county, I warrant. When you think about it, he'd need them if he's up to no good. Their news is vital if he don't want to risk being caught.'

'He won't like the advent of a Bow Street Runner then,' Lucinda said drily.

'A Runner, miss?'

'Lord Frensham has promised my uncle that he will send to Bow Street for help in apprehending the highwayman and I believe the Runner, when he comes, is to stay at the inn.'

'That will put Mr Partridge's cat among his pigeons.' Molly gave a shout of laughter. 'But if we're to have a policeman from London close by, thank the Lord you won't be running any more dreadful risks.'

Lucinda didn't reply, her face deliberately blank, and her maid was instantly alarmed. 'You won't, Miss Lucy. You can't!'

'I must, Molly. My uncle is adamant that he'll not help to release my brother and I know I will never persuade him otherwise. I have to get the money for Rupert.'

'But miss, you cannot risk another ride. Lord Frensham is in the house – the man you tried to rob! And now a Runner will be at large.'

'The earl is already suspicious of me, so I would seem to have little to lose in that quarter. In any case, he will be leaving very soon.'

'But you can't have considered – '

'I have, endlessly. I cannot see any other way. Partridge has talked loosely in the past, he may do so again. Go to your mother tomorrow and tell her that we need information – just once more. Then we will make our plans and this time I will get it right.'

The maid wore a despairing expression and Lucinda took her by the arm and sat her gently down on the bed.

'I know this is a dangerous enterprise, but I have to do it and do it now. My uncle has refused Rupert all help and my brother is daily growing weaker. The earl is beginning to suspect me and a policeman will soon be here. There is very little time. The next ambush has to work and I cannot do it without you, Molly. Are you with me?'

'Yes, Miss Lucy,' she mumbled unhappily. 'You know I'd never let you down.'

Lucinda gave her a quick hug. 'You are the best of all friends!' Then sprang to her feet.

'But we must be prepared. The clothes may need mending – I believe I may have torn a ruffle from the shirt. And Rupert's pistol must be cleaned and primed.'

Molly remained sitting on the bed, her hands working nervously in her lap. 'But you dropped the gun, Miss Lucy, and perhaps Lord Frensham picked it up.'

'It's possible,' she agreed, knowing in her heart that it was almost certain. 'But I have the matching pistol from the wall in Rupert's bedroom.'

She marched across to the large walnut chest which sat sturdily beneath the window. 'See here, it's safely hidden within my underwear. I defy anyone, even a wealthy earl, to find it there!'

⌒

The evening meal was a trial Lucinda could not escape, and a glance at her bedside clock told her she must move swiftly. Sir Francis could not bear to be kept waiting, least of all for the six course dinner he favoured. Molly had disappeared to her attic room with a sewing box and Rupert's shirt and, without waiting for her return, Lucinda dragged the first dress she saw from her wardrobe. It was a gown of white satin matched with an overdress of jonquil gauze. With white satin slippers on her feet and a single string of pearls around her neck, she hoped the ensemble would pass her uncle's scrutiny. A brush pulled roughly through her hair and a modest aigrette to pin back the unruly blonde curls and she was ready as the first stroke of the gong sounded.

Its chime was like the summons to an execution. Her execution. She tried to steady her breath and still her nerves. She must behave as though nothing untoward had occurred; bluff it out until the earl drove away. That could not come soon enough, she told herself, trying hard to ignore the whisper of regret.

The first course was being laid when she arrived – soup à la Flamond, glazed sweetbreads in sorrel sauce, a raised pie and a chine of mutton with removes of fish and veal. Her uncle was happily tucking a napkin around his neck and greeted her jovially. He seemed to have forgotten the morning's disagreeable interview.

'Lucinda, come and sit down. I have some good news. Our guest is to do us the honour of staying a little longer. Will that not be pleasant?'

If it were possible for spirits, already abject, to dip further, then Lucinda's did. 'How is that?' she asked in a voice so brittle it almost snapped.

In leisurely fashion her uncle began to spoon soup from a huge silver tureen, and it was the earl who answered. 'My coachman has been unable to find a saddler willing to do the work immediately, Miss Lacey. I must postpone my departure until Monday next.'

Monday! Lucinda looked fixedly down at her soup dish, crushing disappointment leaving her unable to playact. She would have to run the gauntlet of this man's suspicion, should Molly's mother bring new information. In addition, the Runner from Bow Street might well arrive before the earl left and she would then have two enemies with which to contend. Everything was going wrong and it was all Jack Beaufort's fault.

'Will that not put in jeopardy your visit to Lord Merrington?' In desperation she hoped he might be urged to hire another vehicle.

'It means only a small change to my plans,' he said easily. 'I may arrive in Hampshire a little late, but think how much I've gained.' His hosts looked nonplussed. 'I will have even more time to discover the delights of Verney.' Jack's smile was guileless.

Was he playing a game with her? What other discoveries was he hoping to make? But perhaps the remark was innocent and her surmises wrong. Perhaps he harboured no suspicions and had told the truth when he'd said that he was in Rupert's room to enjoy the downland views.

'We are sorry for the inconvenience to your good self, but delighted to have your company a little longer.' Francis oozed. 'What say you, Lucinda?'

Her uncle's minatory look demanded only one answer. 'Indeed, yes, it will be delightful.'

The baronet puffed out his chest expansively. 'You will have time to explore a little further afield, my lord, and Lucinda will be happy to act as your guide for she knows every country lane for miles around.'

'I imagine she does.'

The slightly crooked smile told Lucinda everything she needed to know. She had not been wrong – he suspected her! But surely he would not denounce her at the dinner table – he would wish to be private with her uncle. She took a quick glance at him. The smile was still there. Could it suggest something else – that Jack might just keep her secret? Lucinda could not be sure. If only he had kept from prying, she would have been safe since he'd not recognised her as his assailant. But now, she thought wrathfully, she was to dance to his tune.

'Yes, Lucinda will be able to ride with you most days,' Sir Francis said smugly, busily making new plans for a niece

79

who had so far proved unsatisfactory.

'You are too kind,' Jack murmured.

The second course had now made its appearance – two chickens, a duck, French beans à la crème, fried artichokes, macaroni and a ratafia pudding. The earl looked stunned as his host slowly ate his way through this bounty. A few more of Uncle Francis's prodigious meals and perhaps he might be persuaded to walk to Hampshire, Lucinda thought tartly.

By the time a final course of nuts, jellies, creams and small cakes had made their way to the table, her uncle's consumption had slowed, though what passed for his conversation had not. Lucinda wondered how long it would be before he talked himself to a standstill. He had exhausted land reform and farming techniques and was now embarked on his bitterest hobby horse.

'The voting system in Sussex is entirely corrupt, you know,' Francis droned. 'The Pelhams are very powerful landowners and they make sure that a family member is always returned to Parliament.'

It was a refrain Lucinda had heard often. Sir Francis was constantly made miserable by the knowledge that he could never bribe as well as his neighbours and therefore never sit as a member. Surreptitiously she stole a glance at Jack. He was finding it difficult to stifle a yawn, but somehow managed to rouse himself to say, 'It is a sad fact of life that representation is still dependent on deep pockets.'

'Indeed, your lordship, that is just my point. If I could tell you how much money the Pelhams have expended on buying up local votes! But then they have the resources to do so. And those men who have their own ideas for the betterment of the country will never have the chance to bring them into being. And why? Because by a quirk of fate they were not born to inherit an immense fortune.'

This time his guest did not respond and began idly to pick at the sweetmeats. Francis sniffed in annoyance and, as if to puncture the earl's indifference, he changed tack abruptly.

'You know, Lord Frensham, I have this minute had a splendid thought. Our entertainments are modest in this small corner of Sussex, but we do boast the occasional public assembly. I happen to know that such a one is to be held tomorrow evening in Steyning. As you are staying with us a little longer than expected, we should all attend. What do you say, Lucinda?'

She was furious with her uncle. His unwelcome suggestion would drive a coach and horses through her plan to keep the earl at arms' length. But she found her anger draining away when she saw their guest's expression. Suave gentleman though he was, Jack Beaufort could not conceal his anguish at being dragooned into attending a rural romp.

She wanted to laugh aloud, but said in the coolest voice she could muster, 'What a clever idea, uncle! It should prove a most entertaining evening.' And a satisfying one, she added silently to herself. Seeing Jack Beaufort discomfited at a public ball might provide her with some small revenge.

He was glaring across at her and she could not resist a further provocation. 'I imagine public assemblies are not much in your line, Lord Frensham.'

'It is some time since I attended one certainly. But I'm sure it will prove yet another interesting addition to my visit.' His smile was sardonic and Lucinda quaked. She should have kept silent, should have kept her head well below the parapet.

'I am delighted that you are enjoying your sojourn with us,' her uncle interjected. 'I must confess that I had a concern you might find it a trifle flat here – after the diversions of London,' he added condescendingly. 'But Verney is a beautiful village and the Towers a most historic house in which to stay.'

The earl's stupefaction was a delight to behold but Lucinda dared not laugh or even smile. That would be to invite retribution.

'You are right, Sir Francis, my stay has been fascinating. In my ignorance, I had thought the Sussex countryside a tranquil haven where little happened.' He looked pointedly in her direction.

He was intent on a game of cat and mouse, but Lucinda had no intention of indulging him. This was the moment to make her escape. Rising from the table, she pinned a gracious smile on her face. 'If you will excuse me, gentlemen, I will say good night and leave you to your port.'

The earl's answering scowl was some compensation for one of the most uncomfortable meals she had ever endured.

Chapter Ten

Jack Beaufort awoke feeling at odds with the world. The rain had been hammering at his window throughout the night and, clambering out of bed this morning, he saw grey skies and sodden lawns. Another day to get through and the prospect of an appalling evening to come. Irritably, he shrugged himself into the coat his valet was holding. At least Lynton was here now.

The man had arrived late last night, after every door had been locked and bolted, and been forced to listen to the butler's loud complaints of folks who turned up at unreasonable hours. Lynton had been forced to waste considerable time in placating his fellow servant and, when he finally ran the earl to ground, he'd found his master severely ruffled.

As a guest Jack could hardly gainsay his host, but only good manners had secured his attendance at a ball that in other circumstances he would have laughed at. A public assembly! He couldn't remember the last time he'd submitted himself to such a trial – the world and his wife lumped together in the hot stickiness of a crowded dance floor.

He'd been made angry, too, that Lucinda had so readily agreed to her uncle's suggestion. That had been quite deliberately done, to spite him. She had not forgiven him for the trespass in her brother's room, but surely he deserved credit for his forbearance. Where was her gratitude? Over the dinner table he'd signalled as clearly as possible that he had no intention of revealing what he knew of her nefarious conduct. There would be little point: she had succeeded in delaying his journey, nothing more. Not one penny had she gained from her ambush, nor one injury inflicted. He had no idea why she'd been driven to engage in such madness, but it was none of his business.

As an older and presumably wiser head, he could have offered advice. Suggested, perhaps, that she look elsewhere to find the excitement lacking in her life. But that would have tasted too strongly of hypocrisy – he had never been a pattern of good behaviour himself, and right now the less than honourable feelings she evoked placed him on even shakier ground.

Impatiently, he turned to the window once more and looked out on the dripping landscape. Then, with a shrug of his shoulders, he grabbed his benjamin and beaver hat and made for the door. He was decided. He would miss the ritual of breakfast and go walking. It was a crazy idea, but the inclement weather would ensure that he was on his own and as far away as possible from the risk of meeting either Sir Francis or his wretched niece.

In minutes he was splashing through puddles and beginning to descend the first of many flights of stairs. Most of the garden was meticulously arranged in levels, each sculpted geometrically with clipped hedges growing as straight as a yardstick and interspersed with assorted circles and squares of flowerbeds set at precise intervals. It was the brainchild of a man intent on imposing rigid order on his world. Only when Jack had negotiated at least a mile of steps, or so it seemed, did he come to the rolling lawns which were his goal.

The rain continued to slice down, silver shards in a colourless world, and the grass squeaked beneath his boots. He must have taken leave of his senses, he thought. But there was not a breath of wind and the air was fresh and cool on his face. He felt oddly intoxicated – a sense of freedom, a sense of liberation, from an almost malign presence. What was it about Verney Towers that cast such a long shadow?

He had squelched his way downhill for some while when he saw a belt of trees in the distance and between their half-covered branches, the narrow reaches of a river. The water evidently marked the boundary to Sir Francis's property. The line of ash trees offered little more shelter than the open parkland, but the river flowing beneath them was a lure. The sight of its pristine waters glittering diamonds of light, even beneath the overcast skies, filled him with a quiet satisfaction.

He stood for some time on the river bank watching small fishes playing chase in and out of the curled pond weed, when the sound of a female voice came to him. It was a curse, a mild curse, but most definitely female. He peered around the wide trunk of the nearest tree and saw a flash of olive kerseymere – the dress appeared to be impaled on a large bramble. Reluctantly, he went to help.

'Good morning, Miss Lacey. May I assist you?'

It was clear from her face he was not the knight errant she would wish, but circumstances had left her little choice.

'Good morning, Lord Frensham. I would be glad of your aid,' she said grudgingly. 'I seem unable to escape.'

It took Jack a few seconds only to unhook the bramble and Lucinda step hastily to one side. But in doing so she almost plunged into the river. His arm shot out and grabbed her by the waist – for a moment she teetered on the edge of the water and then landed safely by his side. Her scent, her softness, the warm curves so close – for a crazy moment he tightened his arms around her, wanting to feel the answering melt of her body.

His heart beat more quickly, his breath grew more jagged. The shawl protecting her head tumbled around her shoulders leaving her hair exposed and his chin tickled by soft curls. He felt an overwhelming urge to bury his face in that hair, to caress the soft white neck with the most delicate of kisses. When he dared to look down into her face, a pair of deep blue eyes looked back at him, and a pair of full lips formed themselves into a sensuous curve. For an instant his mouth hovered over hers, but only for an instant. Then good sense prevailed. Jack swiftly withdrew his arm, leaving the air between them bristling with tension.

'I wonder to see you out and about on such a day, Miss Lacey.' His was a poor attempt to cover an awkward moment.

'Why is that? Do you think me such a hothouse flower that I cannot withstand a little rain?' She had been as shaken as he by the sudden temptation, he thought, and decided on attack as her best defence.

'A little rain is something of an understatement.'

'It could be worse and it does wonders for one's complexion.'

The tone was deliberately flippant but she was the living embodiment of her words. Her skin, gently flushed and shimmering almost to translucence in the rain, was beautiful to behold.

'Then I must be grateful that ruining my second best pair of boots will be worthwhile.'

'This is the countryside. It is frequently wet and muddy. Why venture out on such a day if it displeases you?'

'For much the same reason I suspect as you,' he said shrewdly. 'To pass the time and forget what lies ahead.'

Lucinda appeared to take some time to decode this cryptic remark while the rain fell steadily through the branches above, tumbling and trickling from the few remaining leaves. 'You refer to this evening, I collect. You don't anticipate pleasure from the dance?'

'From a public assembly? That would be a little too optimistic.'

'Of course, you would say so. I doubt it's a setting in which James Mountford Gillespie Beaufort would ever find himself at ease.'

'You think me snobbish and I am not.'

'I think you spoilt, your lordship. The world must be arranged to your liking or you'll take no part in it.'

'On the contrary, I shall be playing my part this evening.'

'Unwillingly,' she said crisply.

'But playing it nevertheless and saving you from unpleasantness.'

She seemed taken aback and stared at him. 'And how is that?'

'If I were to tell your uncle that we have no intention of marrying, I would surely be excused from this evening's expedition, but you – you would suffer a painful scolding, I imagine.'

'I had not realised how much I have to thank you for! But please don't hesitate on my behalf – tell my uncle the truth. I will suffer reproach in any case, so why not spare yourself the ordeal?'

'I have accepted your uncle's invitation. I do not go back on my word.'

'Naturally not – you are a gentleman. As a woman, of course, I can go back on my word at any time. It's well known that we are without honour.'

'I was not –'

But he never got to say what he was not, for Lucinda swished her skirts to one side and stalked past him, walking swiftly away in the direction of the house.

Jack was left to fume. She was impossible – and she knew no shame. He'd kept silent on the ambush he'd suffered, protecting her from the consequences of a night of madness. But all she'd done was rail against him. It was infuriating that he felt so strongly attracted to her – whenever she came within inches of him, he seemed powerless to stop his body flaming with a desire he could not satisfy.

That stuck in his throat. He was not accustomed to

being any woman's puppet – he was the one who operated the strings. He brooded a while by the river before turning back to the cold comforts of the house. He needed to strike a blow, if only for his own pride. Perhaps, after all, he might rescue something from this evening. Perhaps he could use it to turn the tables on her.

He could fascinate as well as she, and Lucinda was not as indifferent as she liked to pretend. He'd not imagined the softening of her body in his arms nor the lips parting for his kiss. He would hit her with every ounce of charm at his disposal, enchant her until she was unable to pretend any longer. He would send Lucinda Lacey spinning with passion before the night was out.

Chapter Eleven

Molly began opening and shutting cupboards and drawers a good hour before her mistress was due to leave for the dance. She was enjoying herself hugely, casting a professional eye over Lucinda's wardrobe, selecting one gown after another, only to reject each in turn. Her mistress took no part in the foray. Lucinda was in a state of the greatest uncertainty, with no idea how she was to get through the evening.

This morning she had chosen to walk in the rain so that she could be alone; she'd had some foolish idea that it would steady her nerves for the evening. The river had proved a calming influence until she'd managed to get herself trapped in the bramble patch. And then he'd materialised out of nowhere. Jack Beaufort seemed to make an art of appearing where he didn't belong. Stupidly, she'd allowed herself to fall into a pointless quarrel with the man. A man, she reminded herself, who could denounce her at any time.

Why had she been so unbearably angry? He'd intruded on her solitude, true, but she must be honest. It wasn't simply his intrusion that had triggered the quarrel – it was rage with herself for entertaining feelings she shouldn't have, determined as she'd always been that she would never allow passion to make her vulnerable.

Not like her poor, dead mother. Remembered lines from Agnes's diary were lodged for ever in Lucinda's head. One rainy day years ago, she had climbed to one the furthest attics and discovered in a dark corner a battered trunk filled with her mother's possessions, doubtless returned to the Towers at the time of her death and then abandoned. Lucinda had been no more than twelve at the time, on the cusp of womanhood, and had no idea of what she held in her hand. All she knew was that it was her mother's book, a book the dead woman had touched. She'd stroked the worn, leather cover and brought it lovingly to her lips. Then prickling with anticipation, she'd opened its pages: this was her mother's message to her from beyond the grave.

At first as she'd read Agnes's passionate declarations, breathless with the dizzying splendour of love, her cheeks had flamed. But embarrassment had been short lived, turning quickly to dismay as she'd read on and the downward spiral of an unhappy marriage became only too clear. Lucinda would never forget the heartbreak recorded in that one small book – the lies, the deceptions, the infidelities. She had vowed then that no matter what temptation she faced in the future, she would remain chaste and above the fray.

But here she was consorting with a man who in all likelihood was as fickle as Captain Lacey. And consorting was a mild description for what had passed between them. Yesterday when he'd thought her in danger on the church tower and held her so there was not an inch between them, she had savoured – there was no other word for it – the warmth of his body. Not just the warmth either, but the hard planes of his form fitting themselves to her as though they belonged, and her body beyond her control, growing weak and boneless. And today his touch had lit a thread of passion which even now was heating her blood. It was very disturbing.

Disturbing, too, the fact that more and more she was finding it difficult to avert her eyes whenever he was near. She enjoyed looking at him: his brown eyes so smooth, like pebbles beneath a clear stream, but on occasions fired by flame; the lock of dark hair that fell carelessly across his forehead despite all the attentions of his valet; and that scar, surely a sign of the marauder. He was like no man she had ever met, silken as alabaster on the surface but dangerous and risky beneath.

Molly was bobbing around the room in increasing excitement, entranced that she was to have the opportunity of displaying her skills to the world, and in front of such a connoisseur as the Earl of Frensham.

She lifted a dress of delicate blue embroidered cotton over Lucinda's shoulders and slipped jewelled slippers onto her feet. Nothing more elaborate could be contemplated since this was a public dance and too much ornament was frowned upon. Anyone who could afford the price of a season ticket could attend. But then she set to work on her mistress's hair, humming happily to herself as she twisted and turned the blonde curls into a cascade of ringlets, their softly waving tendrils framing Lucinda's face. A garland of small blue flowers woven into the curls completed the ensemble. The result was all the maid could have wished.

Francis Devereux and the earl were already in the hall as Lucinda came into view.

'Good, good,' her uncle said fussily. 'We need to be off. The rain has stopped at last and we have a full moon to light us on our way.'

He turned to address his guest who was standing a pace or so behind him. 'The narrow lanes can be quite dangerous at night, you know.'

But the earl was not attending. Lucinda saw his fixed gaze and inwardly cursed that she had allowed Molly to persuade her into the blue dress. She had wanted to avoid attention, to slip effortlessly into the background, and had thought the gown simple enough to escape comment. Instead it served only to make her eyes bluer and her hair fairer – and to highlight her figure. Jack Beaufort was taking full advantage of that, she thought.

'Shall we go? The carriage is at the door, I believe.' Her guardian sounded fretful. Sir Francis was normally an imperceptive man, but even he seemed unnerved by the tension emanating from his companions.

They travelled to Steyning in silence – for the first time since the earl arrived, Francis Devereux had nothing to say. The windows of the small town were ablaze with light as the carriage rumbled its way noisily across the cobbles. Despite the nerves which plagued her, Lucinda began to feel the first thrum of excitement. It was an age since she had attended a dance, any dance, for since Rupert's misfortune she'd become impatient with such trivialities.

Very soon the horses turned off the main thoroughfare

into a long, winding carriage way, where brightly lit lanterns dangled from trees standing sentinel on either side. Within a few minutes they had drawn to a halt at the front of the town's imposing assembly hall. Built in the classical style, it boasted twin staircases, their stone steps reunited at the grandest of entrances. Large torches on either side of an open door flared in welcome.

Lucinda went immediately to the small withdrawing room kept solely for the ladies' use. As she entered, there was a sudden silence among the young women, their busy gossip interrupted. She understood perfectly. It wasn't every day that a member of the *ton*, and a magnificent specimen at that, patronised this humble dance floor – and Lucinda had been the one to accompany him.

He *was* magnificent, she had to confess. When she'd first seen him tonight, replete in black tailcoat, satin knee breeches and embroidered satin waistcoat, she had felt her skin smart with pleasure. Lynton had brought with him a clutch of new cravats and at the earl's neck nestled a folded square of the whitest starched linen, a single diamond stud at its centre.

Lucinda took the passage that allowed the ladies to reach the ballroom without having to traverse a draughty entrance hall. Hundreds of blazing candles greeted her, their light reflected by crystal pendants hanging in a row from the ceiling and by mirrors that lined each wall. Between the mirrors, more candles glowed from numerous wall sconces. And in the centre of the room, a confusion of colour: women and girls, dresses in every hue, tripped lightly between and around their fellows, weaving the complex patterns of a country dance.

Lucinda took a seat between her father and their guest, trying to stop her feet from tapping. The music was filling her with a bubbling energy. On either side, matrons in more sombre dress, brightened only by an occasional rich shawl or feathered headdress, sat out the dance while keeping a wary eye on their offspring. Lucinda did not want to be sitting among them; she wanted to be dancing. And she wanted to be dancing with Jack.

'Miss Lacey, will you do me the honour?'

The country dance had come to an end and a cotillion was being called. She had known that she would dance with the earl – it would have been considered unmannerly if she had not – and she had readied herself for the ordeal. But now the music was pulsing through every vein, sending her senses skittering, sending her to clasp hands with the most elegant man in the room. An ordeal it was not.

She accepted his invitation as demurely as she could, restraining an almost overwhelming impulse to skip on to the dance floor. Instead she walked gracefully towards the other dancers, her arm resting lightly on his. The painful wrist had almost healed and was no longer a constant reminder of that dreadful episode. She wished she could start again. She wished it was not so complicated.

For a while the cotillion took all her attention. It was some time since she had danced and the elaborate footwork and series of changes made her concentrate hard. But she was captivated by the feel of the boards springing beneath her feet, by the sound of fiddles dancing in her ears and the sheer delight of being alive and young and moving to music. Jack Beaufort proved a practised dancer, following the figures easily, his muscular form weaving in and out of the square with languid grace. He was always just where he should be.

'Feet are fascinating, are they not?' he teased, as they came together to dance as a pair.

'I am minding my steps,' she excused herself.

'You have no need. You dance beautifully.'

His arms were around her and his embrace firm, as he twirled her into the pirouette that ended each figure. For a few seconds she felt his warmth enfold her before they were separated by the patterns of the dance. It hurt to let him go.

When they next came together, he pulled her just a little closer until their figures touched at every point. A molten heat began somewhere inside her and flowed slowly and inexorably through every fibre until her entire body was tingling with sensation. Then he was gone, following the movements of the dance, but leaving her yearning. By the time all the figures of the cotillion had been worked, her body was weak with desire and her mind in tumult. What on earth was happening to her?

'You like dancing, Miss Lacey?' It was hardly a question he need ask.

Somehow she found her voice. 'I do, Lord Frensham. And you?'

'Always when I have such a charming companion.'

He was just too smooth. What was she doing allowing herself to be seduced by his obvious charm? 'I should find my uncle,' she said as firmly as she could.

'Of course. We will return to him immediately.'

He had barely delivered her to her guardian when another partner presented himself and was bowing hopefully over her hand.

'You must dance again, Miss Lacey,' the earl insisted. 'You find such pleasure in it. I will bear your uncle company.'

Reluctantly, she returned to the dance floor, fixing an agreeable smile to her face. The set that was just then forming was for another country dance and with a sigh she prepared herself for a lengthy exile. It seemed to her that the music would never stop and, when finally she was reunited with her guardian, it was to find Sir Francis alone.

'Our guest is walking in the gardens – he has found it necessary to take the air.' Francis Devereux was disapproving. 'I had hoped to fetch refreshments, but I do not wish to leave you alone in such a public place.'

'A glass of lemonade would be most welcome, uncle. No harm will come to me – we are surrounded by familiar faces and I will be perfectly happy until you return.'

For a few indecisive moments Sir Francis fidgeted in his seat before disappearing in the direction of the small room that had been laid aside for refreshments.

Chapter Twelve

L ucinda wandered to one of the long windows that had been left slightly ajar. The evening was unusually mild and a gentle breeze provided a pleasant cooling from the intense heat of the ballroom. The moon was riding high, washing the garden silver and silhouetting the stark black of nearly leafless trees.

She opened the door a little wider, her eyes drawn to the marble statue which stood at one end of a narrow gravel path. It was of a naked Greek goddess and the full moon had blanched it to a startling whiteness. Lucinda's gaze travelled to the left and she glimpsed a small red light which glowed intermittently. Someone was smoking out there in the shadows and she had a good idea who it was. No wonder her uncle had been disapproving of the earl's absence. She remembered how Rupert's first attempts at 'blowing a cloud' had brought retribution from his guardian.

Lucinda found herself opening the glass door wide and stepping out. The small red circle was a beacon urging her forwards. She was bewildered by her feelings, frightened by them, but the enchantment she felt was too powerful to resist and she gave herself up to it.

'You have not endeared yourself to my uncle,' she said, trying to speak with composure.

Hearing her voice, Jack walked from out of the statue's shadow and into the moonlight. She could see his rueful smile as he stubbed out the half-smoked cigarillo.

'I'm sorry I abandoned my host, but the crowded room became a little too much.'

'Or was it my uncle who did?'

He didn't deny it. 'Sir Francis is unusual, shall we say. Something of an acquired taste, I feel.'

'He is the taste of a true Devereux.'

Jack raised his eyebrows. 'Would it be impolite to observe that you must be glad then to be a Lacey?'

'It would be mightily impolite, as I'm sure you know. But I would have to agree.' There was laughter in her voice. Why did it feel so right to be here, alone with this man, when in truth she should be as distant as possible? She leaned back against the rough bark of one of the ancient oak trees which dotted the gardens.

'And are there Laceys elsewhere?' he asked.

'There are only the two of us – Rupert and myself.'

He looked thoughtfully at her, seeming to weigh up the significance of this. Her gaze fell on the gleaming white ruffles of his shirt and the pair of strong hands they encased. A tremor of desire chased its way up and down her spine and she tried desperately to control it.

'Your parents had no family?'

'Sir Francis is our only relative. He is my mother's brother. She died shortly after we were born.'

'That is sad – and your father?'

'He had no family to speak of. At least none that ever recognised him. In truth, I know little about him since he, too, died when we were still babies.'

'Sadder still.'

'I doubt that anyone else thought so.' Her voice was impassive but a shadow passed over her face.

'You are severe, Lucinda.' His use of her first name seemed inevitable.

'From what I've learned, Captain Lacey was not the most reliable character. If I tell you that he was killed in a drunken brawl, you might better understand my sentiments.'

A skein of cloud floated across the moon, plunging the garden into sudden shade. For a moment she could not see his face but his voice came out of the darkness.

'Yet your mother loved him,' he mused. 'Theirs was not a marriage of convenience, I imagine.'

'No,' she said sadly. 'It was a love match.'

She had never understood how her gently born mother could have fallen so desperately for such a man. But then she had never been in love and never would be.

The earl's unspoken sympathy washed over her and she was moved to say, 'In the end it was a love match that killed her. I believe she spent most of her short married life chased by creditors, moving from lodging to lodging. She died when we were only a few weeks old – there was not enough money to pay a doctor.'

'But surely her family could have intervened? Her parents, her brother?'

'The marriage severed my mother from her family. They gave her an ultimatum and when she refused to give her soldier up, *they* refused to acknowledge her.'

'That was harsh. Yet they were willing to give you and your brother a home.'

'Whatever else, the Devereux are scrupulously moral. They do what is right or what they see as right. My grandparents considered it their duty to look after two small children who had no other home. And when they died, they left Uncle Francis to continue that duty.'

'Is that how it felt – a duty?'

'Oh yes,' she sighed. 'We were constantly reminded of our good fortune. You can have no idea how depressing that is.'

The October cold was beginning to penetrate her thin cotton gown and she shivered involuntarily. Before Lucinda could protest, he had slipped off his evening jacket and arranged it around her shoulders. The touch of his hand, slight though it was, sent her nerves tingling once more. She bit her lip determinedly.

'And now it's your duty to marry someone of your uncle's choosing?'

'I shall never do so however.' Her denial admitted no wavering.

'You are wise. From what I've seen, arranged marriages rarely prosper. They crush the spirit and destroy dreams.'

'You are talking perhaps of your own family?' she suggested tentatively.

'They are not far from mind,' he admitted. 'Two of my sisters married to oblige the family.'

'And are they not happy?'

'Who knows? I doubt it. They enjoy the wealth and status that such liaisons bring, but happy? Their married lives appear to me cold and formal, hardly conducive to joy.'

'I remember that you named three sisters.'

'Yes. Maria is the youngest and still single – and like to remain so. She was sacrificed on the family altar, too. Expected to nurse our mother until the poor lady died.'

The toe of his dancing shoe dug viciously into the soft turf and she wondered if she dared ask more.

'Your mother was very ill before she died?'

'She was broken, physically and emotionally. My father was a serial adulterer,' Jack said tersely. And written on his face, Lucinda saw the misery he must have witnessed as a boy – the cold silences, the screaming reproaches, his father's bored indifference, his mother's ravaged face.

Lucinda wished then that she hadn't asked and tried to keep the shock from her voice. 'Was theirs also an arranged marriage?'

'It was, and typical of that generation – they expected nothing else. I doubt my mother anticipated undying love from the husband chosen for her but the lack of kindness, the lack of respect...'

The unfinished sentence revealed a well of unresolved pain. Jack Beaufort had always seemed self-contained, carefree even, and in complete control of his life. But this was a very different Jack. For an instant, he'd allowed her a glimpse of what had made him the man he was and she marvelled that so much lay hidden beneath that smooth exterior. Now she understood his absolute determination not to be coerced into a marriage of convenience. Why *would* she not understand, since it mirrored her own feelings precisely?

For a long time he stood, not moving, not speaking, a dark figure against the brightness of the moon. At last, Lucinda said quietly, 'One's choices in life are a gamble, are they not? If I were to judge from my own mother's experience, falling in love would seem to bring little more happiness than a marriage of convenience.'

'It doesn't.' She was shocked by the finality in his voice – it was clear that this was something of which he would not or could not speak.

There was another long silence and then in a complete change of tone, he said, 'I'd like to apologise again, Lucinda – you were right to be angry with me yesterday.'

Was this the chance for her to clear the air between them, to acknowledge her guilt and his silence? She hesitated a second too long and the moment vanished.

He was speaking again. 'I had no right to be in your brother's room. I hope you feel able to forgive me.'

'I have forgotten it already,' she lied. If she could pretend that it hadn't mattered, she might dampen the suspicions he held.

'Thank you. I would wish to leave Verney Towers as a friend.'

'That would certainly please my uncle,' she said lightly.

'Would it please you?'

He walked towards her shelter beneath the tree and stood close beside her. She could feel the sigh of his breath on her cheek as he spoke and the warmth of his body as he drew nearer. She should make her excuses and return to the ballroom. But he was reaching out, his hand caressing her hair, his finger wrapping itself in one of the curls that Molly had so carefully combed into place. Lucinda could not stop herself looking up into a pair of dark eyes; in the play of moonlight and shadow, a flame danced in their depths.

'You have beautiful hair,' he said softly. 'Like spun silk.'

She felt her pulse beginning to beat too rapidly and her breath tangle in her throat. His lips brushed gently against her forehead, then slipped downwards to her cheek.

'And skin to match,' he murmured.

His mouth traced a lazy line along the curve of her cheek and nipped gently at her ear lobe. She felt her skin burning beneath his touch but was powerless to escape. The jacket slid from her shoulders and was replaced by a pair of strong arms. His hands skimmed her waist and drew her body against his. She was as close to him as when they had been dancing, closer even for the hard planes of his body were melding themselves to her softness. She closed her eyes, drinking in the scent of him.

Very gently his lips found hers, a feather light touch that was achingly sweet. She lifted her mouth to his and was shocked how much she wanted this. Firm lips fastened on hers and the kiss that followed was long and hard. She was falling into a delicious darkness, into a cradle of warmth, of acute sensation.

'Lucinda, are you there?'

From the corner of her eye she glimpsed the figure of

her uncle, black against the lighted window, and swiftly slipped from Jack's hold. He stooped to retrieve his jacket and followed her down the pathway.

'What are you thinking?' her uncle scolded. 'To be walking alone at night. And in such flimsy attire.'

'I was not alone. I went to find our guest.' She could not pretend otherwise.

Sir Francis did not look gratified and was still muttering angrily when the strains of a waltz filled the air, causing excited chatter among the guests. The dance had previously been thought too daring to be performed at a country assembly.

'You must forgive me, Sir Francis.' Jack had appeared at their side. 'I persuaded Miss Lacey to walk with me a while and the gardens proved far more extensive than I realised.'

'You have missed most of the ball,' his host said testily. 'We shall have to leave very shortly.'

'A final dance then.' The earl was unperturbed by his host's annoyance. 'Do you waltz, Miss Lacey?'

Lucinda had no idea how to answer. She could waltz – she had taken secret lessons. And she loved the freedom, the vitality of the dance. But whether she had permission to waltz, she doubted. She had never had a Season, had never been officially 'out' and she knew that her uncle, stern moralist that he was, would not approve. But before her guardian could give them the benefit of his views, Jack had whisked her on to the floor to join the venturesome couples undeterred by the monstrous immorality of this latest craze.

'You should not have done that,' she remonstrated.

'Why ever not? We are friends, remember. And friends may dance.'

'It has made my uncle cross.'

'Then let us make him even crosser and enjoy ourselves.'

Lucinda could not stop a small giggle escaping and, at the sound, he smiled down in a way that made her heart shift in alarming fashion. She should have refused to dance, she knew. After that kiss in the garden, she should definitely have refused.

But she hadn't and she was once more in his arms, being floated across the polished boards. The strains of violins sang through her heart, their harmony resonating through every nerve and fibre. She must focus on her steps, she told herself, forget the strong male body that cradled her so intimately, the firm chin resting lightly against her hair, the tempting lips inches from hers.

They were dancing closer and closer together, until their two bodies seemed fused into one single entity, sweeping and swaying across the floor in a sensual delight. Their fellow dancers, the matrons lining the wall, her uncle glowering from a distance, faded into obscurity. All Lucinda knew was light and air and movement – and intoxicating pleasure. She felt Jack grow hard against her and a wild desire to fling off her clothes and dance naked against him burnt its path through her. Then the music stopped.

For minutes, neither of them moved. They were almost alone on the dance floor, Lucinda realised, and every pair of eyes in the room appeared trained on them.

'We should return to your uncle.' Jack Beaufort's voice had lost its customary self- possession.

'Yes,' she said in a whisper.

Her uncle's glowering expression had been replaced by wrath and he could barely bring himself to speak as they approached. 'The carriage is waiting.' The words were almost hissed. 'We should leave immediately.'

Sir Francis must be nursing a bitter regret for championing the earl's courtship. After that shameless waltz, the London gossip he'd dismissed so lightly must be rioting through his mind. Lucinda was sure that, if he could, her guardian would have his exalted guest packed and out of the door by morning light. One thing was certain: he would no longer be encouraging her to spend her days with Lord Frensham.

And her uncle would be right; she must stay away from Jack. That stolen kiss, those intimate caresses, could not signal a greater warning. He was a temptation she must flee. She might know him a little better from this night's encounter, but he was still the same person. By the earl's own admission he was a man who rejected any notion of love – she was sure that women for him were an easy pleasure and as easily discarded. Hadn't he come to Verney in part to escape an affair of which he'd tired?

Lucinda followed in her guardian's wake towards the entrance hall, a sudden blast of cold wind through the open door making her shiver. This time Jack did not leap to protect her. His face was a mask and his thoughts evidently elsewhere. The spell had been broken and the intimacy they'd shared had fled. She wrapped the shawl of Norwich silk around her shoulders, as much to keep out unwelcome thoughts as to offer protection from the cold.

Now that she was no longer in his arms, Lucinda realised how foolishly she had behaved and blushed for the liberties she'd allowed him. She had fallen under his spell so completely that she'd been ready to fling herself, reputation and all, at his feet. How could she have been so stupid as to forget her vow? He was charming, utterly charming. But of course he was: he had not gained his name as a ladies man for nothing. Lucinda felt sick inside as she remembered what he'd said of his father. It seemed that the earldom was not the only thing he had inherited from his parent.

They were making their way to the Devereux carriage, waiting for them a short distance from the front entrance, when she became aware of the stares. People looking at her, following her with their eyes. She had become notorious! The magic of the evening unravelled, shrivelling like snowdrops in ice. All that was left was humiliation. She could see more and more people she knew whispering behind their hands. What were they saying? *Miss Lacey, so measured, so well-conducted! Who would have guessed?* How would she ever live this evening down?

The return home was as silent as their outward journey. Lucinda sat unable to say a word or even raise her eyes. She had a vague sense of her uncle's figure, stiff with outrage, but she dared not look at the earl who lounged lazily in one corner of the coach. Instead she stared determinedly at the floor – it was time again to find her feet fascinating.

Chapter Thirteen

As soon as they reached the Towers, Lucinda hurried through the hall with only a murmured goodnight to her companions. Tomorrow she would be flayed by her uncle, but at this moment all she could think was to escape to the sanctuary of her bedroom. She had her foot on the first stair when Molly glided out of the dim shadows that filled every corner of the house and laid a hand on her mistress's arm. Lucinda's heart gave a little jolt. Something was very wrong. Molly should be above stairs waiting to put her mistress to bed, but this evening she could not wait for Lucinda to climb even a step before thrusting into her hand a crumpled and stained envelope.

Lucinda glanced down at the handwriting and turned chalk white. All thought of the dance and its mortifications vanished in an instant. Quickly, she stowed the letter away in her reticule and ran up the stairs caring little for what the men in her wake might have seen. Molly followed almost as swiftly.

Once in the room, she kicked jewelled dancing slippers to one side and tore at the envelope.

'When did this arrive, Molly?' she asked tremulously.

'About an hour after you left. It was brought from the village. Seemingly it's been in the carrier's cottage a day or two before he found time to send his youngest up with it.'

Lucinda was anxiously scanning the single sheet of paper she had drawn forth. 'There's no date to it – Rupert could have written any time this last week.'

'What does it say, Miss Lucy?'

The maid's voice was unsteady and, with an equally unsteady hand, Lucinda held the message to the light. Black, spidery characters, misshapen and stumbling, crawled across the page as though they would fall off its very edge. Her terror increased – Rupert would not have written so if he were not in the most desperate trouble.

Dear Sister, she read aloud

I am ill with typhus fever and the ague worsens. The money you gave me is gone and I have sold our father's fob. Nothing is left and without money there is no medicine. Go to our guardian – he must send funds. Only you can help, Lucy. Help me. Please.

Rupert.

The signature was barely legible and Lucinda's face held a ghastly expression as she sank into a chair, her hand frantically clutching the dreadful missive as though the two were welded one to the other. Rupert was sick, very sick, and without money he would die. She must go to Sir Francis, show him the letter, and once more plead with him. He *must* help her brother. Surely he could not refuse.

But he would. She knew in her heart he would not veer from his conviction that prison was a rightful punishment for his disgraced nephew. He'd uttered his last word on the subject, her uncle had said, and she understood him well enough to realise that he would not retract his pledge. If by some miracle she persuaded him to read the message, he would say Rupert was shamming, that the letter exaggerated his plight and the boy would try anything to avoid just retribution.

Her brother's fate was in her hands and hers alone. Guiltily she realised how far she'd allowed the threat to Rupert to fade from her mind. Had allowed herself to be waylaid by a plausible charmer. While she had dallied with the seductive earl, her brother had fallen very sick and she had done nothing to aid him. What kind of sister was she? The kind that would move heaven and earth to rescue him, she vowed silently.

Lucinda turned towards her maid and, when she spoke, her voice was firm and clear. 'Did you see your mother today, Molly?'

The girl nodded her head, her expression uncertain.

'And you asked for new information? Has Mrs Tindall heard anything that might be useful to us?'

The maid's eyes were downcast and she refused to meet Lucinda's gaze. In some agitation, she began to smooth imaginary creases from the well-ironed bed linen.

'Well?'

'Ma did overhear something but I don't rightly know if I should say.' Molly's voice dragged with reluctance.

'Look, look at this letter.' Lucinda sprang across the room, shaking the sheet of paper at her maid. 'Read it for yourself and then say nothing, if you dare!'

'I'm sorry, Miss Lucy,' she said miserably, 'but Ma was right flummoxed about whether to tell or not.'

'Let me be the judge. Tell me this minute what your mother heard.'

Molly's sigh appeared to come from the depths of her small, leather boots. 'There's a convoy of wagons making its way to London. It's carrying the tolls from every turnpike for a hundred miles around.'

'Yes, I know. I saw it with –' Guilt returned with a hefty thump as she remembered the church tower and the pleasure of being with Jack Beaufort. 'But you cannot be suggesting I ambush this convoy. It's sure to carry a veritable army of guards.'

'If I had my way, miss, you'd never ambush another thing. I wouldn't have mentioned it except that you were so keen for me to tell and Ma said as how one carriage has got separated from the rest. It lost a wheel and had to stop for repair, so it's travelling alone and there's only a driver and a guard with it.'

Lucinda's face brightened considerably. 'A driver and a guard?'

She began to walk up and down the room, her mind busy with possibilities. 'If the wagon is travelling solo and is only lightly armed,' she said at last, 'I cannot see why I shouldn't take it by surprise. After all they are the same odds that I faced before – only this time I'd not make the mistake of riding too close.'

Lucinda resumed her pacing, running through the plans in her head, gaining confidence as she walked. A few days ago she had been successful in bringing a travelling coach and horses within range of her pistol. If it had not been for the earl...

She turned impatiently towards Molly. 'Why were you so reluctant to tell me this? It's an excellent scheme. Even better than when I rode out against Jack – against Lord Frensham – since this time I need feel no contrition at robbing a fellow being. The tolls are hated by everyone!'

Molly continued to hang her head.

'What is it?' Lucinda felt infuriated with her maid.

'You shouldn't go, Miss Lucy. Ma says it ain't right.'

'What do you mean, not right. I have to act now and it's the best chance I'm going to get. If you're thinking that Lord Frensham will be a problem, he won't. He knows already that it was I who held him up.'

Molly gasped. 'He knows, but – '

'But he will say nothing.'

'Are you sure, miss? Has he made you a promise?'

'Not exactly, but he won't.' How could she explain that she knew Jack would keep her secret? The way he'd smiled, the way he'd spoken? It was too fanciful to put into words.

'But if he discovered you were going to rob again, he'd be forced to report you.'

'I suppose so,' Lucinda said thoughtfully. 'Even Jack Beaufort's tolerance must know a limit. But he won't find out. What is to tell him? And tomorrow he'll be too busy keeping out of my way and out of my uncle's to concern himself with what I'm doing.'

Her maid looked questioningly at her.

'It doesn't matter why, Molly. Suffice to say, that this evening's ball was eventful.' Eventful was an understatement and it was only the shock of Rupert's letter that was stopping Lucinda dwelling on her likely disgrace. 'Do you know the route the wagon will take?'

'Tomorrow it's due to pass nearby. Ma said that likely it will leave Storrington mid-morning, and after Steyning take the Horsham road.'

'Then it's settled. I can use the same clearing in the forest. That's good – I know the terrain and so does Red. I will lose myself for most of the day and in late afternoon slip away. You'll need to make sure that Jem has the mare saddled and ready by four.'

'You mustn't go,' the maid burst out suddenly. 'Ma thinks it's a trap.'

'How can it possibly be a trap?'

'She thinks Partridge ain't to be trusted, that he deliberately spoke of the convoy when he knew she was listening.'

'Why on earth would he do that?'

'Because he means to plot against you.'

'That is ridiculous, Molly. What has Humphrey Partridge to do with me?'

'He suspects you or at least he suspects Ma. She were the only other person who knew about Lord Frensham travelling in the district. And he knows I'm your maid. She's certain he's put two and two together. Very angry, he was, Ma said – talking about thieves encroaching on his patch and making a mull of it, and likely bringing the Runners down on him.'

The maid's words stopped Lucinda in her tracks. The man from Bow Street! She had forgotten him, but he would not now be far away. For a moment Lucinda felt herself stifled by a mantle of trouble. But then annoyed with her timidity, she said staunchly, 'If he were so angry, he would surely be more careful to guard his words.'

'Not if Ma were meant to hear 'em.'

'Even so, to hatch a deliberate plot against me!' Lucinda shook off the last vestige of doubt. 'I wonder if Mrs Tindall has been reading too many romances,' she joked feebly.

But Molly was in no mood for jokes, feeble or not. 'That innkeeper has got a very big chip on his shoulder,' she warned. 'He hates the nobs. There's a rumour he were valet once to a fine gentleman and got dismissed for stealing. He were made to leave without references and never able to get another post in service. It were only marrying the old inn keeper's widow that saved him from the poor house.'

'That's all very interesting, but I doubt a general dislike of the *ton* would stir him to plot against small fry like us.'

'I think you're wrong, miss. He hates this family in particular – he's fallen foul of your uncle. It were several years ago so you might not remember, but Sir Francis laid charges against him for breaking the rules of his licence and the magistrate investigated.'

'I do remember.' Lucinda's brow furrowed. 'But such a small thing.'

'It's never a small thing to Partridge if it brings the authorities snooping around The Feathers.'

Lucinda turned to face her maid, laying her hands squarely on the girl's shoulders. 'I cannot let any of this weigh with me, Molly. My brother is in the most extreme distress and I am his only hope.' Her tone invited no further discussion.

She slipped out of her dress and into her nightgown

while her maid remained where she was, unwilling to move, her lips stubbornly pursed.

'I must sleep now and you must go.' Her mistress took her gently by the hand and led her to the door. 'There's no question in my mind, Molly – tomorrow I ride.'

Jack had been forced to attend the assembly very much against his will, but he could never have guessed at the evening ahead. He might have guessed, of course, when he'd seen her coming towards him in that dress. It was so simple and yet so devastating. The pure blue of cornflower threw into relief her own wonderful colouring, and the tight swathes of the gown enwrapped a figure so lithe and curvaceous that he'd felt his hands itching to reach for her. A few hours earlier he'd vowed to render her weak with desire, but he had not bargained on being himself bewitched.

Nor had he imagined that he could feel such temptation. The impulse to make love to her wasn't new. Its power had been clear from their encounters on the church tower and by the river, but both times he'd managed to walk away. On the dance floor, though, there had been no escape.

A multitude of fair-haired, blue-eyed beauties had crossed his path over the years, but this was different. Was it her frank manner, the sparkle in her eye? Or the sheer energy that she gave to everything, including the cotillion they had danced? He didn't know. But he did know he'd delighted in feeling her close, feeling her body soft and light pressed against his, his face buried in the sweet smell of her hair.

Kissing her had seemed inevitable. From the moment she had followed him into the garden, he'd known that he was going to kiss her, that he had to kiss her. What he hadn't known was how much he'd want to continue. In the moonlight they had been transformed almost into figures from fairy tale, figures that could kiss and live happily ever after. A likely fable! But for those moments when he'd held her in his arms, when he'd fixed his lips on hers and kissed her long and deep, it had seemed that happy endings were not so fanciful.

It was as well Sir Francis had appeared when he did. As well that he'd been so offended by their waltz together that he'd made it impossible for them even to speak. The waltz had set the seal on their desire, the dance stripping from them any pretence – they could no longer conceal from each other their true feelings. Nor, Jack thought sardonically, conceal those feelings from an interested audience watching them locked in such a shocking embrace.

But that was last night.

Chapter Fourteen

This morning heralded another day and, though he'd not felt so fiercely for a woman for a very long time, he had no doubt the feeling would fade. He'd fallen head over heels in love with Julia, had he not? Yet love had died. As a twenty-year old stripling, he'd been so sure he would be different from the rest of his family. He would wed for love and live out his life with the woman of his dreams. But the dreams had hurtled to the ground, shattering and splintering on the way. For years his sisters had searched for a woman who could make him forget the shame and humiliation that still lingered, until a stray remark from a dying aunt had them pondering the snippet of family history that led them to Lucinda Lacey.

Lucinda must have appeared sent from heaven, an inexperienced country girl, content with rural pleasures and delighted to welcome into her life a suitor of the first stare. How very wrong they'd been on all counts. Lucinda had no more wish to marry than he. She was daring, audacious and passionate. She was exciting to be with and utterly desirable. But daring and passionate were also unpredictable and perilous. He would never marry to please his family but neither would he allow himself to be drawn into another supposed love match, whatever the allure.

Nevertheless, this morning found him plagued with restlessness. He was surprised at how badly he wanted to see her again. He suspected it was simply lust talking, but he hoped it was not. Somehow it felt important to smooth the jagged edges of their relationship before he left for good. He could reassure her of his intentions, make clear that though he'd revelled in her kiss last night, she need have no fear he would present himself anew as a potential suitor.

Shortly after a solitary breakfast, he sauntered to the stables and asked Jem to saddle Sir Francis's stolid mount. A ride on the Downs might clear his head and might, if he were lucky, lead to the meeting he desired.

But it did not and, though he rode for nigh on two hours, he met no-one. Disconsolately, he turned the horse and began to wander back towards the house, but found himself on a path he had not ridden before. If he followed its circular route, it should lead him to the village and perhaps Lucinda. Would she once again be playing lady of the manor? The girl, who last night had danced with him so shockingly, could even now be at the bedside of a sick villager. The thought caused him a twisted smile.

There were few people to be seen as he trotted up the village street and no sign of Lucinda. She seemed to have vanished from the world as though from the stroke of a magician's wand. Perhaps it was as well. Before he saw her again, he must make certain he was in command of himself.

For the first time in years he was unsure he could master the force of his desire. Only thinking about her roused the most powerful emotions in him and the smallest flame, he knew, would set them ablaze.

He consulted his fob. He would have to brave dinner this evening and with it an angry Sir Francis, but at least he had managed to miss a dreary luncheon. To idle away more time, he followed a track running due east from the village. It snaked into the distance, bending and twisting for miles, though appearing to travel in the general direction of the house. If he continued along it, he would surely take longer to reach the Towers. The reprieve would be welcome.

He rode on seeing no-one. The hedgerows on either side were now bare but for the fluffy seed heads of Old Man's Beard and the splashes of red and orange rose hips, while further in the distance trees still carried their bright dress of autumn leaves. The peaceful scene was bathed in the glow of a misty sun sitting low on the horizon. He swung around one particularly wide bend and saw in front of him the shoulder of a hill, guessing that he was approaching the house from an unfamiliar angle and that this must be the hill which sheltered the east side of the house. The hillside blazed with autumn colour but it was the shape of the trees that he noticed, trees that appeared to be planted in a strange configuration, standing atop each other in a fashion which was unnatural.

Intrigued, he turned off the lane to take a closer look and saw at the bottom of the hill, a cluster of overhanging branches. They, too, looked strange as though they had been carefully trained in place rather than allowed to grow as nature intended. The gardens of Verney Towers had been planned, chivvied and manicured into ruthless order. But it appeared the wilderness on its perimeter had known a human hand, too. Why should that be? Jack was about to dismount and explore the mystery when he heard the faintest sound of a footstep behind him.

Lucinda at last! He wheeled the horse around but rather than the mistress, he faced her maid. .

'Molly! Good day to you.' His greeting was coolly polite.

'Good day, sir.'

The girl looked apprehensive and seemed hardly able to get the words from her mouth. Why was that and what was she was doing so far off the beaten track?

'Are you returning from the village?'

She appeared to hesitate. 'I am, your lordship.' Then as though to convince him, she added, 'I've been to see my mother. She works at The Four Feathers.'

Jack was unsure of what to make of the maid's nervousness. Was she an innocent among the den of thieves that, according to his coachman, inhabited the Feathers? Or a woman complicit in their villainy? And was it usual in the countryside for a servant to be paying private calls in the middle of a working day?

'Would it not be easier for you to take the lane which runs directly to the Towers?' he asked.

'Most times I do.' Molly seemed to be growing more confident. 'I walk to the village and back plenty, so some days I like to take a different way. The weather is that lovely, too – and it's a pretty path.' She indicated a small track that ran to one side of the mass of branches.

Jack could not argue with the sentiment but he was still suspicious. The track Molly had pointed to might eventually lead to the house but it was a very long way round, and when he looked ahead he could see that in parts thick undergrowth narrowed it to no more than a foot which would make for difficult walking. Molly was here for something else, he would warrant, but he could not fathom what.

'Can I perhaps give you a helping hand – take you home a little more quickly?' He indicated the horse's saddle.

'Thank you kindly, Lord Frensham, but no.' The maid seemed alarmed rather than embarrassed. 'I shall walk. It ain't far.' And she stood back for him to regain the lane and continue on his way. He had little choice but to ride on, though he would have given much to double back and discover just why she was loitering in that lonely landscape.

He walked the horse slowly back to the stables and handed him over to Jem. As the boy began fetching water and brushes, he strolled to the end of the stables. Lucinda's horse was busily chewing its way through a small trough of rolled barley and did not respond to Jack's salute. He walked on to the furthest stable, thinking to greet the splendid chestnut.

The stable was empty. Someone was riding Red. Did he really need to ask who? For a split second he was about to challenge the stable lad but thought better of it. If the boy knew anything, he could put him in danger of losing his job by insisting that he spill confidences. Jack bid him a brief goodbye and walked towards the house, his mind teeming.

'Your lordship has missed luncheon. Should I arrange for refreshments from the kitchen,' Lynton asked deferentially as his master strode through the bedroom door.

'No, I'm not hungry, thank you.'

Jack wasn't hungry. He was beginning to feel decidedly uneasy. Striding to the window, he stood for some time looking blankly ahead, his fingertips drumming a rapid tattoo on the sill. Lucinda was still nowhere to be seen and had evidently not been home for the midday meal. Her horse was stabled, she wasn't in the village – and her maid was not with her. What the devil was she up to? Was this another trick she was about to play? Surely she would not dare to contemplate a further hold up! He'd allowed her to escape justice, imagining it had been a silly spree she'd engaged in thoughtlessly. But now it appeared she might be playing him for a fool and he felt a gathering anger.

It was Julia all over again – a different girl, a different context, but the same need to put herself in jeopardy, the same uncontrollable urge to risk hazard. Lucinda had ridden out on Red, that was certain, and why would she do so unless intent on mischief? But what did she hope to gain and why act now? Had last night's unsatisfied lovemaking spurred her to this madness? He could have satisfied her, he thought savagely. He could have crept to her bed when the household slept – she would have been as eager as he to taste fulfilment. But he'd played the honourable man and maybe she'd been left aflame and wanting. Was this then the result? That she sought excitement of her own making.

Where was she? His fingers drummed ever more loudly as his thoughts roamed over the paths and byways of the district. In his mind he retraced his steps of the morning. And then it came to him. That unnatural looking cluster of bushes and a maid where she was not expected! The place would host no ambush but it had to be important. Clear as crystal, the thought arrived. It was where she would return and when she did, Molly would be waiting. He spun around from the window so suddenly that Lynton, who had been carefully brushing a coat of the finest kerseymere, dropped the brush in surprise.

'Is everything all right, my lord?'

'Probably not,' he said shortly. 'Lynton, I'm going out but I want you to stay close to the house. I may have need of you.'

The valet looked bewildered but bowed his head in acknowledgement. 'Naturally, I shall remain here, sir.' Before he could retrieve the brush, his master had strode to the door and was already clattering down the staircase to the front entrance.

⟿

It took much longer than Jack expected to return to the place he'd seen earlier that afternoon. On foot it was far more difficult, the lane being rough and overgrown, and he wondered how long it had taken Molly to make it back to the Towers. More likely she'd not continued on the path since he was certain there must be another way into the house. He was out of breath and slightly dishevelled when once again he stood facing the cluster of overhanging bushes. He was about to get a great deal more dishevelled. Hastily he began to pull back the torrent of greenery, trying to loop one branch behind another, to make headway into the space they guarded.

His anger at Lucinda's foolhardiness had not abated but, alongside, there was a growing fear, a sick lurching to his stomach whenever he thought of the outcome. He had been a strong adversary and had overpowered her before much harm could be done. Only her wrist had suffered. But what if she met a very different coach, one whose inhabitant was nervous and armed? It did not take much for a cocked pistol to explode. What if the carriage horses took fright and bolted, trampling her underfoot or Red, terrified by gunfire, threw her from the saddle?

A dozen different possibilities haunted him as he worked his way through the branches until he bent back the last bough to reveal a wooden door, splintered in places and mildewed from the damp, but a door nevertheless.

He had been right. This is where Molly had been headed. Her mission had not been to walk a circuitous route to the Towers but to find her way into the house through this entrance. He grasped the rusted iron ring and pushed the door ajar. Sure enough a long corridor stretched ahead, dividing at its furthermost point into two narrower passageways. They had been cut into the hillside and he guessed that the left hand path led to the house, and the right to the stables, in fact to Red's stable. That was the meaning of that odd circular door, the one that Jem swore had been locked since he started work at Verney Towers.

Jack closed the door behind him and settled himself on a tree stump, hoping its rough bark would not snag his knitted pantaloons so badly that Lynton would demand an explanation. Lighting a cigarillo, he drew deeply on it. He would wait for Lucinda's return, wait for her and confront her. And this time there would be no mistaking his message: he would tell her uncle all he knew if she refused to stop her outrageous activities. The threat of homelessness might deter her when the shadow of the gallows had not.

But then she would not be thinking of the gallows – she would not imagine the law would punish her as harshly as any low thief. But it would and she could hang, whether she were gentry or not. The image of the Runner he had himself called in, flitted across Jack's mind and he felt even sicker. A note from Bow Street had arrived only yesterday to say that Didimus Black, one of their best men, was even now on his way to The Four Feathers.

Jack stubbed out his cigarillo and paced up and down to keep himself warm. It was not yet twilight but an October cold had begun to creep into his bones. Looking back at the wooden door, he realised it would be visible from anyone riding in the lane and since he'd no wish to signal a warning that the trap had been sprung, he grabbed several of the bushes, allowing them to swing back into place and shield the door once more. He stamped his feet. He was ready. How much longer would he have to wait?

Not long. He heard the soft patter of hooves, echoing in the sharp, clear air, well before the horse came into view. He was surprised that the mare appeared to be walking very slowly: a fugitive should surely arrive at a gallop or a brisk trot at the very least. But she was here and his sigh of relief was heartfelt. Then the horse came into view around the bend in the lane and he could see why Red was moving so slowly. There was no rider! He peered again through the dusk. No rider, but a figure slumped across the saddle. Lucinda!

Chapter Fifteen

Jack flew towards the horse and grabbed at Red's bridle, steering the mare off the lane and into the undergrowth. Then frantically began to undo his work of a few minutes ago. The entrance was swiftly uncovered and the wooden door wrenched open. He ran back to the horse and slid the inert body of the girl from the saddle, feeling a damp river spurt down his chest. My God, she was bleeding and bleeding badly. He hefted her into his arms and the blood gushed even more strongly. Her right arm hung limp and useless at her side.

He was through the door and into the passage, sending a prayer heavenwards as he spied the dim light which glowed ahead.

'Molly,' he called softly. 'I need your help.'

There was no response but he saw the lantern waver.

'This is no trap, Molly,' he said harshly. 'Your mistress is injured. I need your help to get her to her room.'

There was the sound of running feet and the light grew steadily brighter. 'Lord Frensham, is that really you?' The maid's voice quivered in fear. 'I don't understand.'

'There's no time to explain. Your mistress has lost a

deal of blood. You must guide me into the house and then come back for the horse.'

'Oh, Miss Lucy!' The maid burst into a storm of tears at the sight of the lifeless body. 'Didn't I tell you?' Her voiced cracked, sending hoarse whispers bouncing off the stone walls.

'Whatever you told her, she didn't heed,' Jack said grimly. 'Let's go and quickly.'

Molly choked her tears to a standstill and hurried ahead, the lamp's uncertain beam casting distorted shadows on roof and walls. Where the passage divided, they swung left and continued the walk uphill. For Jack the journey seemed unending. Cradling Lucinda in his arms, he glimpsed her lips blue, her pallor a livid white, a terrifying contrast to the scarlet stream cascading down his shirt.

Now they were at a staircase, cunningly hewed into the rock of the hillside. Up the stairs and through a door into one of the cellars, Molly leading the way, trembling so much she could hardly keep the lantern aloft. Another two flights of back stairs, Jack's breath becoming ever more ragged, and they were at last in Lucinda's bedroom.

'Quickly, Molly. We must get her jacket undone and the shirt sleeve cut.'

'But your lordship,' the maid began to protest.

'Do it girl!' His voice grated. 'This is no time for modesty. Your mistress is bleeding to death.'

Molly ran for her scissors and, hand shaking, cut the jacket open, then sliced through the right sleeve and finally the sleeve of the cambric shirt. Hardly an inch of white remained, for the cloth was soaked scarlet.

'The mistress will surely die.' Molly sobbed in anguish.

'Not if I have anything to do with it. Get me a petticoat.'

All considerations of modesty had fled and Molly leapt to the walnut dresser and pulled out a tumble of undergarments from one of its ample drawers. A cotton chemise was found and Jack proceeded to tear it into strips, one of which he bound tightly around Lucinda's arm as a tourniquet.

'That should stop the bleeding. Fetch me a bowl of warm water – we must find out how bad the wound is.'

'Has she been shot, sir?'

'Yes, she's been shot,' he said levelly, trying to mask his fear.

Molly disappeared towards the kitchens. Only a few minutes elapsed before she was at his side again carrying the bowl, yet in his state of alarm they'd seemed immeasurable. The maid was now moving rapidly to his orders but his next command had her hesitate again.

'I will bathe the arm. You must return to the passage and retrieve the horse.'

'But the mistress –'

'I will engage to keep my passion under control while you're gone,' Jack said caustically.

Molly fled without another word. He slowly bathed the arm, removing layer after layer of blood until the water in the bowl was as scarlet as the discarded shirt. He could see now that the bullet had gouged the arm deeply but had not passed through or buried itself in the flesh. Relief flooded through him. If he could stop the bleeding, Lucinda would live with only a small scar to tell the story.

By the time the maid returned and reported that Red was safely back in her stable, the bleeding had dribbled to a halt. Lucinda's face was still horribly white but her breathing appeared more even. Jack pulled a small flask from his jacket.

'Have you bandages? The brandy will stop the wound becoming infected and binding the limb tightly should ensure that the bleeding will not begin again. You must undress your mistress but without disturbing the arm. Keep her warm and fetch some rice water from the kitchen. I fear she may suffer some fever.'

'Should we not call the doctor?'

'Yes, let's do that,' he said acidly. 'There must be any number of reasons why Miss Lacey should have a bullet wound in her arm.'

Molly nodded numbly while the earl twisted and turned the strips of bandage as tightly as he dared.

When he had finished, he stood back to view his handiwork. 'That will have to do. I must go now and show my face at dinner, else Sir Francis will become suspicious. Send one of the footmen to the dining room with a message from your mistress saying that she has the headache and has taken to her bed. That should suffice for tonight.'

'And tomorrow, your lordship?'

'We can think on that later. I'll return here as soon as I'm able.'

'She's much worse, sir.' Molly almost ran towards him, her hands twisting in anguish. 'She's that hot and nothing seems to cool her.'

The room was in near gloom with only a single branch of candles placed high on the corner chest. Just enough light for Jack to see his way as he crossed swiftly to the bedside. As he'd feared while he sat through an interminable meal with Sir Francis, the fever had taken hold and had Lucinda in its powerful grip. Her cheeks were flushed a bright red while her forehead, pale as ivory, was speckled with beads of sweat.

'Have you given her the rice water?'

'I've tried,' Molly said despairingly, 'but it's difficult to get her to take it. She fights me off, poor lamb.'

'Then you must fight her back. She has to drink.'

He took Molly's place by the bedside and raised the slight figure from the pillows. 'Come, Lucinda, you must have this.'

The girl's glazed eyes looked up at him, trying to focus on his face, but the effort must have proved too much and, with the smallest shake of her head, she lowered her eyelids and turned into the pillow.

'You must drink,' he repeated, 'then you may sleep. Open your mouth and take what is in this cup.'

The stern command appeared to have an effect for she allowed her head to be raised and took several reluctant swallows.

Jack lay her gently down on the bed and turned to the maid. 'It is imperative that she takes rice water throughout the night. You must be firm with her.'

'But the poor mistress – she's so ill.'

'Do as I say and all will be well, I promise.' He sent an impassioned plea to the gods that his words would prove true. 'We will take turns to nurse her through the night, Molly, but first I want you to fetch Lynton to me.'

The maid wore a scared expression. 'But Lord Frensham, no-one must know. Miss Lucy...' She struggled to find the words. 'If someone should tell what they know...'

'I will vouch for Lynton – he is completely trustworthy,' Jack soothed, 'and we are likely to need his help. Now go quickly.'

Once Molly had scurried out of the door, he walked slowly back to the bedside, aware of darkening shadows beyond the flickering gleam of the candles, and was filled with an acute sense of isolation. At the best of times, this was a room bare of comfort. He remembered the absence of keepsakes, of remembrances, from the day he had trespassed. That day when he'd looked for Rupert's gun seemed a world away. He'd been struck then by the loneliness that was almost tangible and now, at this bleak hour, in the shadowed half-light, with a young girl fighting for recovery, the gloom was overwhelming.

It would be a very long night, Jack thought. He would do his best, but he was no doctor. He had suffered the occasional bullet graze, the occasional wound from a sword fight, and had needed little in the way of medical attention. But he had never had an accompanying fever and he couldn't be sure that this fragile girl would have the strength to fight it. He looked down at her slight form huddled beneath the sheets, so helpless, so broken, and his heart surprised him with an unpleasant thud. His anger at her defiance had vanished and all he could think of was to see her safe and well.

Lynton was waiting for him on the landing and he relinquished his post to tiptoe quietly to the door. A hurried conversation later and he returned to Lucinda's bedside, speaking quietly in Molly's ear.

'It is decided that Lynton will go to the village early tomorrow. He will say that he goes to fetch a doctor, but in fact will go to purchase ingredients for a salve that will help Miss Lacey's wound to heal more quickly.'

'But won't Sir Francis want to know what's happening?'

'He will, of course, and you will be the one to tell him. You will say that your mistress has developed a fever and that I have offered Lynton's services to fetch the doctor. You can add that you fear her condition may be contagious. If I've read my host correctly, that should ensure he stays clear of this room. It will give us the opportunity to invent whatever medical diagnosis we please and, at the same time, allow your mistress time to recover sufficiently before she meets her uncle again.'

'She *will* get better, sir?' He could see that Molly's spirits were very low and in urgent need of reassurance.

'It's a surface wound and that is a great advantage. It means we'll not have to dig a bullet from the flesh and so cause infection.'

'But the fever?'

'I imagine that it comes from the shock of losing so much blood and, with luck, it should soon abate.'

⤙

But Jack's pronouncement proved a shade too confident and the fever continued to mount throughout the night. As time passed, he found his optimism squeezed thin. It seemed to him that with every hour that struck, Lucinda became hotter and more restless. He tried to make her comfortable, gently plumping the pillows beneath her head and smoothing the disturbed sheets into some order. But the next minute she had thrown back the bedclothes with her one good arm and was clawing and kneading at the counterpane with rigid hands. He took turns with Molly to sit by the bedside, bathing Lucinda's brow with lavender water and coaxing her to drink whenever she opened her eyes.

'I am so very hot,' she said at one point, surprising him with a moment of lucidity.

'You have a fever but it will pass,' he said gently. 'Come, drink again – for me.'

She did as she was asked, but then became suddenly agitated and grasped hold of his hand so tightly that it hurt. 'Don't leave me,' she whispered and, with a sigh that was hardly audible, sank back onto the pillows.

A wave of protectiveness swept through Jack so fiercely that if he had not been sitting down, he thought it would have knocked him from his feet. 'Have no fear, Lucinda, I shall keep you safe,' he found himself saying. And for that moment, he meant it.

He soaked the handkerchief in lavender water once more and passed it across her forehead, then bathed the delicate white skin of her inner wrists. He would like to kiss them into coolness, he thought, then scoop her into his arms and magically transform her fevered body to the healthy, vigorous young woman he had last seen.

As the night progressed her threshings became wilder

and Jack was riven with anxiety, though he dared not openly show it. Molly was by now almost beside herself and the last thing he wanted on his hands was an hysterical maid. He understood her fear since the situation in which they found themselves was terrifying. He had only the most basic notion of how to treat a fever. What if Lucinda were far more ill than he imagined, and he had failed to call a doctor. What if... but he refused to allow his imagination to contemplate this most terrible outcome.

Around dawn Molly, who had retired to the window seat, fell into a fitful doze, and Jack could no longer stop his own eyelids drooping. He slumped, crumpled and worn, in the small chair by the bedside, until a sharp kick to his knee brought him back to sudden wakefulness. Lucinda was tossing and turning more violently than ever, attempting almost to fling herself from the bed.

He'd thought the fever had reached its height, but this was worse. He tried very gently to restrain her, fearing she would break open the wound, but all the while his mind was churning. Soon Lynton would be scratching at the door awaiting orders. Should he get his man to summon a physician to the house? What were the likely consequences of such an action? The doctor would feel it his duty to inform Sir Francis of his niece's true condition and the whole dreadful episode would be out in the open: Lucinda's transgression, Lucinda's crime, and his guilt in aiding and abetting her.

Then, quite suddenly, she ceased her violent tossing and turning. Her limbs no longer twitched and her hands were stilled. Jack moved nearer and studied her face intently. A pair of sapphire eyes was looking up at him and generous lips stretched themselves into a wavering smile. The fever had broken! Lucinda had come through! He felt the breath rushing out of him, desperate for release, as though his whole body had been held in a constriction of terror.

'Jack?' she queried softly, putting out her hand to him. 'Is that really you?'

'It is.'

'But –'

'Later. We will talk later. Now you must rest.'

With the softest of sighs, she closed her eyes again and lay with her hand nestled in his. Watching her fall asleep, he noticed the smile did not leave her lips.

Chapter Sixteen

Lucinda woke to soft light spilling its way through the curtains. It seemed that she was on a bed and that together they had been on a long journey. But how strange. And why was she lying here? Surely she should be on horseback, riding hard. She should be in the woods, at the clearing. She saw it in her mind's eye, a mist-filled space surrounded on all sides by dense black foliage, still dank from yesterday's heavy rain. And there was Red, the mare carrying her gallantly into the attack. But then – a shuddering halt, uncertainty, bewilderment. There were men, dozens of them it seemed, men shouting and heavily armed. How could that be?

A loud gasp escaped her and she felt someone move closer. She opened her eyes and saw a ceiling, a plaster ceiling snaked with cracks. It seemed familiar. She was in her own room! There was no doubting it, but how had she got here? She turned her head. Jack Beaufort! The world was topsy-turvy. His face bent over her and she could see his eyes were tired and concerned.

'Don't be frightened, Lucinda, you are safe.' The tenderness in his voice made her bite back tears. But why was he in her bedroom? And where was Molly? She struggled to sit up and he put out a restraining hand.

'You have suffered a bad fever and you must rest.'

A fever? Nothing made sense. Yesterday she was perfectly well – perfectly well, her mind kept repeating. She had taken Red from the stable, ridden through the woods, found the clearing and…now she remembered…she had ridden into an ambush. The men, their guns, bullets coming thick and fast, singing over her head and past her ears. She had wheeled the horse around but not before she'd felt a biting pain in her arm so agonising that she could scarcely breathe. And then she and Red galloping for their lives. And then darkness.

'There were guns,' she began, her voice stumbling over the words.

'And one of their bullets hit you. You have suffered a flesh wound. It's a nasty gouge but fortunately nothing more. You were very lucky.'

The searing ache in her arm felt anything but lucky. She looked down at her nightdress and saw a bulge protruding from the right sleeve.

'These are bandages?'

'Looking a little disreputable, I fear, but when Lynton returns from the village, we'll have fresh linen and a salve to help the wound heal more quickly.'

'We? *You* bandaged my arm?'

'I did and if it feels a trifle tight, I apologise, but I had to stop the bleeding.'

'You undressed me?!' Even in her weakened state, Lucinda's voice chimed with indignation.

'Don't distress yourself.' His smile was mischievous. 'I had not that pleasure. I may have bandaged, but Molly saw you into bed.'

'But how –'

'It's a long story and, for now, one that should not worry you. There will be time to talk when you're feeling stronger.'

With enormous effort, Lucinda raised herself into a sitting position. 'I *am* stronger. You said yourself that the fever has passed. I'm well enough to get up.' She had to move, had to act. Her brother was mortally sick and the realisation that she'd failed him again was slowly entering her consciousness.

'Indeed you are not. You have lost a great deal of blood and will find yourself very weakened.'

She sank back, frustrated by her frailty. 'You seem to know a great deal about such matters.'

'My murky past, Lucinda. Sometimes it has its uses.'

'But where is Molly. I want Molly.' She managed to sound both tearful and cross.

Her fretfulness met understanding. 'Molly will be here very shortly and she will keep guard over you.'

'Am I to be a prisoner then?' He did not to respond and her indignation soon turned to alarm. 'Does anyone else know about... apart from Molly and yourself?' Her voice faltered at the enormity of what had happened.

'Only my valet, who is completely loyal. You need have no fear on that score.'

'But my uncle?'

'He knows you have a fever. Later today Molly will tell

him that it's not after all infectious as she first feared, and that if he wishes to pay you a visit, he may. I doubt, though, he'll bother you for a few days.'

She managed a lopsided grin. 'Uncle Francis is very protective of his person.'

'That was my assumption.'

Lucinda fell silent, willing herself to think through a haze of weariness. At last she managed to discover what was worrying her. 'But Sir Francis will want a doctor consulted, if only to tell him that the house is safe from the smallpox. Then what shall I do?'

'I hope we may have pre-empted that small problem. When Lynton returns from the village, he will pretend to the staff that he has brought back a doctor. Hopefully they will be too busy with their work to pay much attention. Your uncle will be locked in his library and will not know the truth or otherwise of the tale. He will believe whatever Molly tells him.'

'You seem to have thought of everything.' Her eyelids drooped and she felt fatigue swell into an all-engulfing wave.

'I hope so. My head is as much on the block as yours.'

'Tell me...' Lucinda made a valiant effort to keep her eyes open but her face was etched with strain.

'Not now. I am going to wash and change out of these clothes – I feel as though I have worn them for a sennight. And I must show myself downstairs as soon as possible. That will stop unwelcome questions as to my whereabouts. But I'll be back.'

The door clicked open and Molly bustled into the

room, but at the sight Lucinda's ashen face, she promptly burst into tears.

Jack frowned at her. 'Your mistress is very tired. We should let her sleep, but when she wakes bring her toast and tea.'

'Yes, my lord. And thank you, sir.' The maid bobbed a hasty curtsy and then burst into another round of tears.

Jack took the opportunity to slip quietly from the room.

Lucinda was sitting propped against three huge pillows when he returned later that evening. She was still pale and had dark circles beneath her eyes but, as Jack came into the room, she smiled with something of her old sparkle. For a moment her gaze lingered appreciatively over his tall athletic figure. He was wearing a newly pressed blue tailcoat, its gilt buttons gleaming in the candlelight, a delicately striped silk waistcoat and dove-grey pantaloons. He was quite beautiful, she thought, but she wasn't going to let him know that.

'You are once more the elegant Lord Frensham,' she teased. 'I was worried this morning that you might be losing your reputation for being all the crack.'

Jack smiled wryly at the forbidden slang. 'So was Lynton. But any sacrifice for a lady, even one whose tongue runs away with her.'

He sat down by her bedside and she felt warmed by his closeness, perhaps a little too warmed. Memories of their dance together rose unbidden and had to be forcefully banished.

'Have you seen my uncle?' she asked quickly.

'Not only seen but eaten my way through an extremely lengthy repast with him.'

'An act of true bravery! And how was he?'

'Very concerned for his health, as you can imagine, but slightly mollified by your maid's report of the doctor's visit. Though he still managed to talk for thirty minutes on the dangers to middle-aged men of contracting any kind of infectious disease.'

'How did you get away from him? I presume you didn't just flee the dining room.'

'Naturally not. I'm a man of address, Lucinda. I simply mentioned that I was feeling a little under par myself and that perhaps an early night would be of benefit. After that, he could hardly get rid of me quickly enough.'

'And are you feeling unwell?'

'Not at all. I've slept for a few hours and feel restored to full health. I will tell him tomorrow that it was all a false alarm.'

'Poor Uncle Francis.'

'Not so poor. He is blissfully unaware that, but for good fortune, he would be facing the most fearful scandal imaginable. He has escaped lightly, I feel.'

Her downcast lashes masked the apprehension in her eyes. She knew that the moment of reckoning was approaching. Jack Beaufort had risked his reputation to help her, was still risking it. He would want to know just what she had been doing and she owed him a full explanation. Or at least something that would pass as full.

'So the bullet that you were unlucky enough to encounter,' he said firmly, 'how did that come about? It's hardly usual to suffer a gunshot wound while out riding.'

'It was my fault.'

'That is no surprise.'

'I thought to run another ambush,' she began with difficulty. 'There was information – Molly heard that a wagon had become detached from the main convoy of toll coaches. You remember we saw the convoy from the church tower?'

'I remember,' he said grimly.

'The wagon was supposed to be travelling alone with only a driver and a guard to defend it. It seemed a perfect robbery.'

Jack's face was impossible to read and she felt forced to continue a story she would have done anything to forget. 'The information we received was wrong.' Her voice began to shake and she had to swallow hard. 'It was wrong. The wagon was not alone, it had not become detached. It was the whole convoy that I ambushed.'

'My God!'

He jumped up from the chair and began walking backwards and forwards across the room. Lucinda tried to ignore his agitation for she needed to finish her story. Her voice was still shaking when she said, 'There were armed guards everywhere, two for each coach. I don't think they could quite believe that a single rider would dare a hold-up, but it didn't take them long to realise what was happening. Then they began shooting.' These last words were delivered almost in a whisper.

'I bet they did.' The earl had come to a standstill and was looking down at her, his expression appalled. 'Are you aware that the punishment for robbing tolls is death by hanging and that there is no reprieve, no matter who the perpetrator?'

Lucinda stared at him in horror.

'To take such a risk, you must have had a trustworthy source for your information. Who told you that the convoy had divided and that a wagon had become detached?'

'Molly's mother – I trust her completely.' Lucinda thought it best not to mention Mrs Tindall's fears.

'And Molly's mother is a chambermaid at The Four Feathers, so whatever she told you must have come originally from Partridge and Partridge, from all accounts, is a villain.'

'It didn't come directly from him,' she protested. 'Mrs Tindall overheard him talking.'

'Are you telling me that you trusted your life to information that a less than honest landlord "accidentally" let slip?'

Jack was too clever, she thought unhappily, or perhaps too knowing of the kind of world in which the inn keeper moved. He had found the fault line which had almost destroyed her.

She nodded miserably, but he had more questions to press home. 'Did you not realise that it was an entire convoy that was passing through the clearing? I'm presuming it was the same clearing in which you attempted to relieve me of my worldly goods.'

'Yes,' she said sheepishly. 'It seemed a good place.' He shook his head in disbelief but Lucinda wanted to keep talking, wanted to share the terror she had felt. It had been the most frightening moment of her entire life and she wanted Jack to know.

'I was expecting a single wagon, and when the first one drove into the clearing, I assumed it was on its own. The light was dim. There was no moon this time and when the coach emerged from the covering of trees, I saw only its outline. I started to ride forward before I realised there were others following.'

'And Red?'

'She couldn't easily stop. I wheeled her around as soon as I saw what was happening but by then the guards had their guns up and were shooting.'

'She got you away.'

'She is a most wonderful horse. She didn't panic at the barrage, but simply turned at my command and galloped towards home. At least I guess that's what happened. I don't remember anything after we flew into the woods, except an excruciating pain in my arm.'

'Your guess is right. She brought you safely home and is now enjoying a well-earned rest in her stable.'

The shadow on Lucinda's face disappeared and she said almost jubilantly, 'Thank goodness. I couldn't bear for anything bad to have happened to her.'

Jack walked back to the bedside and sat down beside her once more. She could smell the fresh lemon of his scent mixed with the warmth of his body and wished she wasn't so easily distracted. But he was very close and the room had taken on an unusually intimate air. She must be sure to keep the conversation flowing.

'So how did I get here?'

'I was waiting for your return, waiting at the entrance to the tunnel, when Red appeared with your lifeless body.'

'You found the secret door?' Lucinda could hardly believe it.

'No longer so secret. I was waiting outside the passage and Molly was inside – between us we got you up to this room unnoticed.'

'But why were you waiting there? How did you know Red would arrive? How did you find the door?'

He held up his hands in mock surrender at the volley of questions. 'That's another story and you're getting tired. You must rest again but tomorrow, if you're very good, Dr Beaufort might allow you to leave your bed for an hour or so.'

Lucinda was feeling unequal to more explanation and thought it wise to agree. So far he'd not asked her the most important question – just why she had risked her life in such a foolish fashion. He would want to know sooner or later, but she found herself reluctant to tell him the truth. He would think very badly of Rupert, express his disdain, and she would find that hard to bear. *She* knew what lay behind her brother's compulsive gambling, but she could not expect a stranger to understand.

And in reality that was what Jack was. His touch might leave her breathless, but he *was* a stranger. She had met him barely a week ago. So why did she feel she had known him a lifetime, that she wanted to share with him every secret she'd ever had? This was a secret, though, that was not hers to tell. She had failed Rupert miserably and the only thing now that she could do for him was to stay loyal and keep silent.

She would say nothing to the earl, but could not forget what she owed him. He'd risked much in aiding her and was risking it still by saying nothing of what he knew. In effect, she had made him her accomplice.

'Jack,' she said suddenly. 'You've been protecting me ever since you came to the Towers and now you've saved my life. I cannot begin to tell you how grateful I am.'

'And so you should be,' he retorted, his smile more sardonic than ever. 'If this scandal were to see the light of day, what little reputation I have would be in shreds!'

She bowed her head guiltily. 'You're right. I've involved you in trouble that was not yours.'

In response he bent towards her, his warm breath fanning her cheek. For a moment she thought he would wrap her in his arms and she longed for it. Just once more. But instead he reached out and clasped her by the hands.

'Sleep well, Lucinda Lacey,' he said softly. 'I will see you tomorrow.'

Chapter Seventeen

T he earl put his signature to the invitation with a
flourish. After the drama of the last few days, it
would be a suitably flamboyant way to say goodbye
to Lucinda. And say goodbye he must. It was clear that
Sir Francis wished him miles away. Since the evening in
Steyning, his host had gone into hiding, burying himself
in his library and emerging only to take his meals. Jack
had sat through several lengthy dinners with him in almost
complete silence. But for his rigid social code, he knew, Sir
Francis would have shown him the door long ago – in his
host's mind, he must figure as a dangerous seducer.

Jack couldn't blame him. Since his guest had arrived
at the Towers, it must seem to Sir Francis that the world
had gone haywire. The marriage proposal he'd so much
desired had not materialised. Instead, he'd been shocked
to the core by his niece's conduct at the ball, a grievance
compounded by the frightening infection following hard
on its heels. It was a distressing state of affairs for a man
who'd invited into his home the biggest catch of the *ton*.
If anyone had been caught, it had been Sir Francis, Jack
thought dryly.

But there was a more pressing need to say good bye than the travails of the baronet. When this morning Fielding had arrived with the news that the carriage was at last ready and they could leave for Lord Merrington's whenever his master pleased, Jack had felt sadness and relief in equal measure.

He knew he must go for Lucinda's sake. There would already be gossip aplenty – her neighbours had been shocked by the brazen waltz they'd danced together. But life could become even more disagreeable for her if he stayed longer. The village would expect an announcement of their betrothal and, when it failed to come, Lucinda would be judged a hussy.

And if he were honest, Jack needed to leave for his own sake. The overwhelming desire he'd felt that night at the ball still resonated, though he knew well that such passion had little currency beyond the moment. But if passion was all, this farewell would be easy. And it wasn't.

It wasn't just sensual appetite that Lucinda awoke. He had been angry with her for duping him, playing him for a fool, furious that she'd been foolhardy enough to attempt another ambush. But when he'd looked down at that pale and fragile form, so small in the huge bed, his heart had hurt. He'd wanted to scoop her into his arms and keep her from all harm. He'd wanted to fight the world for her, and that was a very, very dangerous feeling. He was on a precipice and close to its edge, close to falling in love with her, and that must not happen.

The years had taught him vigilance and this time he would protect himself from harm. Lucinda was bold and beautiful and he delighted in her company, but in the end he must accept that she was no different from the fiancée who had broken his heart. His only option was to bid her a gracious farewell and drive speedily to Merry's, where he could lick his wounds amid the gaiety of that gentleman's house party.

⌒

After a cursory breakfast, he escaped the gloom of the Towers to stroll in the direction of the hot houses. It was another perfect October day – windless and cloudless. The sun was not yet high but already the trees were burnishing their few leaves in its glow and the succession houses, when he reached them, were fairly basking in its warmth. On his visit with Lucinda to pick flowers for the church, he'd noticed that a conservatory had been attached to the furthest building to take full advantage of the panorama of terraced garden and distant parkland spread below. He remembered having seen a table and comfortable wicker seating, a perfect place for tea and goodbyes. He would discover what more might be needed – extra cushions and a blanket perhaps – to make it comfortable for Lucinda's first convalescent outing.

This afternoon he would settle her in the softest chair, ply her with tea and then broach the subject of his departure. He suspected the news might upset her badly, but he was sure she would recognise the rightness of his action – better by far that he left before they fell into something they would both regret. These last few days temptation had been avoided, but it had not gone away. Once Lucinda was returned to her customary good health, it would be only a matter of time before powerful feelings broke free and cast both of them adrift.

'Lynton,' he called to the valet when he returned to his bedroom, 'can you take this message to Miss Lacey?' He pulled the invitation from his pocket and waved it in the air. 'And do it discreetly.'

Lynton was tidying the room in a flurry of pillow shaking and curtain twitching and didn't look up.

'Then organise cushions and blankets for the succession house that overlooks the gardens.'

At this, his valet raised his head.

'Miss Lacey and I will be taking tea there,' Jack said. 'And though the sun is shining, she must be kept warm.'

'Have you seen her today, my lord?' Lynton's voice was edged with curiosity.

'Why do you ask?'

'Only that Molly reports her mistress a great deal better. The salve we had made up in the village has brought about a noticeable difference in how quickly her wound is healing.'

Jack nodded but said nothing and his valet was encouraged to continue. 'As Miss Lacey is making such excellent progress and the travelling coach is now repaired, are we likely to be staying on at the Towers?' Jack felt the man's eyes on him and knew that Lynton as a trusted servant saw a lot more than he would wish him to see.

'We'll stay this one day and then be on our way to Lord Merriman. When you've organised the conservatory, send a message to Fielding to have the carriage at the door for ten in the morning.'

Lynton's face fell. Whatever Lucinda's misdemeanours,

Jack thought, his valet admired the girl. It was evident his man had been wishing for a more satisfying ending to their stay at the Towers.

⌐⌐

Lucinda looked at the elegant sheet of cream vellum and raised her eyebrows questioningly at Molly.

'It were Lynton who gave it me. From the earl.' A conspiratorial smile spread across Molly's face until she saw her mistress's expression.

'It's merely an invitation, so you can spare yourself the blushes. He wants me to take tea with him in the conservatory.' Lucinda looked puzzled. 'Why not in the house?'

'Perhaps he wants to talk privately with you, Miss Lucy.' Molly was not giving up easily.

'Or perhaps the conservatory provides a warm environment with beautiful views – just the place for an invalid who has been incarcerated in her room for days.'

Her mistress's tone was caustic but the maid wasn't listening. She was already riffling through Lucinda's dresses to decide on the most suitable apparel for what she clearly considered a lovers' tryst.

⌐⌐

At four o'clock Lucinda walked alone to the conservatory and was met by a smiling Jack, as always elegantly clad. She was glad she had taken trouble with her appearance, allowing Molly to dress her in the apricot crêpe gown with a matching string of beads threaded through her hair. A shawl of Norwich silk was around her shoulders, but the warmth of the room rendered it superfluous.

The earl took it from her with a gently mocking smile. 'Where is the shawl of many colours? I've been looking forward to its reappearance since our first meeting.'

Lucinda smiled back. 'It's consigned to the furthest corner of my closet and will not see the light of day until Christmas.'

'Why Christmas?'

'Because that's when the vicar holds his annual party and I will have to prove to his wife that I'm still entranced with her tasteful gift.'

'Evidently one of those community obligations of which I'm so ignorant! But you're looking well, Lucinda, surprisingly well.'

'I've had some excellent nursing,' she said a trifle shyly. 'Yours - and Molly's too, of course.'

'And now you're ready to relinquish your sick bed for good?'

'Thank you, yes. I must be up and about every day, otherwise Uncle Francis might suspect he has more than a mild infection to worry him.'

Jack guided her towards the huge glass window that overlooked rolling lawns. An array of cushions lay scattered on the seats with several blankets folded to one side ready to repel any draughts foolish enough to invade. A tray of porcelain china had been placed on the white wicker table and out of nowhere, it seemed, Lynton appeared, bringing tea, milk and cakes.

The earl settled her into one of the large wicker chairs, adjusting the cushions behind her. She felt his hands move gently across her shoulders and linger for a second on her neck, as he released one of her ringlets to hang free. Lucinda found herself wishing he would keep touching. That his hands would move to rest on her shoulders, that he might even allow them to wander.

She was shocked at the thought, shocked that her body was already tingling with expectation. Accepting his invitation had not been wise, Lucinda realised. Lying sick in bed, she'd felt pleasure in having him close, but now that her health was much improved and they were together in this beautiful setting, desire had returned with bewildering force.

For a while she struggled to regain her composure, gazing through the window at the landscape which lay prostrate beneath the sun, the garden and the far parkland illuminated in its glow. In the distance she glimpsed the trees which lined the river, itself glistening like a sheet of tin. She remembered how they'd quarrelled beneath those very trees and the way that animosity, every scrap of it, had dissolved with the first step of the dance.

That evening! That kiss! She felt the same ache now, the same unsatisfied yearning. But she'd vowed then that she would not become another name in the earl's long list of lovers and her determination to mount guard on her emotions had not wavered.

'Your invitation was a surprise,' she said rather too brightly. Lynton had disappeared and she wondered what was coming. The earl had not set up this elaborate tea party on a whim.

He took a seat beside her. 'I thought this a pleasant place for us to meet. A pleasant place to tell you my news.'

An unexpected panic came out of nowhere and gripped

her hard. 'What news is that?'

Instinctively he reached out to reassure, holding her hand between his in a firm clasp. Without meeting her eyes, he said, 'Your local saddler has at last repaired the broken traces on my carriage and it's now fit to travel again.' The words came rapidly, his usual smooth address deserting him for the moment.

'You're leaving?'

'I am. Sir Francis at least will be relieved. I finally intend to join Lord Merrington's party – a little late but hopefully not too lamented.' He tried to speak cheerfully.

'And when do you go?'

'I have instructed Fielding to be here at ten tomorrow morning.'

'I see. As soon as that.' Lucinda felt leaden, as though her shoulders had suddenly acquired an enormous burden.

'But we won't speak of it. Instead let us talk about your return to good health.'

'No, don't let's.'

'Then what?'

'Who will you meet at Lord Merrington's?'

Jack looked puzzled. 'I'm not entirely sure – the usual crowd, I expect.'

'More brides to be?' Lucinda cursed her stupidity. What on earth was she thinking, blurting out such a question.

She tried to make a recovery. 'I was thinking... I imagine your sisters must have been busy again. They will have realised by now that your expedition to the Towers has been unsuccessful.'

'If they've been busy, I have no notion. Who knows –

Verney may have been their last throw. I can only hope.'

Jack leant over the table and poured her a cup of tea. 'I'm sorry if I've surprised you. Tea is good for soothing the nerves, I believe.'

'Thank you, I will take a cup. But my nerves are quite calm,' she said as airily as she could. 'Your visit was always going to be brief and I'm grateful you've stayed as long as you have.'

'It's been a most interesting experience. Certainly not the visit my sisters contemplated!' He picked up the dish of cakes and offered it to her. 'Try one of these dainties – Cook tells me they are madeleines and bound to do an invalid good.'

Lucinda declined but sipped her tea slowly as the earl bit into one of the cakes. For minutes, she sat absorbed in thought. She'd been numbed by his announcement, but now the first shock was wearing off, frustration had taken its place. She was annoyed with herself for ever imagining that he might care for her, that his feelings might be enough to persuade him to stay longer. It was mortifying to realise that she'd been so mistaken – he didn't care for her, even a little. He was intent on leaving at the first opportunity and for a house party that would be no different from a hundred others that he'd attended.

Yet in the days since her injury, he'd been nothing but caring. He'd been sensitive, warm, thoughtful – she could think of a hundred adjectives and none of them had prepared her for this sudden departure. Was it that he was scared, perhaps, scared of growing too close to her? After what he'd told her of his childhood, it wasn't surprising that his face was set against a marriage of convenience. But why had he discounted so completely the possibility of a love match?

'Why are you so against marrying?' she asked suddenly. 'Do you not think that one day you might fall in love?'

He blinked in surprise, clearly discomfited by her question. Lucinda knew she was on dangerous ground, for though their bodies had come close to intimacy, they had never confessed their innermost feelings. But something was pushing her on; she wanted badly to discover what lay behind his stubborn resolve.

Jack said nothing for some time. Then he looked across at her, holding her in a steady glance, as though judging how much to reveal. 'I *was* in love once,' he said quietly, 'and I ended up a fool. I have only just lived down the ignominy.'

'Were you planning to marry the lady you loved?'

'I was. In my youthful innocence I thought I'd met the woman I would stay with for the rest of my life.'

'What was her name?'

'Julia.'

The sound of the word on his lips drove a splinter of jealously into Lucinda's heart, but she said as unconcernedly as she could, 'It's a beautiful name.'

'She was a beautiful woman, or so I thought. But then I thought a lot of things that turned out to be mistaken – I thought she would give me a future that I could be proud of, that she would bring me the kind of joy my family had never known.'

Lucinda tried to ignore the harsh twist in his voice.

'That must have been a very special feeling. '

'It was – for a while.'

He sat wrapped in thought while the minutes ticked by. Then he bent towards her, his face close to hers, trying it seemed to pull her into his very soul, to see for herself the pain he could not lose.

'From a very young age I'd witnessed the disaster that was my parents' marriage and been horrified at the sight of two people tearing each other apart. Then as I grew older, I saw the cold liaisons that satisfied my sisters and felt nothing but disgust. The Frenshams had made dynastic marriages for centuries, but that was not going to be for me. I was a new generation. I was going to do things very differently.'

'It was a noble sentiment.'

'Noble maybe, arrogant certainly. There I was smirking with superiority that I'd found the answer to lasting happiness, throwing myself body and soul into a love affair I believed true. Such a foolishly romantic image of life! At least Julia cured me of that.'

Lucinda thought it wise to step prudently. It was clear he was still very bitter and love was a delicate subject. She should probably let it go. But somehow she couldn't.

'Did the lady find another that she preferred?'

'Nothing so mundane. I think I could have borne that better. She played me for a fool and shamed me before the world.'

'But how?'

'She was a thief. She stole from me and stole from my friends.'

Chapter Eighteen

Lucinda's gasp was almost loud enough to rattle the teacups. This was a confession she could never have foreseen.

'For months I turned a blind eye to what I suspected,' Jack went on. 'I refused to think about the necklace that went missing from my mother's jewellery or the expensive fob that Julia liked but which I'd worn only once before it disappeared or the heirloom vase that mysteriously vanished from the country estate we'd visited as weekend guests.'

Lucinda's lips parted in astonishment. She was finding it difficult to take in his words. He looked at her appalled face and said, 'It's hard to believe, isn't it? My friends had difficulty, too, but then they realised what was going on and tried to warn me. But I refused to listen. I was besotted. I kept pretending to myself that it wasn't happening, but when my man of business told me that he would need to sell funds to cover the huge debts I'd run up – Julia had falsely pledged my credit around London – I had to face the truth: I was betrothed to a thief and a defrauder.'

'Did you confront her with her wrongdoing?'

'I didn't have to. As soon as she realised I knew the truth, she vanished. Once Julia had gone, my friends began to trickle back. I was fortunate to find them sympathetic and considerate of my feelings, but I knew that privately they thought me a fool. My humiliation was complete.'

She wanted to say that there was no humiliation in loving truly but she knew from her mother's sad account, that it was not always so. Agnes's diary brimmed with the indignities of loving a man who could neither protect her nor remain faithful.

But it was Julia that was the conundrum. 'Why on earth did she steal, why defraud? Was she so poor?' And when Jack made no answer, she said in her most practical voice, 'If she had married you, she would have wanted for nothing.'

'She wasn't poor. Her family was not precisely wealthy but they were comfortable enough. She had no need of money. What she had instead was a desire for excitement.'

'How extraordinary!'

'You don't understand that?' He was looking at her a little oddly, she thought.

'Why would I? Why would anyone risk such a thing for excitement? Julia lost a glittering marriage and a man who loved her. It makes no sense.'

She saw a deeper puzzlement flit across his face and wondered at it. But then he was saying ruefully, 'My foray into matrimony was calamitous, as you can see, and I wouldn't recommend it. In comparison the plans you have with your brother seem almost utopian.'

It was her turn to be disconcerted and her gaze faltered.

For days she'd been unable to think of Rupert. He could be dead by now for all she knew. And if he were not, what good was she to him, weak as she was? She felt the tears begin to well and tried to breathe deeply. She must not cry, must not alert Jack to the trouble she was in.

When she looked up again, her eyes were pearly with unshed tears and, seeming to mistake the source of her distress, Jack said, 'I hope Sir Francis is now convinced that I'm wholly unsuitable as a husband for you. I wouldn't wish you to face his scoldings once I'm gone.'

She pushed her dread for Rupert to the back of her mind. 'I won't,' she said stoutly. 'At least no more than usual.'

'Is a state of siege normal between you?'

'I suppose it must be. I hardly notice any longer. My uncle leads a narrow existence and expects – has expected – us to share the same life. He insists we conform to his ways, but that isn't always easy.'

'We? That is your brother and you?'

'Yes,' she said so quietly that the word was hardly audible.

'You told me once before that your brother was not allowed to fence or go to prize fights or join the army. Is that part of conforming to the ways of Sir Francis?'

'Rupert has always been a little wild – he has inherited the Lacey temperament, I fear – and our guardians thought to tame him by keeping him close. My grandparents first and then my uncle.'

'And did it?'

'No,' she said dejectedly. 'Rupert is quicksilver. And a mercurial personality needs some outlet.'

'I would have to agree with you.' Jack lifted the teapot and began to refill their cups. 'So despite being twins, you and your brother are quite different in character?'

'Not so different.' Lucinda smiled inwardly at the thought of the horrifying risks she had run and the fierce desire that even now was plaguing her for the man sitting so near. She might show a calm face to the world, but her emotions were every bit as fervent as her brother's. 'Women are taught to be obedient, are they not? They rarely defy openly as a young man might. If they get their way, it's by more duplicitous means.'

That was probably not the right thing to say to a man whose fiancée had practised duplicity to a remarkable degree. But Jack merely smiled in his laconic fashion. 'I'm beginning to have some sympathy for Sir Francis.'

'Does he know yet that you leave tomorrow?' Lucinda was glad to change the subject.

'He does and was hard put to it to suppress a smile. He will be delighted to see me from the premises.'

My uncle is alone in that, she thought sadly, but that was something she could not say. She must keep her dignity, bid her rescuer a calm farewell and only allow the tears to fall when his carriage had swept down the driveway of the Towers and was out of sight. The image brought with it an overwhelming weariness.

'I'm a trifle tired, Jack. I think I would like to return to my room now and rest.'

He jumped up immediately. 'I've been thoughtless in keeping you here so long. Allow me to escort you back to the house.'

163

He helped her to her feet and stood facing her. She smiled up at him a little weakly. 'Thank you for arranging our tea party. It was a most kind thought.'

He reached out to smooth her cheek, unable it seemed to forgo this one small touch. 'Don't repine too much, Lucinda. It is the right moment for me to leave.'

'Of course,' she agreed, but her eyes were lowered.

His hand tipped her chin upwards and he looked down into her eyes. 'You must believe me. In time you will see I am right.'

'Of course,' she repeated. She dared not look into his beautiful, dark eyes or she would cry long before the carriage left. She must return to the house before she shamed herself.

But he was looking at her as he had on the night of the ball and she found her knees grow weak and her body crave his touch so insistently, that she raised her hands to his chest in mute surrender. He seemed to feel the same desperation since in a second his arms were round her, enfolding her in the tightest of embraces. He kissed her forehead, a light butterfly kiss which barely grazed her skin, then her eyelids, then her cheeks. His mouth hovered over hers and she lifted her lips to him. This would be the last kiss she would know and she felt agony at the touch of his mouth. A last kiss, yet she wanted him to kiss her forever.

His lips took hers in tenderness, another kiss followed, firmer this time, then another and another, stoking their passion until his tongue was teasing open her mouth. More kisses, hard and hot. He had his hands in her hair and the ringlets were tumbling around her face. He was kissing her into ecstasy.

They staggered back and she was crushed against the wall, the cold glass at her back but the rest of her body ablaze. His hands were moving down her figure, nimble fingers slipping open the front of her gown. She felt a piercing ache as he cradled her bosom, stroking her, caressing her, tracing the swell of her curves. She strained towards him and in response, he raised her breasts to his lips, kissing her over and over until liquid with desire, she felt her body melt to nothingness. She was dissolving, annihilated by fire. The conflagration coursed through her with such force that a jagged moan escaped her.

The sound seemed to splinter the air. He raised his head and she saw a dazed expression on his face. He was breathing heavily and his body felt hard against her. It was a moment that flew free of time, a moment when the world seemed to hold its breath. Then he was quickly buttoning her gown.

'That should not have happened.' He was barely able to speak.

'No,' she whispered, 'it should not have.'

His usual carefree manner had vanished and she could see he was thoroughly unnerved. He said nothing more but offered her his arm and together they made their way from the conservatory in silence. Through the rose garden and along the flagged terrace without speaking a word, too overwhelmed by the maelstrom of emotions they had ignited. Once inside the Towers they paused amid the vast expanse of the hall, dazed and bewildered still, not knowing what they should do. Then as though by unseen agreement, they bobbed their heads in farewell and walked away in opposite directions.

Chapter Nineteen

The carriage was at the door at ten o'clock, the luggage almost loaded and Lynton waiting to take his seat opposite his master. A half an hour earlier Jack had bid a chilly farewell to his host and there was nothing left for him to do but climb into the lavish travelling coach and be on his way. But he hesitated. He'd not spoken to Lucinda since he'd escorted her from the conservatory, too stunned to think clearly. This morning, though, had brought wise counsel and he'd thought it best that he disappear today without another word. But now as his foot hovered on the carriage step, he found he could not leave before he'd said a proper goodbye.

That was what he had meant to do yesterday, of course, until an explosion of passion had destroyed all his plans. Their lovemaking had made it crystal clear that the sooner he left the Towers, the better. He could no longer trust himself to be alone with her and he placed no better reliance on her discretion. She wanted him as much as he wanted her. He'd longed to strip her clothes from her and feel her naked form against his, but he was sure that she would have undressed him with equal alacrity. He'd seen her eyes haze with desire, felt her soften against him, heard her groan with passion.

He was no longer teetering on the edge of love, he realised, he was part way down the abyss. But it was not too late if he left now. And he must leave now: he would not be disgraced again, no matter what the temptation. Yet the pain slicing at his heart made it impossible to leave without a last look at her face, a last touch of her hands.

'You must wait a while,' he ordered his men. 'I'll not be long.' And he disappeared around the side of the house. Fielding was lashing a last piece of baggage in place and glanced after his master in puzzlement, while the valet kept his thoughts to himself and looked impassively into the distance.

Jack had a good idea where he might find her. Lucinda would not have walked far, he thought, for although she had more energy every day, a stroll on the terrace was still sufficient exercise. It was an ideal place for her to walk: close to the house but out of sight of her uncle. *And* she could keep her feet dry! He smiled to himself as he rounded the rear of the house and looked along the flagged way. It was empty. He walked to the end of the terrace and through the brick arch into the rose garden. It was empty, too. Where was she?

He was about to turn tail when a small noise reached him through the still air. It was barely audible but he could swear it was a muffled sob. It came from the far corner of the flower garden where he remembered seeing a small arbour that sheltered a simple wooden bench. He headed in that direction, weaving in and out of rose beds and coming finally to the most distant of the paths intersecting the garden.

He saw her almost immediately. Her head was bent and one hand held a crumpled handkerchief. As he watched, she blew her nose in a determined fashion.

'Lucinda?'

She jerked her head up sharply and hastily hid the damp square of linen.

'I'm sorry. I didn't mean to disturb you and I won't detain you long. I came only to say goodbye – my carriage is waiting.'

'I know. I saw it.' She sniffed loudly, trying to swallow her tears. Should he simply ignore her distress, trust she would soon recover, and go? He found he could not and walked quietly up to her and sat down on the bench.

'Tell me what ails you?'

It was a dangerous question. What if she was crying over him and chose to speak of love? How could he respond?'

'I'm in low spirits, that is all.' She smiled a little crookedly. 'It must be the after effects of the fever.'

'If that really is all...' But his tone was doubtful.

Jack was certain that it wasn't all and her unwillingness to confide acted as a spur on him. He wanted to soothe, to share her trouble, to make things right for her. 'Low spirits have not so far afflicted you, so why now? What has happened to upset you so badly?'

'Nothing. Nothing that's new.' She looked at him with tear-swept eyes. 'My failure is an old one. Indeed it's become quite comic.'

He felt bemused. It was evident she was not about to

declare undying love for him. Some other cause for her grief must be found.

'How have you failed?' he asked, hoping for enlightenment.

'Abysmally.'

'But failed at what, and why does it trouble you so?'

Her shoulders slumped even further and every ounce of fight seemed to have drained from her. It was the first time he had known her so utterly defeated.

'I have failed Rupert.'

He saw new tears start up in her eyes and struggled to make sense of her words. What the devil did her brother have to do with anything? Rupert had always been the missing piece in the jigsaw that was Verney Towers, hardly spoken of by Lucinda and never mentioned by her uncle. Jack had thought the mystery of the boy's whereabouts a strange business but in the end unsurprising, since his entire visit had rung with oddity and Rupert's unexplained absence was only a part. He tried again to wrest some meaning from Lucinda's confession.

'In what way have you failed him?'

'I am sure he will die,' she wailed, 'if he has not already.'

It was a wail of blind terror, coming from a place far removed from the beautiful garden in which they sat. It was as though she'd stumbled into another world, Jack thought, a world of pure suffering. Her tears started afresh and this time they flowed in earnest. His heart gave an uncomfortable lurch and he wanted desperately to put his arms around her and circle her with his protection. But he dared not embrace her.

'You are making little sense.' His voice was deliberately severe and it had the effect he desired. Her sobs hiccupped to a close.

She blew her nose again. 'I'm so sorry, Jack. I am a sad case and you must not heed me. Please accept my apologies for embarrassing you.' She offered her hand to him as a gesture of goodbye. 'Your servants will be waiting – you should go.'

'Damn my servants! I cannot leave you in trouble. I must know what ails you.'

The beginnings of a smile wavered faintly on her lips. 'Now you are sounding as arrogant as the Lord Frensham I first met.'

He pulled a wry face. 'And you are sounding as though you're a little recovered.'

'I am fully recovered and you have no need to worry. It was a stupidly weak moment, nothing more.'

'A weak moment that had you sobbing from the depths of your heart? A weak moment that caused you to bewail your brother's death?' He took her by the shoulders and shook her. 'You must tell me, Lucinda, what is it that troubles you? Tell me everything.'

She gave a sigh of resignation, or was it despair?

'I suppose now that you're leaving...' She left the sentence unfinished and he had to prompt her. 'Now that I'm leaving...?'

'I can tell you – since we are unlikely to meet again.' Her hands fidgeted in her lap, pleating and unpleating her handkerchief. There was an intake of breath before she said in a halting voice, 'I woke this morning feeling truly

171

despondent. It was more than a fit of the blue devils – everything was mired in gloom – my future, Rupert's. It came rushing at me, I don't know why. Perhaps because you *are* leaving – I know that you must – but it made me feel very alone. Alone and futile. I have struggled so hard to save Rupert but my efforts have come to nothing.'

'Why have you needed to save him?'

'I didn't want to tell you – I didn't want you to think badly of me, or of my brother. But I suppose it hardly matters now.' There was a long pause and then she hurried to get the words out. 'It's easy enough to explain, though difficult to say. Rupert is in a London prison for debts he cannot pay.'

'In prison? In Newgate?' Jack was taken aback. It was hardly the usual fate of gentlemen who did not pay their bills, but it explained her brother's puzzling absence and the refusal of everyone at the Towers to speak of him.

'Yes, Newgate,' she murmured, her voice slightly breaking. 'He is very ill – he will die if he remains there. And there is nothing I can do to save him.'

'But how is this possible? Surely your uncle if he knew –'

'He knows but will do nothing.'

Jack felt his mind gyrating wildly. Sir Francis was a fussy, unattractive man with delusions of grandeur, but surely he would not knowingly allow his nephew to suffer incarceration in one of the foulest prisons of London. Not when he had the means to extricate him.

'How can that be?' he asked in a dazed voice.

'Rupert has transgressed. He has always outrun his allowance but in recent years there have been very large gambling debts, too. In the past Uncle Francis has paid them. But that was while Rupert was a minor and the debts were unenforceable. It was a matter of honour, you see – the Devereux honour. But our uncle swore that he would not continue to rescue Rupert once he reached his majority. If he got into debt again, he would be on his own. And uncle has kept his word.'

'But Newgate!' Jack protested.

'Uncle Francis considers that time in prison will teach Rupert a lesson and eventually reform him.' The handkerchief, Jack noticed, was now in shreds. 'But I know that it will kill him long before he is reformed.'

The events of the past few days were gradually beginning to make sense and Jack felt the frown leave his forehead.

'And how have you tried to save him?' he asked, though certain that he already knew the answer.

'I sold my mother's jewellery to Partridge, but it turned out that it was worth very little.'

'Now why do I find that unsurprising? But that's not all, I imagine.'

'No, of course not. That was my first attempt to raise money. My second was to rob you.'

'I wish now that I had let you.'

'I wish you had too, then I would not have been tempted to ambush the toll coach.'

'Ah, yes, the toll coach. That rates another black mark against our genial landlord. Don't think I have forgotten his part in your injury. I've left a written document for the Runner which details in full my suspicions of that gentleman.'

'You said nothing about the toll convoy?'

'Naturally not. In any case, no real attack took place, nothing was stolen.'

'No,' Lucinda sighed despairingly. 'Nothing that I've tried has worked.'

But the very fact that she *had* tried, put a different complexion on events. He was being forced to reorder what he'd believed to be the truth.

'So riding out as a highwayman was not simply because you were bored with life at Verney Towers?'

'Are you quite mad, Jack?'

'I may have been. I thought you so desperate for excitement, that you would take colossal risks simply for the thrill.'

'What! I could have been killed – and but for you, I might have died. It was Rupert's catastrophe that pushed me to such extremes. How could you think otherwise?'

'I had my reasons,' he murmured, 'though now they seem very stupid.'

Lucinda was not what he'd thought, not a careless, hedonistic thrill seeker but an intensely loving sister. Such courage, such loyalty! This girl had risked her life, had loved her twin so much that she had braved the gallows to save him. Would he have risked such a thing for his sisters? He hardly need ask himself the question. But nor would anyone he knew have taken such a risk – it was too great a sacrifice. It had not been for Lucinda, though. She was an amazing girl: he looked at her with new admiration and a sudden freeing of his heart.

It spurred him to jump to his feet, knowing there were

plans he must set in motion. 'Wait for me here. There is something I have to do.'

'Yes, it's called making a journey. Have you forgotten that you're about to leave?'

'There are arrangements I must first make. Don't move. I'll be back in seconds.'

Her face showed bewilderment but Jack had no intention of explaining. Instead he raced through the rose garden, back along the terrace and round to the front of the house. The carriage, the horses, Lynton and Fielding were still patiently waiting.

'Fielding,' he hailed his coachman. 'I wish you to carry a letter to London for me. Lynton, fetch me paper, quill and ink. And be swift – I will write the letter here.'

For an instant both servants looked at him in dumb astonishment, but then the valet bustled into the house to find the necessary writing materials and, a few minutes later, the missive had been scrawled and handed to Fielding.

'I wish you take this letter to Mr Lowell in Chancery Lane. I have told him what I want done and he will give you his instructions. Once you've carried out his commands, you will return to The Four Feathers.'

Fielding scratched his head. 'Begging your pardon, your lordship, but most times you send a courier to your man of business. I can't be driving to London and Hampshire at the same time.'

'Strangely, Fielding, that small problem had occurred to me. In this instance I cannot send a courier. The matter is too delicate. I need my own staff, people I can trust. Mr Lowell knows you well and will be happy to give you his orders. And both of you can be relied upon to keep silent on whatever you see or hear.'

Fielding's chest swelled at the earl's words, the praise sufficient to keep him happy and uninterested in enquiring further. For Lynton, though, it was otherwise. He coughed apologetically.

'A small matter, my lord. But while Fielding is driving to London and back, where are we to go?'

'An easy one, Lynton. We will repair to The Four Feathers for several nights. When Fielding returns, we will be on our way to Lord Merrington's.'

'But your lordship!' Lynton's face was aghast. 'The Four Feathers!' He had heard enough of that hostelry from his companion to consider his master had taken leave of his senses.

'It may be better to find some place else,' the coachman interjected. 'That landlord is in a fearful temper. The Runner from Bow Street has arrived – an odd cove, name of Didimus Black – but he's been prying into every corner of the inn and old Partridge has worked himself into a fair fury.'

It was the longest speech Jack had ever heard his coachman make. 'You have my promise that it will be for two nights at most,' he said smilingly. 'Once you return with the carriage, Fielding, we will be on our way. In the meantime, take Lynton and the bags with you as far as the inn. I will follow shortly on foot.'

His two henchmen looked at each other in mute disbelief and he guessed they were privately deciding that this time their master had run completely amok. But they were far too well trained to raise any further objections and Jack was able to return to the rose garden feeling assured that his instructions would be carried out to the letter.

Chapter Twenty

The prolonged farewell had not been good for Lucinda. Instead of slipping quietly away from the Towers, Jack had insisted on saying goodbye – in fact two goodbyes. And they had broken her heart. She recognised now what she'd long suspected. She loved him. She'd known, of course, that he could rouse her to a passion she could never have imagined. But she'd made up her mind that though desire might strip her naked and leave her temporarily defenceless, it was a weakness that would eventually pass and leave her unscathed. The certainty that Jack was a professional charmer and that she was just another of his flirts, had made her determined not to succumb.

But when she'd ridden into danger, he had become her saviour, a protector who'd treated her with the utmost delicacy and who had cared nothing for the risk to his own reputation. He had won her trust and won her heart, too. During those sick room days, she'd tried to pretend to herself that what she felt for him was grateful affection, but their passionate lovemaking amid the teacups had destroyed the fiction. It was not grateful affection she felt but a living, breathing, demanding love, a feeling from which she would never be free. Love was here to stay, even if Jack was not.

When he'd returned to the rose garden, it had been to reassure her that all would be well. But what was so well about a brother in prison and the man she loved about to leave and never return? His final farewell had been brief, almost business like. She'd not expected an outpouring of emotion, but some acknowledgement that they were parting forever would have been balm to a bruised heart. Instead it seemed as though he hardly noticed he was saying goodbye, as though he were thinking about something else entirely.

Yet he had been right to go. When he was close, she became another person – one who was ready to fling any number of bonnets over the windmill. She knew herself overwhelmed by his charms and made weak by his tenderness. In her daydreams she had begun to believe him the perfect man for her. How very stupid! He wasn't for her and she should never have allowed herself the fantasy. Years ago he'd met with a disaster that scorched him so fiercely he would never allow himself to love again, refusing to see it was not love at fault but a fallible woman.

Lucinda wished he'd not found her crying: that was not the way she would have chosen to say goodbye. She'd had to pretend that Rupert was the source of her grief – he was in any case a constant sorrow – but in reality she'd been crying for Jack. She had known him little more than a sennight, yet when he drove from Verney Towers, a light would be switched off and the pillars of her life crumble.

Without him, all she had ever known felt meaningless. She was used to being the strong one but in Jack she had found someone as strong, stronger even, someone in whose arms she felt safe. He had made things right with the world.

But not any more. Very soon he would be in Hampshire while she was back where she started. Not even that, since she no longer had any hope of rescuing Rupert and had gained her very own broken heart with which to live.

Weary hours ticked by: a book was taken up, pages listlessly turned, but she could not bring herself to read. Her maid appeared to dress her for dinner but Lucinda refused, saying she would prefer to stay where she was and would take a light supper on a tray. All evening she sat at the window, looking blankly over the landscaped gardens until the light thickened and the distant woods became a brooding darkness. When Molly returned to help her to bed, the maid tried to talk dresses, give her news of the stables, pass on the village gossip, but nothing interested Lucinda. Her mind was miles away, travelling the road to Hampshire along with Jack.

She was sitting in her room the next morning, toying with the tea and toast her maid had fetched for her in lieu of breakfast, when the sound of voices, loud in their greeting, rang out from below. For the first time since the earl's departure, Lucinda woke from her reverie and listened intently. She'd learned from Molly that Sir Francis had left for Steyning that morning and she was puzzled at the unexpected arrival. The greetings faded away, to be followed by subdued murmurs and finally silence. Molly had in her lap one of her mistress's gowns and, needle poised, was about to mend a torn flounce when without warning the door flew open.

Lucinda's pulse grew disagreeably rapid and she started up fearful of a new mishap. But then amazement, happy joyful amazement!

'Rupert,' she half whispered. It must be a ghost, she thought. Rupert had died as she'd always feared and returned as a ghost. But Molly was staring, too. If it was a ghost, they were both seeing the same apparition.

'Can't you welcome a fellow home, Lucy?' The voice was hardly spectral and she ran towards him.

'Rupert, is it really you?'

'Of course it's me. Did you think my spirit had come to haunt you?'

It might as well have, she thought. He looked very thin and very pale and when she put her arms around him and hugged him tight, every one of his bones seemed honed to sharpness.

'You're not looking your usual bright self, Luce.' He kissed her lightly on the hair. 'What's up?'

What's up, she wanted to scream. For weeks I have been sick with foreboding, risked injury and even death to save you and now you appear out of the blue, emaciated but alive, and ask what's up!

'Won't you sit down, Rupert,' she said aloud, 'and tell us how you come to be here. Tell us everything. No,' she corrected herself, 'first Molly must bring refreshments. Have you eaten today?'

'I had a pretty good breakfast on the road, but some

beer and a slice of ham would go down sweetly.'

Molly had sat motionless throughout this interchange, as though held captive by a spell.

'Molly!'

The maid rushed to put the needle down and stabbed her finger, drawing blood. 'I've stained your dress, miss,' she wailed, her mind seemingly disordered by Rupert's sudden appearance. 'I'm so sorry,' and she started dabbing furiously at the material.

Lucinda went to her and took the dress. 'Don't be upset. It really is Rupert who has come home – bring him a little food and drink and then we'll talk.'

The maid's face twitched in response as though she still couldn't believe what she was seeing and, bobbing a curtsy to Rupert, she fled through the door.

'Is Molly all right? She's not become dicked in the nob, has she – from living here?'

'She will be fine. You have given us both a shock, Rupert, you must know that. It's hard to believe that it's really you who has come through that door.'

'It's me all right.' Her brother threw himself into a chair, stretched his thin legs and yawned.

'But how is it that you have been released from Newgate? Did Uncle Francis pay your debts after all? And how did you get here?'

'Hey, hold on. Give a chap a chance. Our beloved uncle paid not a penny – you should know him better than that. Someone else did, but don't ask me who.'

Lucinda gaped at him. 'An unknown benefactor? Someone you don't even know paid your debts? That makes no sense.'

'Whether it does or not, that's what's happened. The chief keeper came to my cell last evening and jerked me awake. Then he marched me to the sheriff's office and told me I was going.'

'And you just walked out of the gates? How astonishing and how wonderful! But where did you go once you were released? You could not have had money.'

'I didn't, naturally, but when I walked from the prison, there was a hansom waiting. The driver took me to Southwark, the George Inn, and there was a room for me. Paid in advance. It all felt a tad strange – as though I was playing a part in someone else's fantasy.'

'And did the cab driver have instructions for you? Else how would you know what to do next?'

'No. He drove off but the innkeeper at the George had an envelope with my name on it – inside was a ticket for this morning's stage to Steyning.'

Lucinda gasped again. 'Your journey seems to have been planned down to the last detail.'

'Looks like it. Even at Steyning there was another carriage waiting – well, not a carriage exactly, a farmer's cart, but it got me to the gates and here I am.'

Lucinda jumped up again and hugged him joyfully. 'It's so wonderful to see you and such an amazing tale. But who– ?'

'I told you, I haven't the faintest idea.'

She crouched down beside him and looked searchingly at his wasted face. 'Is it possible that you made a powerful friend in Newgate?'

'But obviously – they're ten a penny there.'

'I don't mean an inmate,' she scolded. 'A visitor perhaps who took pity on you.'

'Visitors are pretty rare and why would anyone donate such a honey-fall?'

'They might see you were of gentle birth and feel grieved at your brutal treatment.'

He laughed down into her upturned face. 'Believe me, sis, after months in Newgate, any vestige of my gentle birth, as you call it, had disappeared completely. When you came calling, I could have been any felon – admit it. And after I fell ill, I looked even worse.'

'Thank heaven that you were strong enough to beat the typhus – since your letter arrived, I've been sick with worry.'

'Worry wouldn't have done much good, but I was lucky. There was a man, due to hang, and he gave me some kind of potion. He had it from his grandmother. I think she must have been a witch. Anyway he said it would cure the fever in no time and he wasn't going to need it where he was going. I didn't know whether to swallow it or not, but I reckoned that if I was going to die anyway, it was worth the gamble. And within two days the fever began to wane. I'm still a trifle weak but I'm on the mend.'

'The man who gave you the medicine deserves a place in heaven and if we could find your benefactor, I'd kiss his feet.'

'Steady on. I grant you it was decent of him to pay my debts but I must have done something to deserve his help.'

Lucinda wrinkled her forehead. 'What do you mean?'

'I must have impressed someone or why would they have sported the ready?'

'But you said – '

'That I didn't look gentle born and I didn't. I still sounded it though and, now I recall, I spoke to a cove a few weeks back. He was visiting a sharper who'd just arrived in quod.'

'A sharper? Quod?' Lucinda queried faintly. It seemed as though her brother had caught more than typhus from his incarceration.

'Prison then. Anyway he was glad of my advice. It *must* have been him,' Rupert said with growing confidence. 'I can see that now. Newgate can be a shock – the stink, the pestilence. Do you know that people walking on the pavement outside hold their noses? Anyway I took the trouble to pass on to him what I'd learned – what to avoid, who to avoid – and he was grateful. Some of the prisoners are madmen and you're best not to go near *their* cells. They can reach out through the bars and grab. I've seen it done.'

'I'm sure he benefited from your advice, but would it be sufficient to deserve such a reward?'

'I don't care where the money came from, Luce,' her brother said irritably. 'I'm free and by God I deserve to be. Four months in that hell-hole and not a visitor – except you. And you only came once.'

'That was difficult enough,' she protested.

He shrugged his shoulders and began to wolf down the ham that Molly had delivered while they were talking.

Lucinda felt deflated. She was astonished and delighted to have Rupert home again. An hour ago she would not have thought it possible. But the reality of his homecoming was not living up to the dream and she wondered why his lack of gratitude grated so badly. He had been treated wretchedly and a degree of rancour was to be expected. Yet she still felt ruffled.

Perhaps acquaintance with Jack had unconsciously changed her perspective. She'd called the earl arrogant yet he treated his servants with courtesy, had uncomplainingly shared with Molly the drudgery of the sick room and allowed her uncle to bore him half to death. It was a matter of manners, she decided, a matter of gentlemanliness. But when Rupert had had time to settle, he would become more like the brother she used to know. It could not be easy for him to be pitched so suddenly back into his old life.

'Are they your clothes?' For the first time Lucinda became aware that the jacket and trousers he wore were ones she had never seen.

'No, they were given me by the keeper. Mine were too disgusting to wear beyond Newgate. These were part of my rescue, I imagine, but they don't fit.'

'They look fine to me.'

'That's because you're not wearing them. I guess they'll do until I can get to a tailor.'

'You have a wardrobe of clothes in your room. You cannot need more.' Her tone was reproving and her brother responded with scarcely veiled anger.

'Says who? I've been locked up for months and if I want to draw the bustle a little, I will.'

'How will you do that? You have no money and who will

frank you?'

'You must have some gingerbread, sis. Can't you spare a little?'

'I have none,' she said flatly. 'I had to sell Mama's jewellery to pay for my journey to London.'

Once more Rupert shrugged his shoulders and she could see that she was proving as much a disappointment to him as he was to her. But she must try to ignore his shortcomings since it was clear he carried within him a deal of unexpressed anger. She understood well why that was so and, though he might prove a different twin from the one she'd known, Lucinda was certain she would grow accustomed very soon to the miracle of having him home again.

Even as she comforted herself with the thought, she found her mind wandering. By now the earl would be meeting and re-meeting old and new friends. There would be plenty of them and some would be very pretty friends, she was certain, all too willing to flirt and perhaps more. The nip of jealousy made her physically flinch – she could not bear to think of Jack sharing intimacies with another. What was the chance that he would remember her and turn away? Sadly, very small. Beneath the smooth exterior, beneath the charm and gentlemanly consideration, he was the pirate she'd first thought him and he would seize whatever bounty was on offer.

But yesterday that self-same pirate had listened to her sobbing over the boy who now sat so close. Jack had been concerned for her and very, very kind. When he'd returned a second time from giving orders to his staff, he'd held her hands in his and made her promise solemnly that she would never risk her life again. All would be well, he'd assured her, and she must cry no more. And when she'd asked him how he could know that, he had said simply, *Trust me.*

And he'd been right. Everything had turned out well. But of course, it had – a sudden thought ripped through her brain. It had turned out well because he had made it so. All this – the payment of Rupert's debts, the clothes, the cab, the inn, the stage coach ticket – had been organised by Jack. Such meticulous arrangements! And he'd done it for her. Her heart swelled. Was there ever a more beautiful man? If only he were here and not fifty miles away, she would prostrate herself in thanks. She would kiss his feet, whatever Rupert said.

But how could he have done so much in such a short time and still travel on to Hampshire? The truth was that he could not. Was it possible then that he was still in the neighbourhood? If so, he would have had to take rooms in The Four Feathers since it was the only hostelry within miles. It seemed most unlikely but if there was any chance of finding him, she must try. She must thank him from the bottom of her heart.

Lucinda jumped up and grabbed a woollen cape from the closet. 'I have to go out for a short while, Rupert, but while I'm away you should go to Uncle Francis and tell him what has happened. He will be back from Steyning by now and you'll find him in the library.'

Her brother's face registered a stubborn refusal. 'You must,' she urged. 'You cannot suddenly appear in the house without explanation. And the sooner you speak to him, the easier it will be for you.' And for all of us, she thought.

'What is so urgent that you must leave as soon as I arrive?'

'I have business in the village but I will be back very soon.'

'You are going to the village!' he exploded. 'Your only brother, your twin, returns this very hour after nearly dying in prison and you go to the village!'

Molly was looking at her in astonishment but she refused to meet her maid's eyes. 'This is something that cannot wait,' she said vaguely, 'but it won't take long, I promise.'

And she was through the door before either of her companions could say more.

Chapter Twenty-One

Lucinda hurried along the lane to the village, head bent in determination. The path was uneven and it was difficult to maintain her pace, but she continued to push herself to cover the distance as quickly as she could: half a mile, a mile, and then the first straggling line of cottages came into view. Her breath was coming in short spurts and her limbs were growing heavy. She dropped into a slow walk – she was not as thoroughly recovered as she'd thought. But she would get there, she resolved, though she might have to beg a ride home from a passing farm cart.

She had turned the corner into the final straight of Verney's main thoroughfare when she almost collided with a large black horse trotting towards her in the centre of the road. Its rider swerved but Lucinda had already leapt from its path and found herself teetering unsafely over a yawning ditch. She clung precariously to the narrow grass verge, waiting for her breathing to return to normal.

A hand was at her elbow. 'Have you walked all the way from the Towers? What were you thinking of?' It was a familiar voice.

She spun round and would have toppled from her perch

but for his arm. 'You have not yet left, Jack,' she breathed huskily. 'I thought you would be gone. I walked as quickly as I could, and – '

'No more words. You have exhausted yourself.'

'I wanted to talk to you,' she panted, 'I know why you're still here.'

He looked disconcerted but took her arm and led her towards his mount. 'Come. You must walk no more. We will find somewhere we can talk.'

'Good. I have so much I want to say.'

'Whatever it is, it can wait. You'll need to hold tight to me. Use your good arm.' He lifted her on to the saddle – as though she were no heavier than thistledown, she thought, and then silently scolded herself for her fancifulness.

'I said we would ride but that is an approximation,' he murmured into her ear as the animal slowly lumbered forward. 'I hired this beast from the most cunning of farmers. It makes your uncle's horse seem a veritable Pegasus.'

Lucinda giggled. It felt right to be with him again, right to be cocooned in his arms. In stately fashion they plodded along the street and out of the village, the gentle motion of the horse melding them together. She leaned back against his chest and raised her face to what warmth there was from the autumn sun. For a moment, her grip slackened and in response his arms tightened around her. She wanted this journey to go on for ever and wondered if Jack did, too. But when they came to the stream which marked the southern boundary of the village, he dismounted and turned to help her down.

'This river must be the very one that flows through the park at Verney Towers,' he said. For an instant, as she slid from the saddle, Lucinda was held in his arms again. But then he carefully set her down on her feet. 'Let's hope that history doesn't repeat itself.' He gave a slight smile. 'If you remember, the last time we talked by its waters we fell into a stupid squabble.'

Jack's cool detachment shrivelled the warmth in which she'd been basking. But he was right to stay aloof, Lucinda knew, just as he'd been right to leave the Towers. It was only his kindness to Rupert that had brought them together again.

Tethering the horse to a nearby tree, he shrugged off his riding jacket and spread it on the riverbank beneath a small alder. Lucinda sat down beside him. The river flowed swiftly here, its eddying currents bearing leaves and broken twigs rapidly downstream. An enormous willow on the opposite bank cascaded its branches into the rushing water, trailing leaves into ever shifting patterns of green and gold. And within its protective circle, small fishes played hide and seek beneath the water's clear surface. They sat watching their games in silence, the soft ripple of the river cloaking them in its calm.

At last, Lucinda broke the quiet, impatient to express her thanks. 'I thought you miles away at Lord Merriman's.'

'There were things I had to do,' Jack said evasively. He would not easily admit to his generosity, she could see. 'But you must not think I've been wasting my time. You met me as I was returning from the woods or more precisely, from the clearing. Yes, that clearing! I took Didimus Black – he's the Runner sent by Bow Street – and showed him where I suffered the most nefarious of attacks.'

His words sent a riff of fear chasing down her spine but Jack smiled encouragingly at her. 'I've suggested to him that the highwayman haunting the Sussex byways is no more fearsome than a youngster playing games, and that it's just the kind of spree to tempt a bored youth.'

'Do you think he believed you?'

'He didn't disbelieve me – he's still making up his mind. I pointed out that nothing was taken from me and that it was hardly a sensible place from which to launch an attack. No professional highwayman would have gone for a wood. They prefer open land where their escape is more certain. I didn't mention that the clearing was a perfect choice for anyone knowing every inch of the local countryside.'

She quaked inwardly. 'Let's hope he doesn't think of that for himself.'

'I made light of the incident and acted as though I thought he should, too. After all I'm the victim and if I don't take it seriously, then why should he?'

The sun's rays had strengthened and in the reflected river light the air grew warm. Jack murmured an apology and began to unwind a badly wilting neckcloth. She saw a glimpse of bare chest before he adjusted the ruffles of his cambric shirt and leaned lazily back against the tree. Just looking at him sent a sizzle of pleasure through her veins but wished it were not so.

'If you appear so unconcerned, Mr Black will think he has been called out on false pretences.'

'I suggested that in part he was called to allay the fears

of an elderly gentleman living nearby, but that in any case the presence of a Runner in the neighbourhood would bring home to local striplings the seriousness of their misconduct.'

'You have been busy. But if he should hear of the attack on the toll wagons? I doubt you could explain that as the work of a bored youth.' She was astonished at how collected she sounded, when her body felt anything but.

'So far he has heard nothing of it and I doubt that Partridge will give the game away – it would implicate him in knowledge he's not supposed to have. The Runner is taking a particular interest in our landlord and that's my doing as well. Mr Black won't want to return to Bow Street empty handed and the shady activities at the inn should provide him with a just reward.'

'Are you ever at a loss?' Lucinda closed her eyes to the sun and leaned back, joining him against the alder tree.

'Not often – though I was astounded to see you running down the village street and nearly killing yourself in the process.'

'You exaggerate.'

'I don't like to see my patients relapse,' he teased.

'I wanted to find you if it was possible. I wanted to thank you. No, that is inadequate. I actually wanted to kiss your feet, but Rupert baulked at that.'

'I think I might, too. But Rupert? He is home again?'

'You know well that he is. You arranged it all.'

He did not confirm or deny her suggestion, but she knew it for the truth. She reached out for his hand and lifted it to her lips. 'Thank you, Jack, from the bottom of my heart.'

He took her hand, palm uppermost, and kissed it back. 'Rupert is well?'

'Well enough. I've left him to make his peace with Uncle Francis.'

'That could be tricky, but it's not your problem,' he said softly. 'It's Rupert's. You must leave him to work it out.'

'You think me foolish to be so concerned for him?'

'How could I think that? You have been a most loving sister, and I'm sure he is aware of how much he owes you.'

'I'm not,' she said bluntly. 'Rupert has come to expect my aid, whatever he does. But it's not his fault. I have led him to depend on me ever since we were young children.'

'And why was that?'

'He found growing up without a mother or father very difficult.'

'And you did not?'

'I did, naturally, but I coped. It's strange,' she reflected, 'we are twins. In fact, I believe that Rupert was born first, but I have always felt the elder child.'

'And so you've shouldered his troubles. Was that wise?' It was an uncomfortable question, but there was sympathy in Jack's eyes.

'In retrospect no, but I wanted to protect him. My grandparents treated us both severely but Rupert particularly so. They hated my father and Rupert is very like him – in looks at least. They worried that he would go the same way and ruled him with a rod of iron. They could be cruel.'

'To a small child?'

'That hardly mattered. They saw him as a wicked soul in need of correction. He was imprisoned in his room, denied meals, sometimes even beaten. Our uncle has followed in their footsteps.'

'It's difficult for me to picture Sir Francis administering a beating!'

'He never did in fact.' She thought for a moment. 'But in many ways he treated Rupert as badly. He has meted out punishment differently, that's all – forbidding my brother playthings when he was young or new clothes as he grew older, or a pony when he was desperate to ride. It was my mother's godfather who bequeathed Red to him. He was never allowed friends either – instead he was made to do lessons eight hours a day. He had only to sin slightly and he was chastised.'

'And you were not? You were the golden girl.' Jack reached out to smooth away a wisp of blonde hair that had blown across her face. 'Quite literally!'

'I was as naughty as Rupert, naughtier at times, but somehow his punishment was always more severe. It made me very protective – I felt I had to defend him, shield him if I could. I still do.'

'I understand. But why was your father so hated that his son was made to suffer in that way? He was a military man, I think you said. It's an honourable profession.'

'He *was* a soldier but by the time my mother met him, he had sold out. He existed on what he could win at the gambling tables and from other activities it's probably best not to dwell on.' Her mother's words danced before her eyes. 'Suffice to say he mixed with some very undesirable company.'

Jack gave a low whistle. 'It's hardly surprising that your mother's family was upset by her choice of husband. But how did the two of them ever come to meet? I can't imagine that Captain Laceys were thick on the ground in the Devereux's social circle.'

'I've never discovered exactly how they became acquainted. My uncle finds it impossible to talk of his sister. They were very close at one time, I believe, but then Agnes, my mother, met my father – I suspect it may have been through Uncle Francis or rather a friend of his, so perhaps he feels guilt at the outcome. Though knowing him,' Lucinda said fairly, 'I cannot see him feeling it for long.'

'Nor me.' He grinned. 'Your father's career though – before he took up gaming, that is – might be just the thing for Rupert. He is weak at the moment and will need some months to regain his strength, but the military could be a sensible choice. It's a disciplined life and would help tame his energy.'

Lucinda made no response but became aware that he was looking at her intently, his brown eyes honey warm. She felt her body flush beneath the heat of his gaze. Neither of them moved and neither looked away, their eyes feasting on each other.

Desperately, she pulled herself back to reality. 'How did you become such a sage?' She gave an involuntary spurt of laughter and wished her voice did not sound so shaky. If only he did not touch her, all would be well. If only he would touch her.

'Most of the time, Lucinda, I'm scrabbling for wisdom. Now, for example, I should put you on my horse and walk you back to Verney Towers.' His voice, too, was hardly his own.

'But – '

'But instead I must kiss you. I can do nothing else.'

His hand tipped her chin upwards and in an instant his mouth found hers. She opened to him, her lips knowing exactly what to do. His kiss this time was possessive, hard and intense: he was claiming her for his own. Again and again he kissed her until her lips felt bruised and her whole being ached with longing. Then his hands were skimming her body, caressing every curve, in an unrelenting embrace. She felt the tremors of fire spreading wider and wider through every nerve, every fibre.

He followed her down on to the jacket, his body covering hers, moulding himself to her. The ties of her bodice were loosened and the covering of soft cotton pushed to one side. Without a moment's hesitation she took his head in her hands and pulled his mouth down to her breasts. Slowly and tenderly he kissed her into fierce delight. She felt the cool air on the naked skin of her legs and his hands moving upwards – she longed for him to find her and stay there forever.

The sound of a coach being driven fast along the nearby road burst upon them. His hand was stopped, her lips released and he pulled them both to a sitting position.

'That should not have happened.'

'I've heard those words before, I think.' Her mouth curved itself into a sensuous smile.

'You are a witch and I cannot resist you. But this is a public place and we could have been discovered at any time. I must have been mad.'

'*We* must have been mad,' she amended, reaching out to smooth the face that had become so dear. He was right to say it should not have happened, but she couldn't feel sorry. She would have one last memory to warm her through the years of loneliness.

Jack helped her to her feet and stood looking into her eyes. He seemed to be going to say something, but then turned and went to untether the horse. Lucinda collected his crumpled jacket from their resting place and a sheet of white fluttered to the ground. Picking it up to replace it in his pocket, she noticed that it bore a London address. Surely Grosvenor Square was where his sister, Lady Bessborough, lived.

The earl was still busy adjusting the girths on the horse and Lucinda could not resist the letter's temptation. But as she read, her face grew crimson as each line imprinted itself on her brain. Minutes ago she had been lost in the embrace of this man, had longed to surrender herself gloriously to him. She had wanted him as she'd wanted nothing else in her life. But now – she felt cheated, humiliated, and very, very angry.

'When were you thinking of telling me? Or perhaps you were not,' she said in cold accusation.

He turned around and looked at her questioningly. She waved the letter at him. 'It seems that Miss Hayward awaits you at Lord Merriman's. How very pleasant. And perhaps she is not the only one you can look forward to. Perhaps

Lady Bessborough is even now busily finding a few more virgins for your delectation.'

'What the hell!'

'Tut, tut. You must learn to stifle your curses, Lord Frensham. Other women may be more choosy than I.'

He strode towards her, a tinge of colour in his lean cheeks, and snatched the letter from out of her fingers. 'Is this a Lacey phenomenon, too – reading other people's correspondence as well as spending other people's money.'

He was out to hurt her, Lucinda knew, but all she felt was rage. He had been toying with her. She had thought him splendid, the perfect man. She had ached for his touch and when it came, had been ready to give herself to him in love. And what was her return? A passion that was quickly forgotten and his swift departure to pastures new.

She tried to control her voice but could not keep the tremble from it. 'I confess I had no right to read your letter. But what right had you to make love to me, knowing that tomorrow you will be charming another woman?'

'I know no such thing. Whatever is in that letter has nothing to do with me. My sisters are a law unto themselves. They arrange and I ignore – I thought you realised that.'

'So you intend to disregard Miss Hayward's attractions?'

'I have no notion of who Miss Hayward might be.'

'In the same way that you had no notion of who Miss Lacey might be. It hasn't stopped you getting to know her quite well though!'

'With her blessing.'

It was Lucinda's turn to flush angrily. 'And what do you mean by that?'

'Simply that I haven't noticed too many protests on your part.'

'Is that your excuse for serial seduction?'

'I need no excuse.' He was towering over her, his face a study in wrath. 'Seduction takes two – you have been as eager for me as I have been for you. And you know it!'

The flush died and her face turned a sickly white. She was feeling ill, but when she spoke her voice was steel. 'Let us hope you find Miss Hayward as eager.'

'I care nothing for Miss Hayward. How many times have I to say that?'

'As you have cared nothing for others you've seduced. Your excuses are weak, sir. You are a womaniser, plain and simple, and I have been foolish enough to believe you sincere. But no longer.'

And gathering her skirts together, Lucinda walked briskly away, leaving him in a state of seething resentment.

Chapter Twenty-Two

Jack was still seething the next morning. It had not been easy to obtain Rupert Lacey's release but he had done it. He had pulled strings, paid money. His men had exerted themselves to organise cabs and coaches and accommodation. All for Lucinda – so that she could rescue her beloved brother and know peace of mind. He'd not wanted gratitude, he'd not wanted another intimate encounter. But in the event, he'd got both and more.

Two days ago she had stunned him with the news that her brother was in gaol and that the thrill seeking he so abhorred had in truth been a purposeful campaign. She was not after all another Julia chasing excitement, but a brave, foolhardy girl who had acted out of love and loyalty. He'd not known how to respond and had bid her an almost mechanical farewell, as he very slowly absorbed the realisation that something fundamental had shifted.

Knowing the true situation had changed the very landscape of his mind. The barrier he'd erected against her had been demolished and, in turn, thrown the future he'd planned into disarray. One question had hammered insistently at him. Could he bear to love again? The past was still so vivid – the heartbreak, the shame, the humiliation – and love was a gamble. He had believed he would never venture there again.

And what of Lucinda? Would it be fair to involve her any further when he was unsure of his own mind? She desired him, it was certain, but desire would pass. In a year or less she would forget him. She was fixed on a very different future – from the outset she'd been clear her brother was to be her companion through life. Her every thought was for Rupert and, on the very day of Jack's departure, her tears in the rose garden had been for her brother. Now she had her twin home again and the life she dreamed of could eventually be hers. What right had he to step into that dream and distort it?

She provoked the utmost passion in him, but a lifetime commitment could not be built on passion alone. In time, the urgency would fade and how could he be the husband and companion she needed and deserved? There was nothing in his life that suggested he could. As a very young man he had loved truly, but after that disastrous affair, he'd thrown himself into a world of heedless pleasure: fine clothes, fine parties, fine women. Except for his sporting prowess, there was nothing of which he could be proud, and it was hardly a basis on which to build enduring happiness. Lucinda deserved so much better. Once Fielding returned from London with the carriage, he would go, Jack had resolved. He would leave her in peace.

The decision had been made, the carriage returned, and he'd been on the point of setting out for Hampshire when the business with the Runner had detained him. Before he could make good his escape, Lucinda had come rushing into his life once more, happiness writ large on her face and in every gesture. He should have simply acknowledged her thanks and bid her a final farewell. But he'd lingered, riding with her to the river when he should have ridden away. Talking once more with her, seeing her lovely face, her smile, had lifted his heart in a way that he couldn't explain. He'd been unable to say goodbye, unable to leave. And despite his very best intentions, unable to resist making love to her.

He'd been struggling to impose order on his wayward feelings when he'd seen her with the letter in her hand. A small spurt of anger took hold of him now as he thought of it. How dare she read his correspondence – and then abuse him. His first impulse when he'd opened his sister's letter had been to throw it away. Why hadn't he done just that? The answer was clear. Because he hadn't expected anyone, least of all Lucinda, to come snooping. He could kill Georgina, he could kill Lucinda Lacey. Accusing him of being a womaniser! That was his father, not him. He had a fondness for women, it was true. He would even admit to being a dangerous flirt on occasions – he had the scars to prove it. But a womaniser!

And why had a stupid letter from his interfering sister so enraged her? She knew his family's intentions and knew, too, that their efforts to find a countess for him were doomed to failure. Had she thought that Miss Hayward would be different? But why? And why did it matter to her? He recalled that she'd asked him before whether a potential bride awaited him at Merry's. He had thought it an odd question, but now it did not appear quite so odd. Not odd at all if Lucinda was moved by jealousy.

His thoughts were brought to an abrupt halt. Jealousy suggested love. But was that possible? Lucinda had no wish to marry. And she did not love him. She was powerfully attracted, he knew, and she felt immense gratitude to him for rescuing both her and her brother. But love – that was a very different matter.

He thought back to their times together: the laughter, the quarrels, the sheer enjoyment of being together, and wondered. The tears in the garden. Was it possible they had been for him and not Rupert? The glow on her face yesterday when she first saw him – was that love? He shook his head at the thought. Love was a torment and, like him, she would be well advised to avoid it at all costs. Yet not loving felt just as miserable. He hated that their friendship had ended so sourly, if friendship it was. In truth, it had been a great deal more. It *was* a great deal more for his arms felt newly empty and his heart sore.

He could not go to Lord Merriman's. He'd no wish to fight off the attentions of his sisters' protégées. At the best of times, it would have been a wretched business but with his mind filled with Lucinda, it was impossible. He would return to London instead. He strode to the bell hanging crookedly by the door and then remembered that it no longer worked. He cursed The Four Feathers and all its iniquities. He would have to go in search of Lynton, but at least within the hour he would have put this hated piece of England behind him.

But then he hesitated and walked back to the grime-ridden window, standing irresolute for several minutes. If he went, he would never see Lucinda again. How could he bear that? Perhaps if they had not met yesterday, if they had not quarrelled so badly...she should have believed him when he'd said that he had no interest in Miss Hayward. Or any other woman. It was the truth. It was unlikely that he would ever again feel interest in another woman. The realisation hit him with sudden blinding clarity: the only woman he wanted was Lucinda, troublesome, frustrating, adorable Lucinda. He could not live without her.

He could not live without her! For the first time in years he felt the burden he'd carried for so long float free. He was dazed, filled with exhilaration by a new sense of liberty. A barrier had broken and the memories that oppressed him, the guilt, the dishonour, began to dissolve.

Lucinda was his heart and soul and he knew what he had to do. He would go to her and offer himself. He might not be a prince among husbands, but he would be the truest lover she could ever have.

Lynton had his head around the door, an apprehensive expression on his face.

'Why are you looking as blue as megrim?' Jack was filled with gladness and wanted the world to celebrate.

The valet seemed in a quandary as to whether to speak or not. Ever since they'd come to Verney, his master had been acting out of character. It would be better for them all, Lynton considered, if they travelled immediately to Lord Merriman's. Two uncomfortable nights at The Four Feathers were more than enough.

'I was wondering, your lordship. Fielding and I were

wondering,' he corrected himself, 'whether or not we might be leaving today.' He looked hopefully at Jack.

'I'm aware that you both consider I've taken leave of my senses, but you'll be relieved to know that we'll shortly be bidding farewell to this fly-blown place.'

'We're leaving for Lord Merriman's, sir? Today?' The valet was trying not to sound too eager.

'Not Lord Merriman's. Not today, not any day.'

'But –'

'No buts. Now brush the new blue superfine. I'm going out and, despite my surroundings, I don't wish to look a hayseed.'

Lynton sighed inwardly and fetched the clothes brush. He knew exactly where the earl was bound and he feared for the outcome.

Chapter Twenty-Three

Lucinda was bent low over a flower bed. A small bush had been uprooted and she was making ready to replant it. Her movements were deliberate, as though by attending to every detail she could keep the world at a distance. Rapt concentration left her unaware of the figure winding its way upwards towards the house. The earl had entered the estate through a little used gate and was clambering from terrace to terrace when half way up a flight of steps, he caught sight of her.

'Was it a fox?'

Lucinda spun around, her face filled with confusion. Jack was the last person she had expected to see and it was painful to meet him again. Her voice seemed to her to come from a long way away.

'I'm not sure. It might be a fox but sometimes it's a farmer's dog that strays. My uncle will be filled with murder if he sees this destruction. I'm repairing the damage as quickly as I can.'

'Could Latimer not do it for you?'

'He would volunteer to carry my uncle's shotgun.'

She finished shovelling earth and straightened up. She

could no longer avoid looking at him directly and, without realising, her lips creased into a smile. He was hardly dressed for gardening but his face and figure gladdened her eyes. She was a fool, she chided herself. She had only to see him and she was lost.

'Lucinda, I've come – '

'No, don't say a word. I have to grovel.' She should not have spied on his private correspondence whatever the provocation, she knew, and she had to get her apology out. 'I was so terribly in the wrong yesterday, Jack. I had no right to read your letter and no right to take you to task for your conduct. After you saved Rupert, it was unforgiveable.'

'I must disagree with you,' he said quietly. 'But can we talk somewhere that is not quite so open to prying eyes?'

'The conservatory is near – that is, if you don't mind.' She was horribly conscious of its associations and a blush began to creep across her cheeks.

'It has only happy memories for me.' The glimmer of a mischievous smile lit his face and he offered her his arm. 'Unlike the Towers, which I confess does not improve on re-acquaintance.' He looked over his shoulder at the gloomy mansion hovering in the distance.

'I told you the house was ugly – do you remember? Admit now that I was right.' If they could keep the conversation unexceptional, Lucinda thought, she would manage this difficult visit.

The conservatory was warm and welcoming after the chill of the garden, but Jack remained standing as though he wanted to speak his words as quickly as possible. 'I am sorry that we quarrelled, Lucinda. After what has passed between us, you have a right to be interested in what I do. Every right. I should not have ripped up at you.'

'And I should have believed you when you said you were unaware of the delights in store for you at Lord Merriman's.' She tried to speak lightly but it came out askew and, to cover the awkward moment, she beckoned him towards the chairs which overlooked the park.

'They are delights I could do without, but I seem incapable of controlling my sisters.' He shook his head ruefully. 'Georgina is unquenchable in her search for the right woman.'

'Perhaps she wants your happiness and feels that you need help to find it.'

'It's far more likely she wants an heir for the Frensham title. But even if I were to think her motives benign, her conduct is foolish. She cannot seem to realise that my happiness is in my own hands and that I will be the one to find the woman who suits me.'

Lucinda took a minute to digest his words. Was he looking for a wife after all? The notion flew in the face of everything he'd ever said and she could not stop herself blurting out, 'But I thought there was no such paragon. Have you not vowed to die unmarried?'

'I have, but lately I've been made to reconsider.'

'But you were adamant. The woman you were once to wed...'

'I spoke truly – at the time. I was still plagued in my mind and heart by thoughts of the past.'

She looked perplexed. 'Are you saying that you are now willing to marry?' It hardly seemed possible.

'I believe I am.'

Lucinda felt a sharp stab of pain. Naturally he would marry. His refusal to choose a wife had always been a sentiment that would pass. No doubt the young women at Lord Merriman's would be eager to help him achieve his new ambition. He would have plenty of choice.

She swallowed hard 'But it is not to be Miss Haywood, I presume?'

'Indeed no. But I hope it will be someone of whom my sisters approve.'

The pain twisted and turned inside her so that her whole body felt racked. 'I see. It's someone you have already met?' How on earth was she managing to continue to talk?

He nodded. 'I'm hopeful that the lady will be willing. I've not yet asked her.'

'Then you must do so without delay,' Lucinda said brightly, jumping up from the chair and starting towards the door.

Jack shot out his hand and grabbed her by the arm. 'I will need your help.'

He was impossible. Need her help to propose to a woman she already hated!

'I cannot think I can be of any assistance to you in the matter,' she said coldly.

'You are wrong.' And taking her hand in his, he went down on one knee. 'Will you marry me, Lucinda Lacey?'

She paled. 'Is this an unkind joke? Not one word of love has ever passed your lips, Jack - and why else would you wish to marry?'

'Why else?' he repeated, rising from his knees. 'What

211

other reason could there be? It has taken me time to see what has been staring me in the face. You are a beautiful woman and I desire you greatly. But you are also a girl who has touched my heart in a way that I could never have imagined.'

'What are you saying?' Lucinda's pulse was thudding uncontrollably. Was she really hearing him aright?

'I love you! I am as astonished as you. But it happens to be true. I have found it impossible to leave here – you can see that. I pretended to myself that I needed to stay in the neighbourhood while Fielding went to London, but the truth was very different. I could have stayed elsewhere. I could have hired a coach and taken myself to Lord Merrington's, yet I remained in Verney, in that miserably uncomfortable inn, because I could not bear to leave you. But I couldn't admit the truth to myself. Yesterday, when I had you in my arms again, I needed to quarrel to allow myself to walk away. But it seems it didn't work. I'm still here, still unable to say goodbye.'

She wanted so much to believe him, but could she? Could a man who had forsworn love for so long really want to be with her forever?

'It was only a day ago that you were so sure you would never love again,' she said uncertainly.

'I've been blind, Lucinda, and only now can I see clearly. I think I loved you from the moment I saw you – even in that most dreadful of outfits. But I resisted. I fought against it – you have no idea how hard – but today a lightening bolt struck and made me see that I would never be happy without you. That without you the world makes no sense.'

His words should have sent her floating on a cloud of happiness but she found herself stricken, unable to respond. I must be in shock, she thought. Jack's expression assumed an uncharacteristic nervousness and he reached out for her hands and brought her close to him.

'I know that your brother means everything to you, and that you had thought to stay with him for the rest of your life. But do you think you might change your mind? Is it possible that you could love me back?'

There was a silence so complete that they could hear each other breathing. Then she shook her head sharply as though to dislodge the confusion of thoughts and a small joyous laugh told him what he wanted to know.

'Say it,' he said urgently. 'I still need to hear the words.'

'I love you, Jack. I love you more than life itself, but –'

'But?'

'I had thought never to wed. And neither had you.'

'It will take getting used to, I admit, but we have all the time in the world. I may want very much to marry you but I'll not press you for an answer. Now come to me.'

Without hesitation she walked into his arms and felt his warmth surround her. His hands were in her hair, pins pattering to the ground as he buried his fingers in her riot of curls. He was kissing her again and again, each touch of his lips sweeter than the one before. A slow heat began to uncurl and suffuse her entire body. They clung to each other, weak with desire, their kisses ever deepening. She scrabbled at the buttons of his waistcoat, tore at his shirt, fumbled with the fastenings to his breeches, anything that prevented her touching his naked skin. Her dress and petticoats fell to the same treatment. In moments she was lying body to body with him, stretched full length on the blankets that had been fetched to keep an invalid warm. She was no invalid. She felt powerful and free – free to love this man as he deserved. For he *loved* her!

$$\backsim$$

They lay for long minutes safe in each other's arms, exhausted and half delirious. Eventually he nuzzled her neck and she stroked his body in response. Then his hands were touching her again, slowly and relentlessly awakening her to renewed passion. She felt herself dissolving into nothingness, desire once more blazing its wild path through them both – they must be together, nothing else was possible.

At length a soft, whispered sigh escaped her and caused him to murmur, 'All is well with you? '

'All is well, Jack,' she breathed, her body satiated with love.

But the autumn dusk was encroaching and he felt her shiver and pulled the blankets more closely around them.

'It's time we left,' he said at last. 'Any minute now Latimer will be doing his rounds, will he not, and I shall wither at his glance.'

'That would never do,' she said saucily and wriggled out of his arms and reached for her clothes. They dressed hastily, aware now of the approaching twilight and the likelihood that one of the gardeners, if not Latimer, would be with them at any moment, key in hand.

'Am I tidy?' she asked as she pulled on her slippers.

'You look as if you have fallen through a hayrick.'

'And so do you.'

'Then now is not the time to confront Sir Francis.'

Her eyes shone. 'You wish to see my uncle?'

'Probably for the first time in our acquaintance! But it will have to wait until tomorrow. I shall need to look my very best – I must ask Lynton to pay special attention to my clothes. There is a slight chance then that I might recover my standing with Sir Francis.'

'And that is important?' she teased.

'My entire happiness depends on it. I must persuade him to accept me as a suitor, then woo you with the greatest vigour – until you agree to marry me.'

'In that case I had better not agree too quickly. But don't fear Uncle Francis. I confess I'd prefer him not to take you in permanent dislike, but remember that at one and twenty, I am my own mistress.'

He placed his hands on her shoulders and kissed her soundly on the lips. 'I do remember and I thank heaven for it. I'm not at all sure that I shall be successful in convincing Sir Francis I am sufficiently virtuous to deserve his niece.'

Lucinda gave a small giggle. 'Poor uncle. We have conducted ourselves shamefully. Lynton will have to work particularly hard tomorrow.'

'Poor Lynton. I have now to tell him that he faces yet another night at The Four Feathers.'

Chapter Twenty-Four

Lucinda skipped up the stairs to her bedroom, her face warm with love and her heart beating happiness, though she still found it hard to believe that Jack loved her - even more, that he wanted to marry her. The world had gone mad, but it was a wonderful madness and the temptation to accept his offer had been great. Why hadn't she said yes immediately? She had doubts, she conceded, small but important, and very subtly they were infiltrating her joy. She wasn't entirely sure that Jack was ready to forget the past and neither could she quite expunge her mother's words, lingering like a dark stain on her mind.

But Agnes Devereux had chosen badly, she told herself, and it did not mean that her daughter must follow in her footsteps. As for Rupert... a whisper of reproach clouded her delight again. Jack had said that she needed to let go, allow her brother to make his own way in the world, and perhaps he was right. Perhaps this was the moment when she should draw back.

'Luce, I need to talk to you.' Rupert stopped her at her bedroom door. If it were possible, he seemed paler than ever and his face had grown more haggard.

'Whatever's the matter?' Any euphoria drained away since it was clear that her brother was in trouble – again.

'I need to talk to you,' he repeated dully. 'Alone.'

It sounded bad. She ushered him into her room and closed the door. They would not be disturbed for some time as Molly was busy in the kitchen helping Cook prepare Rupert's homecoming feast.

Lucinda took her brother's hand and led him to the window seat. 'You look as though you really *are* a ghost. What's troubling you? '

'This.' He thrust a crumpled sheet of paper into her hand. Not more letters, she quailed inwardly. Letters inevitably spelt disaster. But she read the note quickly while Rupert drummed his fingers against the window pane in increasing agitation. By the time she had finished, she was as pale as he. This *was* a disaster.

'How can Partridge threaten you like this? Did you ever gamble at The Four Feathers?'

Her brother nodded dumbly.

'But this man that Partridge mentions – he says he died.'

'He was a crook, an ivory turner. He was cheating me. I may have been drunk but I knew I was being cheated.'

'How much did you lose?'

'A lot. Money I didn't have, money I'd borrowed. You know the score, sis.' She shook her head wearily.

'But it was worse than that – I lost the Lacey ring.'

'How could you, Rupert? How could you pledge our father's own ring?'

'I had to, there was nothing else left. But when I realised

he'd foisted loaded dice on me, I refused to hand it over. I was going to walk away – I would have let him keep the money, but he wasn't going to get his filthy hands on the ring. He would have sold it for tuppence.'

Lucinda looked at him, her gaze painfully intent. 'What happened when you prevented him taking the ring?'

'He grabbed me, tried to throttle me, but I fought back. I'm slightly built but the drink was powerful. It gave me strength and he was befuddled by liquor – he'd dipped much deeper than me. We struggled, I remember, lumbering around the room in a kind of bear hug, neither of us able to land a killing blow. It would have been comic except that he lost patience and drew a knife on me.'

Lucinda put her hands to her face in horror. 'Why did you never tell me this?'

'It's hardly the kind of thing you relate to your sister.'

'But did he wound you?'

'He would have done, for certain. But I drew my own knife and threatened him. I had to do it – he was going to kill me.'

Lucinda jumped up from the window seat. 'What knife?' she asked jerkily.

'The dagger I had made. The one with the Lacey motif.'

'But you swore that the dagger was simply decorative.'

'I didn't tell the truth – I didn't want you to worry. It had the sharpest of edges.'

He saw her appalled expression and burst out, 'I'm not proud of lying, but you would have rung a peal over me if you'd known and probably told our uncle. He would have found some vindictive way to punish me for it. And I had to protect myself when I was in London. I ended up in all kinds of dangerous places, but I never thought I'd need the knife in this backwater.'

'So why,' Lucinda asked, her voice trembling, 'did you take it to The Feathers?'

'I always wore the same jacket for gambling. It was to bring me luck.' His grin was ghastly. 'Anyway it was in my pocket that night and when the stranger lunged at me with his knife, I drew mine.'

'A knife fight? Oh my God, Rupert, what have you been at?'

'It never came to a fight. He charged at me like a mad bull. He really wanted that ring, I guess. I did nothing, I swear Lucy. I just stood there with my knife outstretched to fend him off and he ran into it.'

'You killed him.'

She sank down on the bed, her head bowed, her hands restlessly pinching at the counterpane.

'I didn't mean to. It was self-defence, surely you can see that. He killed himself – he just ran into the knife,' Rupert repeated flatly.

There was a terrible silence between them. At last Lucinda roused herself and looked across at her brother. 'Surely the disturbance must have brought people on to the scene. Why were you not arrested there and then?'

'It was odd. The whole thing – the lumbering around the room, the stabbing – took place in complete silence. Except...' and for the first time he faltered in his tale, 'except for his dying. A horrible, choking wheeze kept coming from him.' Rupert put his hands over his ears, as though the sound still travelled in time. 'I never want to hear that noise again.'

His sister shook her head impatiently. 'But you must have called Partridge – why didn't he report it to the authorities? Why didn't you?'

'I didn't call Partridge. I fled.'

'Rupert!'

'Don't look at me like that.'

'Rupert, a man died a violent death – no matter whether or not you were responsible – and you called no-one!'

'I panicked. All I could think was to get away.'

'You must have been seen though. Customers in the public bar, people coming and going in and out of the inn.'

'I wasn't. No-one saw me. There's a back entrance to Partridge's private room – he keeps it locked but opens it when he knows he's to have guests. It's some distance from the public bar. The man was already in the room when I arrived and nobody knew I'd followed him in.'

'Partridge must have known.'

'Yes.' Her brother gestured miserably to the letter. 'Of course he must.'

Lucinda got to her feet again and began to pace up and down the room, forcing herself to think through the grisly events of that evening. She had to help Rupert, but how was she ever to extricate him from this devil's brew?

'Partridge would have discovered the body,' she said. 'He must have known you were coming that night and when he found the man dead, he would guess there had been a struggle between you.'

'I suppose so.'

'So why was the fight never spoken of in the village?'

'Partridge couldn't have reported it.'

'But why would he not? The man would have to be buried. Partridge couldn't just forget he had a dead body in his inn.'

'A story went round a few days later that there had been a suicide at The Feathers. I wonder you didn't hear it.'

Lucinda had heard nothing but others apparently had, and she wondered how such a falsehood had spread so speedily through the neighbourhood. 'Do you think the landlord put it about that the man had stabbed himself?'

'He must have done. Anyway there was no official enquiry. The magistrate must have been satisfied because no-one came asking questions. A few weeks later, those damn London tradesmen put out an arrest warrant for me and I was dragged to Newgate. The rest you know.'

Lucinda was reeling from the shock of her brother's disclosure, but she was also greatly perplexed. Why would the landlord have covered Rupert's tracks by swearing to a magistrate that it was suicide? The scene played out in her mind: Partridge finding the body with its stab wound – it would have needed only a single blow to the heart to kill – testifying to the magistrate that the man had been drinking, that he was in depressed spirits perhaps. He would swear he'd seen no-one else in the vicinity and if, as Rupert asserted, there had been no real fight, there would be little sign of a struggle. The magistrate would be eager to close the case and happy to believe Partridge. What was one drunken vagrant after all? But why had the landlord in effect protected Rupert? Had he really believed at the time that it was suicide?'

'Why do you think Partridge testified it was suicide, if he knew it was you who had been in that room with the man?'

'It's obvious isn't it,' her brother said bitterly, pointing to the letter. 'He always planned to implicate me in the man's death. He would bide his time until the right moment and then strike. My going to gaol was a hiccup but, now I'm back, he's free to do his worse.'

'He says he has objects belonging to you which he'll turn over to the Runner unless you pay up. He means the ring, I presume. But you could have lost that anywhere. So it's his word against yours. You could swear that you had never been anywhere near the inn that night – if no-one else saw you.'

'It's not that simple.' Rupert looked moodily down at the floor. 'It's not just the ring that he has.'

'What else?' She strode towards him, shaking him by the shoulders. 'What else, Rupert?'

'He has my dagger.'

Lucinda looked at him blankly.

'My knife. The one that killed the man. It probably still has his blood on it.'

'But how can Partridge have it?'

'I told you, I fled. I left it behind and he must have squirrelled it away to use against me.'

Her hands went to her face again.

'He is cunning beyond belief, Luce. He saw the decoration – the Lacey motif – and knew it was mine. He hates the aristocracy, hates this family. He must have decided he would keep it and use it when he could benefit most.'

Lucinda began her pacing again. The picture could not look bleaker. How could her brother have got himself embroiled in such a dreadful situation? Debt was bad enough, but murder! For it would be seen as murder, no matter how much Rupert protested his innocence. His plea of self-defence might have been believed if he'd alerted the authorities at the outset, but after all these months no-one would credit his innocence.

Yet time had passed for Partridge, too. Would anyone believe him after such a long period if he did as he was threatening and went to the local magistrate? Lucinda's face brightened.

'If the landlord suddenly comes up with this story, who will believe him? The magistrate will want to know why he didn't report the fight earlier. He will be accused of covering up for you and charged as an accomplice.'

'He's not that stupid, sis. He will have his story ready. He'll say that he saw me there that night sitting with the man. But that he was working all evening in the public bar and saw nothing else until he found the man dead.'

'Which at least has the merit of being true,' she said tartly.

Her brother ignored the interruption. 'No doubt he'll say that he had his suspicions at the time but didn't like to voice them. We are a powerful family in the district and in the past he's fallen foul of Sir Francis. He could say he was worried that if he suggested my involvement, he'd be punished – our uncle would make sure his licence was forfeit and The Feathers closed down. Then he would lose his livelihood, so he thought it best to say nothing. His conscience was tortured, but when I went to prison – not for killing anyone, but at least I was in prison – he could feel I was being punished.'

'And now...' she began thoughtfully.

'Now I've been freed and that's unjust. I should be back in prison at least. He'll make great play, I'm sure, of how difficult it's been for him to come forward, but how the public good demanded he did.'

Lucinda reached out and took his hand. 'Humphrey Partridge is hardly known for his integrity. If you tell your story first, Rupert, you might be able to spike his guns.'

'I won't. Think of it – I've already been in prison and I'm only here because a rich well-wisher paid for my freedom. And I can't even name him. What chance do I have of getting a fair hearing? Who will believe that I acted in self-defence and simply panicked? Nobody. I'll be condemned even before I'm sent for trial.'

Rupert sat steeped in gloom while the minutes ticked by. 'There's only one way out,' he said finally. 'I'll have to escape abroad – go to France – and do it quickly. I'll travel to Newhaven and find a skipper to take me over to Dieppe. That shouldn't be difficult.'

She looked aghast. 'If you do that, you'll never be able to return, Rupert. You will have to spend the rest of your life on the Continent.'

'Is that so bad? Napoleon is locked away on St Helena and Europe is safe again.'

'But how would you live? You have no money and I've

none to give you. How would you pay for shelter and food?'

'I'd have to chance my luck at the tables. But at least I'd have a life. Don't look like that – it's true. If Partridge carries out his threat, the gallows is all that awaits me or, if I'm lucky, a miserable existence as a chained convict half a world away.'

'Perhaps Partridge won't do as he threatens.' Lucinda clutched at straws. 'What good would it do him? It's money he wants.'

'And it's money he won't get, so he'll settle for revenge. That will taste almost as sweet to him.' There was a pause before her brother said thoughtfully, 'I wish I knew who my well-wisher was. He might be willing to tip over the dibs and I could pay Partridge off.'

'No!' Her voice crackled ominously, surprising them both. 'Even if we raised the funds to pay this time, Partridge will demand more and more. That's what blackmailers do.'

'It would give me a breathing space.'

'But you don't know your benefactor's name.'

Rupert was looking at her curiously and she felt an incriminating flush steal over her face. 'Do you know who it is, Lucy?'

'I don't,' she lied, 'and even if I did, I would never ask him. It would be a bottomless pit. And you cannot go to France, you would likely starve to death there. There is no alternative – you must tell the truth.'

Her brother shook his head vehemently. 'I can't.'

He rose from the window seat and began to walk around the room, whistling tunelessly through his teeth for minutes on end. Just when Lucinda thought she could bear it no longer, he stopped in front of her and looked closely at the floor as though the solution to his problems lay beneath the tufted rug on which he stood.

'There *is* something we haven't thought of.' She distrusted the way his eyes refused to meet hers.

'There is a way we could get the dagger back, the ring too.'

'What do you propose? That we should walk into the inn and ask for them?'

He ignored her caustic tone and said slowly, 'I couldn't, of course. I can't go near the inn. I'm too well known there and Partridge will be on the lookout for me. But you could.'

'I am to march into the inn and ask the landlord for your belongings back? Are you quite mad?'

'No, listen, Luce, this is what to do.' Rupert was all eagerness now, his misery temporarily forgotten. 'The ring and the dagger are sure to be in Partridge's private room – he keeps every secret there.'

'And?'

'You break in to the room and you search for them.'

'I am to burgle Partridge? But naturally I am. That shouldn't prove at all difficult – perhaps we could invite the whole village to watch.'

'You go at night, under cover of darkness. The rear door will be locked but there's a small side window facing the woods. If you climbed in there, you wouldn't be seen.'

'Then if it's possible to get into the building without being seen, why don't you go?' She could hardly believe she was suggesting this. It was proof, if proof were needed, of how desperate they were.

'I may be thin but I'm still too large to get through that window. It would be easy for you - you're small enough.'

'You *are* mad.'

'I'm not. It would work. You could go in disguise - lose your skirts and wear a pair of my breeches and a jacket. If they're black, you'll be virtually invisible. And if you go when the inn is bursting with customers, the landlord will be too busy pulling the beer to worry about what's going on at the back of the house. You could be in and out in no time.'

'And what if he keeps his valuables in a safe?'

For a moment Rupert looked worried. 'That would be a problem if it's shut.'

'Of course it would be shut,' she exploded. 'Why would he have a safe and leave it open?' Lucinda couldn't believe she was actually discussing this.

'You could take an iron bar just in case - one blow to the handle would open it.'

'No!'

'Tonight, that's when to go,' he said excitedly. There will be nobody anywhere near that room, I've just remembered.'

'Remembered what? How can you be so sure?'

'Because it's Jeb Farrar's name day and he's holding a celebration. Molly told me. Everyone in the village will be at the front of the bar, including Partridge. It's the ideal time.'

She brought down silent curses on Molly's head. 'I can't do it.'

'You can, Luce, you're agile enough.'

'I mean that I won't do it. I have made a promise.'

227

'What promise?' He was suspicious.

'The details don't matter. While you were away I was given help and in return I made a promise,' she said vaguely.

'I don't know what you're talking about – and I don't want to know. But ask yourself this. Do you care more for your promise or for your brother?'

Chapter Twenty- Five

L ucinda asked herself the self-same question in the intervening hours. Asked it over and over again. It was an impossible situation. Rupert was convinced he would not receive a fair hearing and he was probably right. If he'd had money, an escape to France might have been a way out, though she would never have seen him again. But he had no money and neither did she. He would become a beggar on the streets of Europe and she could not bear to contemplate his eventual fate.

For a short while she toyed with the idea of confiding in Jack and asking for his help, but decided that she dared not. They had survived all kinds of alarms and misunderstandings to arrive at a wonderful place. She could not jeopardise the happiness that had lit her life a few short hours ago. Jack might be a pirate at heart, but he was a gentleman through and through and he would baulk at covering up such a heinous crime as murder, even for her. He would insist on her brother giving himself up. And when Rupert refused and fled the county, the whole loathsome business would cast the darkest of clouds over them, for how could Jack continue to love a woman whose brother was a murderer and a fugitive?

No, she couldn't tell Jack. She was on her own. She had vowed to him that she would never again break the law and she'd made that promise in all sincerity, little dreaming it would be put to such a test. She hated to deceive him but Rupert was facing the gallows. It was a stark choice. She knew well that if her brother were arrested again, Francis Devereux would not lift a finger to aid him; indeed, he would disown his nephew forever.

Round and round her mind travelled, jumping this way and that, thinking, thinking how to escape the trap that ensnared them. There was no way out. But if she retrieved the missing items, then in one stroke she could rescue her brother. For years she had reproached herself for being unable to protect Rupert from their family's cruelty. What that had done to him, she could only guess. And now he was once more under threat, while she herself knew nothing but happiness. No wonder she felt shrouded in guilt once more.

This time, though, she possessed the power to save him, to save his very life – and she must not fail. She had no idea how hard the task would be, but she would have to try. What other choice was there?

With a leaden heart, she went to Rupert's room. Her highwayman's costume had been cut to ribbons and long since burnt and she had once more to search her brother's wardrobe. It took a while but eventually she found out a pair of breeches and a jacket, both made from the dingiest cloth. She would need to fit into these garments as best she could, since this was one exploit in which she dared not involve Molly and her needle.

⌒

It was eerily quiet in the woods. Here and there a slight fog had gathered between the leaves and every noise was muffled. Birds had flown early to their nests and only the occasional bat swooping overhead told Lucinda that she was not alone in the world. The trees on either side pressed tightly in on her, their branches making a gloomy vault but sheltering her from sight as she skirted the perimeter of the woods to arrive at the rear of the inn. In the black suit she was almost invisible, since a crescent moon gave little light and from time to time disappeared altogether behind passing fragments of cloud.

Out of the woods and into the bushes, which grew so thickly around three of the inn walls, that she had to force her way through the tangled undergrowth. It was clear that Partridge had little interest in gardening or perhaps, she thought, it served to keep intruders at bay. It would not deter her. Now that she was embarked on the adventure, she knew she had done the right thing – she had to help Rupert and this was their only chance.

He'd been right about the whole village turning out this evening for a celebration. Once she reached the rear wall of the inn, she could hear raucous singing and shouts of laughter coming from the front of the building. The noise helped to smother the crackle of twigs and the scuffle of leaves as she crept along the wall towards the small window that gave on to Partridge's office. Rupert had been airily certain that the window would present no problem, but he could not have reckoned on the gully immediately below.

Standing in the hollow, Lucinda found herself at least three feet below the sill.

Be resourceful, she told herself, and looked around. A chestnut tree grew a little to the left of the window. It was rooted on higher ground, but several of its branches were long enough to tap their fingers at the glass. She squinted up at it, deciding in the dim light that if she could climb to the second of its branches, she'd be able to ease her way far enough along to be within reach of the window. From there she could pull open the bottom sash as long as Partridge had not secured it from the inside. But surely he would not go to the bother – from inside the room, the window must look inaccessible. She thanked heaven she was in breeches and thanked heaven again that she had misbehaved as a child and dangled from every tree on the Devereux estate.

It was easy enough to reach the branch. She crawled her way carefully along towards its end and leaned forward. Slowly, slowly, she stretched out her hand. She was just short of the window frame. She would have to crawl further along the thinning branch and risk it breaking beneath her weight.

As she edged forward, she felt her breeches catch and heard something rip, but displaying her underwear was the least of her worries. She hung off the end of the branch and with some difficulty eased the bottom sash upwards until she managed to make a space just large enough to admit her. It was a tricky manoeuvre and she almost fell through the window, plumping down on an armchair beneath. The chair skidded under her momentum and there was a screech of wood on tile. She held her breath, but the noise from the front of the inn was deafening.

Where to start? She thrust a spill into the small fire that burned in the grate and lit the one candle she had brought. Holding it high in the air, she could see that the walls of the room were festooned with shelves. Tumbling piles of dusty papers, clusters of broken ornaments, and what appeared to be tools, littered every space. Nothing of any interest, she thought. In any case Partridge would not have left such precious items on full view.

She turned round, candle in hand, seeking a likely hiding place: there was no safe but there was a bureau. She padded quietly across the room to a desk of battered oak and tried the drawer. It was locked. Naturally, it would be. Looking around for something to lever the lid, she thought she heard a slight sound at the door but loud laughter continued from the front of the inn and she returned again to her search.

Holding the candle higher still, she looked more closely along the shelves. Surely there must be some implement she could use. In the half shadow she saw what looked to be a carpenter's chisel at the very top. To reach it she would need one of the wooden chairs that sat either side of the hearth. She had barely reached the chair, when a voice spoke behind her.

'So I've got yer, my fine lad.'

Instantly she blew out the candle and the room was plunged into darkness.

'That won't help yer one little bit. Didimus Black allus gets his man. It's the nubbing ken for you.'

Lucinda's heart was pounding. There was no way back through the window and the Runner, for it was he, had cut off her escape through the door. She should have taken more care, been more aware of the danger this man posed. Jack had told her that Black was still at the inn but she had forgotten.

Jack – she was paralysed by the thought of him. If she were discovered, he would know she had broken her promise to him. Would he forgive her? She could not be sure. She had seen the joy in his face when he'd learned that her misadventures had been for her brother's sake and not simply for thrills. He had been thinking the worst and if he were to know of this exploit, he might think the worst again. He might conclude that she was little different from the woman who had caused him such heartache.

The Runner was advancing on her. She could see nothing, but she could hear the soft shuffle of his feet. Gradually as her sight adjusted, the darkness assumed different tones and from the corner of her eye, she could just see the open door and the unlit corridor beyond.

'Didimus Black 'as ogles that can see in the dark, speshully when there's a bridle cull about.'

He sounded smug, but it was not the tone of his voice that interested her but its location. She would have to make a dash for the door. She had no idea of the geography of the inn but it was her only hope. Quietly she lifted the chair and then with all her strength threw it in the direction of the Runner. There was a muttered curse, and a stumble, but she was through the door and into the passage beyond.

Where to? She lost precious seconds, unsure which way

to turn, but then headed towards the noise. The main entrance must be nearby. An open door loomed to the right of her and she caught a glimpse of a crowded room filled with villagers drinking their way through the evening and too engrossed to recognise the flying figure making for the front door. She could hear Black breathing heavily. He could be only a few steps behind her, but he seemed unfit. She would outrun him.

She tore across the gravelled courtyard and plunged into the woods but the Runner held closely to her. He was not giving up, every one of his footsteps echoing hers. She knew these woods and he did not; surely she could lose him among the trees. She had run a mile at least, or so it seemed, and still the Runner stayed with her.

She was breathless and almost sobbing with the pain in her lungs, for though Didimus Black was rotund, he was remarkably swift. She had to find a way to shake him off – she would trick him by doubling back on herself. She veered to the left, sidestepping the man so close on her tail, but as she did, her foot caught in an exposed tree root and she fell spread-eagled to the ground.

'Got yer, yer varmint,' he wheezed. 'And a merry dance yer led me. I'll see yer swing on the nubbing cheat, danged if I don't!'

⌣

Out of nowhere the air was splintered by a sickening crack and Lucinda felt the hold on her legs relax. She was no longer pinned to the ground. What had happened? She rolled over onto one side and found herself face to face with Didimus Black. He lay inert, stretched out beside her.

'You had best vanish as quickly as you're able.' The voice was coldly expressionless. It was Jack's! She scrambled to her feet, perplexed and fearful. A thousand questions teemed through her brain but *what happened?* was all she could think to ask. She gestured towards the prone figure.

'Mr Black has met a temporary setback.' Jack's tone continued impassive and he made no attempt to move towards her.

'But is he...? Did you...?'

'I hit him over the head. A little drastic, but necessary. He is not dead, if that's what worries you, merely unconscious.'

'But how did you know he was chasing me?' she gasped. 'You must have followed him from the inn.'

Jack nodded grimly. 'I followed you both. I was escaping, too – from the noise, not the Runner – and was about to set out for a walk in the woods when I saw him lurking in the passageway. He seemed about to pounce – as indeed he was. So I watched and I followed.'

'I can't thank you enough, Jack.'

'Don't,' he said harshly. 'I want no thanks for assaulting an officer of the law. You must go before he wakes.'

Lucinda felt sick to the stomach, for the man she loved had vanished from view. In his place was someone she did not recognise, someone who could freeze the very words on her lips. Seconds passed before she faltered into speech again. 'What will happen to you when I've gone?'

'I will wait to help Mr Black back to the inn. He's like to be a trifle unsteady.'

'But might he not think it was you that hit him?'

'Why would he think that, Lucinda?' It was the first

time he had used her name and it sounded almost bitter. 'I am a wealthy aristocrat, as you've often remarked, and the one who summoned him here to investigate a highway robbery – if you remember.'

Her flush was invisible in the misty half-light but she said in a spirited voice, 'If I leave now, you will be the only person in the vicinity. He may begin to have suspicions.'

'I think not. I shall say that I found him lying here and brought him round. I'll show him the broken bough and say that someone must have used it to hit him over the head. He is almost certain to jump to the conclusion that you had an accomplice nearby who helped to free you. It will give him two fugitives to pursue.'

They stood silently across from each other, the body of Didimus Black between them. A gap had opened and it was more than the two feet of grass that separated them. Jack had rescued her in a coldly efficient manner, but without one hint of love. He was judging her, and judging her cruelly.

'I'm sorry,' she burst forth, 'I'm sorry to have involved you again in my troubles. But I want to explain – let me explain.'

'You must go now. I will call on you tomorrow.'

His indifference tore at her. She wanted to reach out and hold him close, remind him that only a few hours ago they had lain in each other's arms. Instead she stood motionless, the sickness threatening to overwhelm her.

The man at their feet groaned softly and twitched his legs. 'He is beginning to stir,' Jack said in that horrible, mechanical voice. 'You must make haste. But when you reach home, be sure to mend your breeches. You will need them again, no doubt.'

The hateful remark sent Lucinda plunging forward into the wood.

Chapter Twenty-Six

Still shaking from the dreadful encounter, she hurried through the trees as fast as she was able and made for the lane leading to the hidden tunnel, intent on regaining her room unseen. But once inside the passageway, her pace slackened until she was barely walking. She was still not wholly recovered from her injury and the escape had taken an enormous toll on her strength.

Flight by flight, she dragged herself up the back stairs, desperate not to faint before she could reach her bedroom door. Exhausted, she fell across the threshold. She'd been lucky – she had reached her room without having seen or heard a soul. It was as though the house had been sleeping for a hundred years.

But Lucinda could not sleep. She was too terrified to close her eyes and, swaddled in a blanket, sat herself down by the window. What if the Runner did not recover properly? What if he recovered but refused to believe Jack's story? What if Partridge, when he learned of the attempted break-in, decided to tell his tale and the trail led back to Rupert and his sister? More and more questions to torment her.

She tried to reason with herself. Jack knew what he was doing. Things would happen just as he said, and as for Partridge, he would do nothing precipitate but would take time to think over his next move. And what would that be? She dared not think, could not think – her head was too heavy. Despite her terror, her eyelids began to droop.

A tawny owl hooted just outside the window and she started up, hearing the beat of unfurling wings as it launched itself into the night. She was very cold even beneath the blanket and crawled into the bed to find some warmth. Almost instantly, though, her mind began its ceaseless churning.

This time the thoughts could not be reasoned away. Jack had rescued her, but at what cost? His voice had frozen her to silence and there had been not one glimmer of love in his face, not one gesture of feeling in his body. It was only a few hours ago that he had been planning to come to the Towers today – it was nearly dawn already. He had be coming to persuade Sir Francis that he was a worthy suitor for his niece. Now, though, it would be to demand an explanation.

He would think she had run mad. No, it was worse than that. He would suspect her, as he'd done before, of adventuring for the sake of sheer sensation. She could never tell him why she had tried to rifle Partridge's office. She'd spoken of Rupert's imprisonment in Newgate, but she could not bring herself to confess her brother's involvement in a man's death. Rupert alone could do that and he would be adamant in his refusal. His confession could be bought only by the knowledge that Jack was plump in the pocket and able to pay Partridge his blood money. Lucinda could not bear to think of it – their love, their pure love, diminished and dirtied in that fashion. For the first time since she'd set out on this ill-starred undertaking, she allowed herself to cry.

⤳

Jack watched as Lucinda stumbled through the undergrowth and disappeared from sight. In the threads of mist that swirled heavily around them, her face had gleamed white, wounded and desperate, but he could not bring himself to comfort her. The heartache of betrayal was too great. He had hardly believed his senses when he'd realised that the fugitive fleeing from Didimus Black was none other than Lucinda. He still could hardly believe it. But if he doubted, the evidence lay at his feet in the shape of the Runner's unconscious form. She had made him a promise that she would never again break the law and he'd believed her without reservation. She loved him, did she not, and love made a promise sacred. But not for Lucinda, it appeared. The call to excitement was too great and her love for him too shallow.

With an enormous effort he pushed away the destructive thoughts. This was no time to be lingering over a lost future when there was a charade to play.

'Mr Black, are you all right?' He bent solicitously over the unfortunate man.

The Runner struggled to life, endeavouring to sit up, his head swaying to and fro. 'Who?' he stammered. 'What?'

'Don't try to talk – you appear to have hurt your head. I am Lord Frensham and I'm staying at the inn. We have already met.'

'I knows yer well enough,' Didimus Black muttered.

'I was taking my evening walk and came upon you,' Jack continued smoothly. 'What has happened to you, my dear sir?'

'What's 'appened?!' The man stroked his sore head angrily. 'I'll tell yer what's 'appened, your lordship. I've been set upon.'

'But who would do such a thing?'

'I 'ad 'im, 'ad 'im in my power. I were almost there. The bridle cull – or maybe 'is accomplice. There's two of 'em.'

'Two highwaymen? Are you certain, Mr Black? I thought they usually worked alone.' The earl was being deliberately obtuse.

'This 'un was a stripling – learning the trade no doubt, but I caught 'im in Partridge's quarters. On the jump.'

'Filling in the time before the next ambush perhaps?'

'Exactly. I 'ad 'im, got 'im in me fambles, and then out of nowhere, this cove appears and floors me.'

'Allow me to help you up. You are still a trifle shaky.'

'I should think I am.' He pointed to the offending bough. 'That's what 'it me. Any man would have gorn down with a blow from that.'

They began to trace a stumbling path back through the wood and towards the lighted inn. 'You didn't 'ear nuffin'?' The Runner's tone was just this side of suspicious.

'No. I'm sorry, I heard nothing. The noise from the inn...' It was fortunate that the riotous party was still in full swing. 'I was trying to escape the clamour and walked into the woods to find some peace. I could hardly believe my eyes when I came upon you.'

'Nor see nuffin'?'

The Runner's job was to be mistrustful, Jack thought. 'Not a thing. Whoever attacked you must have melted into the mist. But can I assist you to your room?'

'I'm much obliged, your lordship, but I'm well enough. I'll be taking a rest just now but tomorrow that office of Partridge needs looking to – the varmint might have dropped a clue, yer never know.'

'No, you never know,' the earl said and walked slowly up the stairs to his room.

He sank down in the single chair furnished by the inn. It was of bare wood and roughly turned, but he felt none of its discomfort. All he felt was misery. Lucinda had deceived him. She had made a binding promise that she would never again go adventuring and here she was, disguised in breeches, and ready to steal. For why else would she have been in a private room and wearing such garb?

Today they had loved each other to the full; today he had offered her marriage. She'd hesitated in accepting him and now he could see why. She *was* the inveterate thrill seeker he'd first thought and a husband would prove a severe curb on her activities.

For years he had guarded himself against love but Lucinda had shot to pieces his determination to preserve his heart. How could he have been so stupid to allow it to happen? The qualities in her that entranced him were the very same that had brought him to Julia. It was so drearily predictable: the moth to the flame. He'd not managed to safeguard himself at all. He had fallen once more for a woman who could only bring him hurt and disillusion.

◷

Jack was at Verney Towers by ten o'clock in the morning and was shown into a drawing room at the back of the house. It was a room he had never visited and the chill struck him immediately. It was sparsely furnished and heavy velvet curtains obliterated most of the natural light. He thought it tomb-like, but perfectly fitted for a day which spelt the death of his hopes. He stood motionless in the centre of the room and squared his shoulders for what was to come.

He wasn't even sure why he was here except that he felt he owed it to Lucinda to hear her out. If he were sensible, he would already be on his way to London. He had left Lynton finishing the packing and Fielding fussing over the horses. By tonight he would be in Half Moon Street and taking his first steps on the long, painful path to a future without her. He had to get on with his life, put the last few weeks behind him. If he repeated that mantra to himself often enough, surely he would succeed. He'd endured the catastrophe that had been his courtship of Julia and he could survive this.

Survive was the right word. He could not compare his youthful love with the feelings that had taken hold of him since he met Lucinda. When he'd fallen for Julia, he had been young, very young, just learning to fly, and in retrospect his feelings appeared mere gentle flutterings in the path to love. But when he'd met Lucinda, he'd been a man hardened by experience, made cynical even, by the world in which he lived. Yet in knowing her, he had grown new wings; in loving her he had launched himself into full, joyous flight. Together they had soared and now together, fallen to earth.

Once he had left here he would go on living – what else was there to do? – but this time there would be no salvation in sport, no distraction from travel, no oblivion to be found in the mindless social whirl. The hurt was too acute. He would survive but not forget, for she would always be with him – a face in the mirror, a figure in his dreams, an ache that would never leave.

A slight sound caused him to turn and Lucinda came slowly through the door, the shadow of a smile on her face. She was simply gowned in white muslin over a tunic of pale blue sarcenet with a blue ribbon threaded through her blonde curls. Her face was still very pale and, as she glided towards him, he thought her almost ethereal.

But the urgent desire to pull her into his arms was far from ethereal and stopped him in his tracks.

'You reached home safely, I see.'

She hesitated for a moment, seeming unable to speak across the cold distance he was putting between them. 'Yes, I thank you.'

Then when he made no further comment, she said in a constrained voice, 'I know you don't wish to be thanked, Jack, but you have my everlasting gratitude for rescuing me from a dreadful predicament.'

'I have already said I desire neither thanks nor gratitude and I meant it. It's an episode I wish to forget.'

The harshness in his voice made her stumble on her words. 'How is Mr Black?'

'Mr Black is alive.'

'And he suspects nothing?'

'You can be easy. He harbours no suspicion of either of us – he is intent on pursuing two fearful rogues.'

She tried to smile but failed. 'Even though I'm not allowed to thank you, I'm glad that you have come. Last night... you must wonder at my conduct. Won't you sit down and we can talk?'

'I would prefer to stand. I must return to the inn very shortly.'

A flush spread across her face and she tried again to defend herself. 'Last night – it wasn't what it seemed.'

'And what was that?'

'I understand why you're so angry. You believe me to have sought excitement by dressing up again and trying to steal from Partridge.'

'And for what other reason would you have adopted that wretched disguise?'

'I dared not be recognised.'

'Why not? Why, in fact, break into his office?'

'I did not play the intruder for the thrill of it. You have to believe me. I was driven to the deed for the best of reasons.'

'And what would they be?' Scepticism was written large on Jack's face, suggesting an unwillingness to believe any explanation she might produce.

'I cannot tell you. It is not my secret to tell.'

'How very convenient.'

'This is not what I want,' Lucinda said desperately. 'I cannot bear that we are quarrelling. I swear to you that I had good cause for what I did. If you truly love me, you will trust that I speak the truth.'

'You have given me little cause to trust,' he said bitterly. 'You made me a solemn vow that you would never again go adventuring. How can I trust a woman who breaks her promise within days of making it?'

Lucinda hung her head and said with difficulty, 'I cannot argue with your anger. You have every right to distrust. But please believe me when I say that only something exceptional, a request I could not refuse, would make me break my vow to you.'

'So exceptional that you cannot tell me what it is, cannot tell the man you have sworn to love. Or has *that* vow, too, vanished overnight?'

'You must know it has not.'

'But that's the rub, I don't. I no longer know what to believe.'

'Believe that I tell the truth. I love you dearly, Jack, and if you truly love me, you will understand.'

'Let me return your words to you. If *you* truly loved me, you would tell me why you have chosen to throw our futures to the wind.'

She started towards him and held out her hands, but he resolutely kept his arms by his side. Crestfallen, she said, 'I want to tell you everything, but the secret I hold is not mine to tell.'

'So you have said – if secret there is! But let us suppose for one minute that your words are genuine. In effect, you are saying that if we were to marry, there would be things that you could not divulge to me, times where you owed your loyalties elsewhere. That is not my idea of a marriage. There should be no secrets between people who love each other.'

Other secrets, old secrets, had come back to haunt him as he spoke. Everyone, it seemed, had known about Julia except for him. He recalled the humiliation of having his bankers' draft refused by a cringing clerk, their hostess's swift removal of unlocked valuables when they came to call, the look on a friend's face when he recounted losing this or that bauble. They had all known the secret while he had not. Or, what was likelier, he had known but refused to confront it. This time he would not shy from the truth, no matter what pain it gave him.

His voice, when he spoke, was without emotion. 'In all our dealings together, Lucinda, I've asked only that we are honest with each other.'

'I have been honest. I've not deceived you. Well, a little perhaps when you first came to Verney Towers,' she amended. 'But I dared not confess then that I was the highwayman. And when you knew, you kept my secret. It did not appear worrisome to you – quite the contrary, since you involved yourself when you could have walked away.'

Jack could feel himself losing the calm he'd maintained with such difficulty. 'I involved myself because I believed in you. And you have been happy enough to accept my help. Indeed, if you had not accepted it last night, you would be kicking your heels in Lewes gaol at this very moment, locked up with every type of miscreant – that is before they stripped you naked to search you.'

He could see her visibly shudder and the tears start in

her eyes. 'It's not an enticing prospect, is it?'

'I owe you an enormous debt but please, I beg you, trust me.'

'The truth is, Lucinda, that I cannot trust you. You have tricked me once too often and there's little more for us to say, except goodbye – but this time we must both mean it. We are not good for each other.'

'You're wrong. We are made for one another. I know it and so do you.'

'I thought I did – for a few fleeting hours. But I can pretend no longer.'

There was a deathly silence and then he said in the most matter of fact voice he could find, 'I am to return to London and, if I wish to arrive before nightfall, I must be on my way. By now my servants will be packed and ready to leave.'

'You are leaving Verney today?'

'I am.'

Lucinda's stricken face was almost more than he could bear. He wanted to take her in his arms and kiss her back to happiness. But his heart was at war with his head – he had spoken truly when he'd said they were not good for each other.

Ever since they'd first met they had been swept along on a roller coaster of feeling: surges of happiness followed by uncertainty and disquiet. He could not live in such emotional turmoil, never knowing from one day to the next what she would be at. Jack had thought his love strong enough and deep enough to satisfy her desire for excitement, but he had been wrong.

He held out his hand in farewell. She looked at it, shocked to utter stillness, as though disbelief had sucked the life from her. Then ignoring the hand, she brushed past him. He could see her tears begin to fall even before she reached the door.

Chapter Twenty-Seven

The walk back to The Four Feathers was the saddest Jack had ever taken. When he'd returned to the inn last evening he had felt ready to conquer the world. All that had been wrong with his life - the unhappiness of childhood, the trial of family, the hurt of betrayed love – all of it had vanished in those moments when he'd loved and thought himself loved in return. A new life was before them both, a sparkling bubble in a mundane world.

But the bubble had burst the minute he'd realised the identity of the slight figure fleeing for its life. He had been staggered, hardly believing what he saw, but he knew that figure too well not to recognise Lucinda - Lucinda in disguise, Lucinda at her tricks. His heart had plummeted even as he lifted the broken bough to lay the Runner low. He had saved her skin, but that was for the very last time. She was on her own now.

Not quite on her own. She had her brother back, though she was unlikely to confess to him what she had been doing. Jack was sure that her fears for the boy's safety had been genuine; she might even have been sincere in thinking she could help him by taking to the road. But her overriding desire had been quite other, and she had used Rupert's plight as an excuse for her wild conduct. He recalled that it was only when he was packed and ready to leave the Towers that she had told him it was for her brother's sake that she'd ridden out on Red. Why hadn't she told him before? There had been plenty of opportunity to do so. It smacked of yet more subterfuge, a last minute attempt to disarm her lover and stop him from going.

Rupert was no longer in danger and she'd had to find another motive for last night's exploit. Her excuse had been flimsy beyond belief and had done nothing to restore his trust. Yet though Jack no longer believed her protestations, it did not stop him loving her deeply and fearing for her future. He had to remind himself that she was not his responsibility. She had not accepted his offer and, though his heart might say otherwise, he owed her no formal commitment.

Perhaps her brother, now that he was home, could succeed in persuading her from the dangerous path she had chosen. Freed from the stigma of debt, Rupert would be keen to restore his standing in the county. It would be hard enough for him to claw himself back to respectability; he would not want a sister bringing him into disrepute. Hopefully, he would convince Lucinda that their new life together was excitement enough.

Jack had always felt a little jealous of her devotion to her absent brother. The still absent brother, he thought. That was a question – where was Rupert? There had been no sign of him since his return to the Towers and today Lucinda had made no mention of him. That in itself was strange and Jack turned it over in his mind. Could the boy still be causing trouble? Now that her brother was freed, there would seem no need for Lucinda to court danger on his behalf. But what if there was something else, something of which her lover knew nothing?

She had spoken of a matter so urgent that she had been driven to drastic action. Was her brother then behind last night's foolhardy attempt to break into Partridge's office? If Rupert had sworn her to secrecy... it would account for her determined silence. Jack's heart began to beat just a little faster and his mind shifted backwards and forwards through a kaleidoscope of thoughts, trying to find a path through the morass. Could it be that Lucinda had made two promises and that only one could be kept? Was her promise to Rupert so critical that she'd been forced to abandon the vow she had made to him? Pure speculation, he thought unhappily, a ruse to exonerate the woman he loved.

He began to descend the slope that signalled the approach to the village. And none too soon, he reckoned, looking upwards. Banks of clouds piled one upon another in a troubled grey sky. He would be lucky to reach the inn before the rain unleashed itself. His stride increased, his mind keeping step with the quickened pace. What *was* Lucinda doing in Partridge's office? It was a far cry from highway robbery. If she was looking for excitement, why had she not ridden out on Red once more? Perhaps she had tired of that game and decided breaking and entering would be more diverting.

Jack tried to think himself back. He had been so

stunned by her betrayal that he'd made no attempt so far to analyse the events of yesterday evening. Now he did. He'd been driven out of the inn by the riot of noise from the public bar and, despite the encroaching night, decided to walk for a while in the woods. He had been descending the staircase when he'd become transfixed by the sight of Didimus Black, crouching by the door to the landlord's private quarters. Standing motionless on the bottom step, he had seen a dim light spilling from the room – a light that moved. It was a candle and whoever held it high was intent on scouring the office.

It had been Lucinda, of course, and the more he thought, the more certain he was that she had been searching for something. She had been searching for something she expected to find. But what? What could Partridge have in that room that had made her willing to risk her life and the future they'd planned together?

Jack crunched across the gravel courtyard as the first drops of rain fell heavily on his shoulders. The sharp sting of water jerked him from his reverie. This would not do; he was entangling himself in pointless conjecture. He must find Lynton and give orders to leave – he needed to be away and to think no more.

The landlord was in the public bar supervising several of the village women who cleaned for him and, after the chaos of last night's party, it seemed they had a monumental task on their hands. Elsewhere an intense quiet hung over the inn. Jack saw the door to Partridge's office slightly ajar and moved silently down the passage towards it. He would put his head into the room, just for a second, in the forlorn hope that he might discover why Lucinda had searched there, if search she had.

It was not obvious. The room was filled with rubbish: nick-knacks long broken, heaps of paper spilling themselves untidily from shelf to shelf, tools left scattered everywhere. It looked as though Didimus Black had already visited that morning to take measurements, for what good they would do him. There were chalk scratches on the floor and on the furniture to mark where the perpetrator had stood and moved. The desk was open and Jack peered inside. There was nothing of any interest. What was it that Lucinda had wanted from this dismal space? Or had it been, as he knew in his heart, simply a senseless spree? It had to be. He clamped his lips together in chagrin and turned to go.

A curtain had fallen half across the open doorway and he tugged it to one side in irritation. The fierce action ripped the velvet drape from its rail and it dribbled to the ground in a heap. He went to pick it up, ashamed of his spurt of temper but, as he bent, he saw with surprise a safe built low into the wall. Clearly Partridge did not want his strongbox to be common knowledge and had hidden it carefully. Was the safe what Lucinda had come for? But the marks on the floor and furniture suggested that she had gone nowhere near it. It might be interesting to look inside, however. Jack tried the handle and unsurprisingly found it locked. He should leave the room; he had no right to pry into another man's possessions, even though that man was as crooked as Dick's hatband.

He walked to the doorway and then looked back at the strongbox. Angered by his own indecision, he strode across the room and on impulse plucked from the desk a heavy iron paperweight which he smashed down on the safe's handle. The noise was extraordinary. He had better make haste, he reckoned, and vacate the room before the whole inn came running. But the safe door had swung open and its interior was awash with shining points of light. Tray after tray of rings, necklaces and bracelets were caught in a stray shaft of hazy sunlight which filtered between storm clouds and pierced the window high above. He pulled out one of the trays – these were real diamonds, he could swear. Another tray, this time of rubies and yet another of emeralds. Even a studded tiara! Stolen goods, Jack was sure, and he wanted nothing to do with them.

He moved to put them back, tray by tray, but as he did so he brushed against a piece of canvas, tucked towards the back of the safe. He withdrew the bundle and began to unfold the cloth. This was something very different and not obviously valuable. A ring again, but a plain, onyx signet with an intricate pattern worked around its edge. He had seen that motif before – a gun, he recollected, Rupert Lacey's duelling pistol. The ring belonged to Lacey. *This* is what Lucinda had been searching for. Her troublesome brother was the reason she had again risked her liberty. He should have listened to his instincts, not his head, Jack castigated himself. He should have trusted her. But why had she tried to retrieve it in this surreptitious fashion? Surely if Partridge had stolen the ring, the Devereux family could have informed the magistrate and been granted a warrant to search the premises.

There was something else in the canvas. Slowly, he drew

it forth. A dagger bearing the very same motif – a crown of acanthus leaves – undoubtedly this, too, was Rupert Lacey's. Jack inspected the dagger closely. It seemed to be an ornamental knife, but for a toy it was looking a trifle begrimed. He whetted his fingers and felt its tip – some ornament, this could do serious damage. And now that he looked more closely at the grime... my God, that was blood!

Out of nowhere he felt a punishing blow to the back of his neck and his knees crumpled. Before he went down, he turned slightly and saw a scarlet-faced Partridge and in his hand the self-same paperweight Jack had used to smash the safe open. His adversary lifted the weight again and would have brought it down on his head this time, if Jack had not lunged out with his foot and kicked him hard on the shin. The landlord hopped back in pain and dropped the paperweight. Jack scrambled to his feet but only just in time, for Partridge had snatched the fire iron from the hearth and was making ready to knock him senseless. It was clear that he had seen too much and the landlord did not mean him to leave the room alive.

Jack parried the oncoming blow, catching the poker between his hands. For a while they struggled for control of the iron bar until, with a sudden wrench, Jack tore it from the landlord's hands and flung it to one side. He grabbed the man by the neck and swung a punch at him. Partridge dived low to avoid the blow, swinging his own punch in return. He was no novice, Jack thought. He must have spent time in the ring, as a prize fighter no doubt. He thanked heaven that he was no mean pugilist himself, but he would need cunning to defeat this very large and very angry man.

He danced around his opponent, trying to keep his distance until an opportunity to attack presented itself. He was unused to bare knuckle fighting, but all the frustration and anger that had been boiling within him since last night, gave him almost supernatural strength and, when Partridge forgot for an instant to raise his left hand in defence, he found the man's jaw with a heavy blow. The landlord reeled and staggered back. Before he'd had time to recover, Jack followed with another punch, and another and yet another. He was filled with fury that this man had hurt Lucinda, filled with fury that he had hurt her himself. He wanted to lash out, to batter the landlord into oblivion, and it was only Didimus Black's voice that stopped him.

'Lord Frensham! What are you about?'

The Runner puffed his way into the room. Jack allowed the supine form of Partridge to drop to the floor. He took time to straighten his neckcloth and pull his jacket into place.

'Whatever are you about, sir?' the Runner repeated.

''e's the thief,' Partridge whimpered from the floor. 'It's 'im you want to arrest. 'e's the one that broke in last night and gave you a blow on the pate.' The landlord staggered to his feet and began to sketch a zigzag path to the safe. He had every intention of shutting it before the Runner could investigate.

Didimus Black threw out his chest. He was about to apprehend a member of the *ton* and it wasn't every day that happened. But before he could begin to recite the words of arrest, Jack intervened.

'One minute, my friend. I have stolen nothing – far from it. On the contrary, I appear to have uncovered stolen goods. Mr Black, would you care to look in the safe and give us your professional opinion.'

''e don't need to look at nothin', Partridge blustered. 'It's as clear as the nose on yer face – you're the thief and yer trying to flim flam yer way out of it.'

In answer, Jack strode across the room to the safe and flung the door wide. 'Do you think a humble landlord could come honestly by such expensive geegaws? For myself, I do not.'

Black peered into the safe and gave a long drawn out whistle. 'My, my, what 'ave we 'ere?'

The landlord had been edging gradually towards the door and, at the Runner's words, he geared himself to flee. But Didimus Black was faster. With the same agility that had worried Lucinda, he reached the door before Partridge got his foot over the threshold.

'Not so fast, Captain Sharp. We've conversations to be 'ad. Plenty of 'em – but they'll be in Lewes gaol. Right now I've got a carridge waitin' fer us, all neat and tidy.' He slipped handcuffs expertly around the landlord's wrists and, without another word, marched him from the inn.

Left alone in the room, Jack pocketed the roll of canvas and shut the safe carefully behind him. He was taking only what belonged at the Towers and the sooner he returned those items, the better. It was clear that Rupert Lacey had been embroiled in something very dark, but he had no wish to know what. He knew all he needed: Lucinda had acted only to protect her brother. He hated himself for having doubted her. Would he ever persuade her to forgive his stupidity? First thing in the morning, he would put it to the test.

Chapter Twenty-Eight

For a second night Lucinda hardly slept. She was steeped in misery but filled with anger, too. Why had Jack not trusted her? He loved her, didn't he, so why could he not accept that she had good reason for the trespass in Partridge's room? The sad truth was that he did not love enough. Even as she'd heard him speak endearments and offer himself in marriage, something had whispered to her that his words were not quite real. A twinge of unease had held her back from committing herself completely.

Yet if she looked deep into her heart, she could not blame Jack for the fragility of his feelings. Memories were still too vivid for him, and she knew that when he'd saved her from the Runner's clutches, he had thought history was repeating itself in a savage mockery. Years ago he had had his trust shattered irrevocably and now the tentacles of that wretched event had reached out and made victims of them both.

When she counted how much it had cost *her* to learn to trust, why would it be any easier for Jack? Until she met him, Lucinda had not realised how great a burden she carried from the past, how much she had been affected by her mother's disastrous marriage and the loveless household in which she had been raised. Agnes Devereux's fate had been inevitable, it seemed, but all marriage was a gamble. Lucinda had never wanted to fall in love and put herself in a man's power. She had thought her affection for her twin was all she needed, all she could depend on. But Jack Beaufort had shown her differently; he had taught her the true meaning of love and, in doing so, had turned her world upside down.

At the outset, she had judged him just another of his kind, one of those arrogant members of the *ton* that she met occasionally at neighbours' country houses. She had taken him in dislike without knowing him and yet, against her will, she had been attracted, mightily attracted. Gradually, she had learned her mistake. Jack's life as a wealthy, pleasure-seeking man was one she'd always despised, but he was so much greater than the caricature she'd created for him. She had fallen headlong in love and with a man she had thought did not exist.

She knew now that her feelings for Rupert were not something on which she could build the rest of her life. All these years she had taken responsibility for her brother and she could do so no longer. Last night, he had come to her eager to hear the good news and she'd had to tell him that she'd returned from the inn with nothing, indeed had been fortunate to escape capture. She had dared not mention the Runner's pursuit and Jack's rescue, dared not intimate that her brother's benefactor was so close.

Instead, she'd told him that she had searched until

she heard footsteps coming towards the office and been forced to flee, but it was clear that Rupert doubted her. He thought she had lost her nerve and, at the first noise, had run. So now there were two men who did not believe her, Lucinda thought sadly, the two men closest to her heart.

Her relations with her brother were subtly changed. Since his incarceration, Rupert had grown harder, less considerate. He was no longer the loving twin he had been; at times Lucinda thought him almost a stranger. Her sense of loss was sharp, but it was as nothing when set against the desolation of losing Jack. At the end of the longest day of her life, she had crawled into bed and lain sleepless between the sheets. For hours she had looked out at the night sky, at the handful of stars tossed like a scattering of crystals and the crescent moon riding ever higher. She had tried to lose herself in the vastness, adrift as she was without an anchor, floating towards an unknown future.

What would happen now? She grieved that Rupert would flee, disappear from her life, before Partridge had an opportunity to tell his tale, and she was certain that once Francis Devereux learned of the vagrant's death, her brother would be banned from ever returning to Verney Towers. The honour of the Devereuxs must remain unimpeachable.

Her mind wandered to her uncle and it struck her that recently he had been unusually amenable. Did he have some inkling of what had been happening beyond his library? He could have no idea yet of the new disaster that had befallen Rupert, but he might guess that it was Jack who had been her brother's saviour. Perhaps it had encouraged him to hope that the shocking conduct he'd witnessed at the ball was about to lead to something a good deal less shocking. He was destined for disappointment, though if he'd learned of Jack's visit yesterday, he must already have guessed the unhappy outcome.

⌒

Come the morning, Molly found her mistress standing by the window and looking aimlessly out on the world. In reality, Lucinda saw nothing, not the sky as clear as polished glass nor the gleaming leaves of evergreens freshened by a night of intermittent rain. Sapped of all energy, she allowed the maid to choose her gown and submitted docilely to having her hair brushed and fixed in a simple topknot. A footman brought tea and toast, but she could only pick at it and she grew increasingly irritated with herself. It was ridiculous to be so afflicted; she was behaving as though she were the doomed heroine from a novel out of the circulating library. Was she, too, about to go into a terminal decline from the devastating loss of her love? Her life was in tatters, it was true, her future a dark, empty space, but she ought at least to pretend that she was made of sterner stuff. When Molly took the breakfast tray downstairs, she settled on the window seat with the intention of reading her way through the latest edition of *La Belle Assemblée*, but it was not long before she gave up and began idly flicking through its pages with even less interest than usual.

Out of nowhere a loud noise from below caused her to drop the journal in a startled splutter – there seemed to be some kind of altercation coming from the hall. She very much feared that it might be Rupert in a bad quarrel with his uncle. They had hardly spoken since her brother came home. Sir Francis had been outraged by his nephew's release and had not believed Rupert when he denied any knowledge of his benefactor. It was only the boy's gaunt figure and ashen face that had convinced Sir Francis his punishment had been sufficient. But relations between them remained strained and, if her brother had dared to broach the dreadful history that Partridge had threatened to disclose, it would easily account for the angry noises ricocheting up the grand staircase.

Her uncle's raised voice slowly dwindled into loud mutters and instead Lucinda heard footsteps running up the stairs, footsteps pounding towards her door – an intruder that Sir Francis had been powerless to stop! Her heart thudded furiously and the blood hammered in her ears. What new alarm was this?

A knock. She rose from her chair and walked unwillingly towards the door. Another loud knock. Drawing herself erect, she opened the door a fraction and was met by a pair of warm brown eyes. They were shining. She could swear they were shining with love, but that had to be a fantasy.

'Let me in, Lucy.'

It was the first time he had called her by her pet name. Her heart jumped again, but this time for the best of reasons. She could not understand why Jack had returned or why he was looking at her with such concern – and yes, with love. It *was* love! Tears started in her eyes and began slowly to trickle down her cheeks. She must look utterly woebegone, she thought, and tried to smile, but it proved a sad effort.

'My darling girl, I am so sorry.' Jack was in the room and leading her towards a chair. 'You must sit down before you fall. You look quite ill.'

She sank into the soft velvet of the armchair, feeling bewildered. But then she bristled. Of course, she looked ill – when he had said the things he'd said, and walked from her door without a backward glance, and left her forever to return to his life in London. What else did he expect?

'I am well enough,' she said stout. 'But why are you here, Jack? After your words yesterday, I thought never to see you again.'

'Yesterday I was a fool. Can you ever forgive me?' He was kneeling by her side, his expression remorseful. 'I refused to trust you. How could I have done that? I refused to trust the woman I love, the woman I had just asked to be my wife.'

Lucinda's small rush of resentment slipped away unnoticed and instinctively she reached out to grasp his hand. He gripped her tightly, saying nothing but holding on to her as though his life depended on it.

She must let him know that he was forgiven. 'I understand why you found it so difficult to trust me. What happened to you in the past...'

He put his finger to her lips and her voice trailed away. 'I've used the past as an excuse for walking away from my true feelings,' he said. 'And that is cowardly. Over the years I convinced myself that I had lost my one and only sweetheart. But that was a nonsense – my first love was a mere nothing. It was the humiliation that came to matter most to me, but I hung on to my grievances as a way of escaping commitment. Until I met you, that is.'

'And fell in love?'

'And fell in love,' Jack repeated softly. 'How could I not love the woman who ambushed me?'

'And from the start I loved you back, even though I didn't want to!'

His expression grew serious and he held her hands even more tightly. 'I should have believed you – I should have known that you had a reason for your actions. I have only the haziest notion what that might be, but you did not break into Partridge's office for the fun of it. How crazy of me to think so.'

Lucinda's smile was stronger now. 'It certainly wasn't for fun. It was difficult and frightening and falling through that window hurt! I want to tell you why I did it Jack, I wanted to tell you yesterday. But I could not and I still don't think I can.' She faltered on the last words.

'There is no need to tell me anything.'

'But you *should* know.'

She sat up straight, her fingers pleating her skirts in some agitation. In rescuing her from the Runner, Jack had courted danger himself and, if he were to stay in Verney, he was likely to face suspicion, maybe accusations, perhaps even arrest. He would need to defend himself and for that he needed knowledge. But, Lucinda thought bleakly, he must not stay.

Jack bent down and wrapped his arms closely around her. 'I hate to see you distressed. There is no need for me to know a thing – let us say that the matter is finally closed.'

'But it will not be closed for others. Bad things could

happen and I don't want you involved. You were right to distance yourself. I think you should go away before the worst occurs.'

'Nothing bad will happen.' He was smiling at her in a way that made her stomach somersault in the most inappropriate fashion. Really she should not feel like this. Instead of melting into a puddle, she should be pushing him through the door.

'You cannot know that. You must go away and go now.'

'Then before I do,' he said gently, 'allow me to give you a small gift.'

'This is not the time for presents,' she scolded, 'and in any case by coming here this morning you have given me the best present I could ever have.'

'There are far better ones to come, darling Lucy. This is a mere pinprick of a gift! But I think when you see it, you will be happy.'

He turned to the bed where he had flung his caped benjamin and delved into one of its roomy pockets, drawing out the piece of bloodied canvas.

'Is this what you went looking for?'

Lucinda gave a small choking sound. Then jumped up and rushed over to the bed. 'Where did you find this?'

'I have to confess that "find" is not exactly the right word. I walked into Partridge's office, smashed his safe open, and took it.'

She looked at him aghast. 'But will you not be in the most dreadful trouble? Even worse trouble now?'

'I fancy not. There was enough stolen jewellery in that safe to keep the Runner happy for months. Partridge is by now in Lewes prison and will soon stand trial for receiving stolen goods. I doubt he'll be bothering this neighbourhood for many a long year.'

She took a minute to absorb the momentous news, for with one stroke Jack had made things right. But she was puzzled. 'When you found this roll of canvas, why did you take it? How did you know it was important?'

'I didn't and I don't wish to know why it matters. I went on a hunch. You were willing to risk your entire world for something in that room and I couldn't for the life of me see what it was. But I didn't think Partridge was the kind of man to store a keepsake such as this, unless it was likely to be useful to him. And if it was useful to him, it was useful to its true owner – Rupert, if I were to hazard a guess.'

'The landlord was threatening him.' Lucinda's expression drooped at the thought of the ruin they had so narrowly avoided.

'I thought that might be the case. But look at me, Lucinda, the threat is no more.'

She did as she was asked and smiled at him through tear-filled eyes. 'I am sorry to be such a watering pot, but I cannot believe that you have rescued me – again!'

'Us,' he said firmly. 'I have rescued us. Unless, that is, you cannot forgive me for doubting you when you needed me most.'

'I think we need to forgive each other, Jack. We have been a sorry pair!'

'And once we have forgiven, what of the future?'

She looked up at him, her face radiant. 'That is for us to make – together,' she said with certainty.

'Then can we begin now?' He delved into his jacket pocket. 'This is the best Steyning can offer but I hope you will find it acceptable. We will buy another as soon as we get to London.' And he slipped a band of glowing sapphires on to her finger.

'It is quite beautiful.' Lucinda held out her hand to him, caressing his cheek and admiring the clustered stones as they caught the morning light. 'I want no other.'

'Then we should tell our news to Uncle Francis. I wonder how he will like me calling him that? Currently he is fuming in the hall. He appeared desperate to bar me from the house and I had to put him aside a little roughly.'

'He thinks you an immoral person intent on seduction.' She gave a small giggle.

'More likely it is because he believes me responsible for your unhappiness. And he is right.'

'But no more.'

'No more, Lucinda.'

His lips caressed her cheek, brushing away the stray tears. She lifted her mouth to his and his kiss was warm and hard and wonderful. She had thought never to feel it again, but life had turned amazingly right and she had a world of kisses ahead.

'Uncle Francis will come round, you'll see,' she said, recovering her breath a little. 'I'm sure he still clings to his old wish that our two families be joined. And when he learns I am to become a countess, he'll be overjoyed!'

'Then we mustn't disappoint him.'

In answer, Lucinda nestled closer. Her lover's hands were warming her body through the fine muslin of her gown, skimming the curve of her waist, tracing the outline of her bodice. 'As soon as I can get a special licence, we will be wed,' Jack whispered into her ear.

An unwelcome thought burst suddenly into her mind and she broke away. 'I will have to tell Rupert. He will be euphoric to know his possessions are safe.' She nodded towards the cloth bundle. 'But I fear he will dislike the idea of my marriage.'

'Then we must tempt him with something even better than a stained piece of canvas.'

Lucinda looked questioningly at him.

'I was thinking of the army. You said that was always his dream. Shall I buy him a commission? The cavalry or the dragoons perhaps? The army will give him plenty of opportunity to exercise those high spirits of his.'

'Would you really buy him a commission?'

'Gladly. I think Rupert would be a great deal happier and a lot less trouble if he were settled in a military career. And I cannot be forever rescuing my wife from the Bow Street Runners!'

'You are the most perfect man, Jack.' She flung her arms around him and his lips once more found hers. This time he did not let her go until they were breathless and tumbled together on the bed.

She tugged at his shirt, but already he was gently disentangling himself. 'The perfect man is in danger of forgetting his situation. We should go and find Sir Francis and tell him the good tidings.'

'Must we? I am just getting used to having you in my arms again.'

He laughed. 'In a few days you will have me in your arms every morning and every night. Though I'm unsure if that's a threat or a promise.'

'A promise, Jack,' she laughed back. 'Most decidedly a promise.'

If you enjoyed reading *Dangerous Disguise,* do please leave a review on your favourite site. Authors rely on good reviews – even just a few words – and readers depend on them to find interesting books to read.

Other books in the Allingham Regency Classic Series:
Duchess of Destiny   (2017)
Dance of Deception   (2017)
Masquerade   (2018)
Romancing the Rake   (2019)

Other books by Merryn Allingham:
The Girl From Cobb Street   (2015)
The Nurse's War   (2015)
Daisy's Long Road Home   (2015)
The Buttonmaker's Daughter   (2017)
The Secret of Summerhayes   (2017)
House of Lies   (2018)
House of Glass   (2018)
A Tale of Two Sisters   (2019)
The Venice Atonement   (2019)

For more information on Merryn and her books visit:
http://www.merrynallingham.com/

And sign up for her newsletter at
http://www.merrynallingham.com/
and receive *Through a Dark Glass*, a FREE volume of short
stories.

About the Author

Merryn Allingham was born into an army family and spent her childhood moving around the UK and abroad. Unsurprisingly it gave her itchy feet, and in her twenties she escaped an unloved secretarial career to work as cabin crew and see the world.

The arrival of marriage, children and cats meant a more settled life in the south of England, where she's lived ever since. It also gave her the opportunity to go back to 'school' and eventually teach at university.

Merryn loves the nineteenth century and grew up reading Georgette Heyer, so when she began writing herself the novels had to be Regency romances.